The Very Best of Quintessentially Quirky Tales

Hilarious comedy stories

by

Iain Pattison

First published in Great Britain in 2020
by DoubleQ Books
www.doubleqbooks.com

All stories © 2020 by Iain Pattison
Cover illustration by Jean Hill
Formatting and design by Peter Jones
Editing by Maureen Vincent-Northam

About the Author

Internationally-acclaimed humorist Iain Pattison has been entertaining readers on both sides of the Atlantic for more than 20 years with a succession of short stories that have won prize after prize, appeared in magazines and anthologies, and been broadcast on the UK's most prestigious speech radio station, BBC Radio 4.

As well as penning quirky tales, he is a creative writing tutor, competition judge and after dinner speaker.

Originally from Glasgow but now living in Birmingham, Iain hates shortbread and porridge, can't abide whisky and has never worn a kilt – not even for a bet. All of which may explain why they didn't give him a vote on Scottish independence.

To find out more about Iain follow him on Twitter @AuthorIain or visit his website at iainpattison.co.uk

Contents

Hue and Cry

Snarling, Doctor Watson stormed out of the offices of *The Strand Magazine*, derisive laughter echoing in his ears.

It was outrageous. How dare the man, he fumed; fighting the urge to return and punch the smirking editor's nose.

The journalist's words stung like angry bees. "You've had a good run, Doc, but we'd look stupid publishing any more of your chronicles. This bizarre new direction Sherlock's taken doesn't exactly grip the punters."

Thrusting the barely read pages back into Watson's hands, he'd mocked: "These accounts are too dull for us. Why don't you try them elsewhere... like Homes and Gardens!"

During the Hansom ride back to Baker Street, Watson harboured thoughts that would have broken his Hippocratic Oath, if not his knuckles. But as the cab eventually pulled up outside 221b, he calmed, realising wearily that the magazine owner was right.

Since taking up his strange new hobby six months earlier, Holmes had lost interest in solving the baffling, glamorous, high-profile crimes that had made his name. And although the eccentric genius was still frantically busy, his forensic eye more tested and probing than ever, Sherlock's exploits could now only in one sense, be described as colourful.

There was nothing for it, Watson resolved. If he and Holmes were to avoid ending up in the Workhouse, the madness had to end. He'd have to demand that his companion abandon this folly. However, any possible stratagem for achieving this goal evaporated as a sudden scream disrupted his thoughts.

The wail of terror emanated from within, and bundling through the door he found Mrs Hudson, ashen faced and shrieking, pointing with trembling hands to the staircase carpet. Following her finger he gasped in apprehension.

A trail of droplets led up the gas-lit stairs, each tread soggy with an ominous splodge of viscous crimson. It didn't take much imagination to grasp its meaning and Watson bolted up the sticky steps two at a time.

Pulling out his service revolver, he gulped at what horrors he might encounter. The sight that presented itself made him gag with revulsion. The apartment was bloody, every inch, every cranny splattered and criminally despoiled.

And standing in the middle of the mayhem, clutching a dripping vermilion roller, Sherlock Holmes – once master detective but now self-proclaimed Greatest Interior Designer in the World – beamed with opium-fuelled satisfaction.

"Behold, behold," he proclaimed. "No longer an office in off-white, a living room in boring beige, but a study in scarlet."

For a second Watson considered shooting his crazed friend. He now understood what it meant to see red.

Yet, Holmes appeared oblivious, dropping the roller and snatching up a bright yellow brush.

"There's just time to give the porch one swift coat of canary before Inspector Lestrade pops round," he announced breathlessly.

Groaning, the doctor realised he didn't need to ask what glossy vandalism Sherlock intended for the hallway. He'd heard it dozens of times already.

"Lemon entry, my dear Watson. Lemon entry!"

The Eden Project

Gabriel gave a melancholy sigh, wings drooping so violently that showers of white downy feathers cascaded from the sky, covering the breathtakingly beautiful gardens like a fall of fresh snow.

Sometimes, he reckoned, being an archangel wasn't as great as it was cracked up to be. Yeah, there was the melodic harp music, the snazzy white frocks, being able to lounge about on clouds all day and the simply divine digs described in TripAdvisor as "heavenly but woefully lacking cable TV". All that stuff. But there were other times when the job was a bummer.

And this was definitely one of those occasions.

Studying the eviction notice in his hand, with its big florid Jehovah signature at the bottom, he told himself ruefully: "Now there really is going to be trouble in Paradise."

The big boss was fuming, angry beyond words, and when his wrath was stirred there was no arguing with him. Adam had to go, he'd declared, thrown out of Eden before the end of the day. And Eve had her marching orders too.

Gabriel had pleaded on their behalf, made excuses, promised it wouldn't happen again but, when it came to Adam's antics, God was - well - adamant.

"They knew the regulations. It was all clearly set out in the tenancy agreement," The Almighty thundered. "They ticked the box to say they'd read the terms and conditions. I'm perfectly within my rights - and being me, I do mean perfectly."

Further debate promised an unholy row, so Gabriel gave up, realising with a sinking heart that he was going to have to act as the first bailiff in history.

As he landed by the verdant entrance archway, he reflected that being the first bad guy in the Bible wasn't quite the starring role he'd envisaged for himself.

It was growing dark, evening on the cusp of turning into inky night, and he hurried down the path between the swaying trees, fragrant bushes and lush grasses. He didn't have time to admire the flowers with their magnificent multi-hued blooms or marvel at the iridescent birds flitting from branch to branch in joyous song. He wanted to get this unpleasant task over and done with.

He found Adam in a distant clearing busily trying on a badly fitting fig-leaf thong as Eve, kitted out in a green foliage bikini, chided: "It's too small. Look, it's pinching. I said you should have got the next size up. Well, I'm not taking it back."

Both seemed oblivious to his approach, until a twig snapped underfoot and they stopped in mid squabble. Spinning round, Adam waved a welcome while giving Gabriel a conspiratorial look that said: "Women? Eh? What can you do?"

Eve blushed, averting her eyes from the winged messenger's gaze. She'd never done that before, not even when she'd been as naked as the day the Lord created her from Adam's rib.

"We weren't expecting company," she said awkwardly, trying to cover her chest with her crossed arms. "You could have given us some warning."

And how could he have done that, Gabriel asked, puzzled. He could hardly text or ring ahead.

"A burning bush maybe? Some sort of portent?" Adam ventured. "Still, don't worry about it. You're here now, Squire. What can we do for you?"

Gabriel told himself to be firm. It had to be done. But his voice quivered a little as he announced: "I'm here to tell you that your occupancy of Nirvana is over. God requires you to vacate the premises as soon as possible and never return. Any money left on your deposit will, of course, be refundable and we'll provide you with a good reference."

The two humans rocked back on their heels.

"Leave?" Eve spluttered.

"And never return?" Adam gasped.

The archangel nodded solemnly.

"Look," Eve began. "If it's about the business with the snake and the apple, I take full responsibility. I can expla—"

But Gabriel held up his hand to silence her.

"It's not that," he reported. "We fully expected you to sample the fruit of the tree of the knowledge of good and evil. It was inevitable that you'd succumb to temptation at some point. That's not what's got The Almighty so hot and bothered."

"Then what is it? What did we do that was so awful, so unforgivable?" Adam demanded.

Turning slowly to view the despoiled paradise garden, Gabriel suddenly understood the seriousness of the first couple's crime and why it couldn't go unpunished.

"You put down decking!" he said, with a shudder.

It's Better to Give

Grinning, Gary shook the tin vigorously. The coins inside jingled loudly. "Must be close on to a hundred quid," he muttered, "not bad for an hour's work."

All that, he thought, just for rattling a tin. Who said crime didn't pay?

Gary had known the Larkwood estate would be a winner. You only had to look at the big cars and glittering fishbowl conservatories to know that the people had loads of money.

Even so, he was amazed how quickly they emptied their purses when he held up his fake ID card. The neatly coiffured women didn't look properly at the laminated plastic proclaiming: Authorised Collector for Save the Elderly. They just wanted rid of him as quickly as possible.

It was an easy number, easier than the distraction burglary game - and that had been a sweet caper. He and Kevin had made a fortune dressed as gasmen. He'd keep the housewife talking in the back garden, scaring her with talk of a gas leak, while Kevin rifled through the dressing tables.

It had been a doddle, until the afternoon Kevin walked into a bedroom and bumped into one housewife's lover - all six foot and fourteen stone of him.

Later, as the police surgeon dabbed at his wounds, Kevin said: "That's it, Gary. I'm going back to ram-raids. This lark is too dangerous."

They'd both got six months. Six months while Gary lay on his bunk, counted the bricks in the cell wall and tried to devise a new, safer scam.

Then, the Sunday before Gary's release, the prison chaplain supplied the missing link. He was babbling on about the Good Samaritan and said the magic words: "It is better to give than to receive. Charity must begin at home…"

It was a revelation. "Oh, you're so right, padre," Gary agreed. "From now on I'm going to devote myself to charity."

The chaplain was delighted, so was the governor. Gary marched out with a biblical slogan bouncing around inside his skull… God helps those who help themselves!

* * *

Gary's grin widened as he remembered their stupid, pious faces. They'd reckoned they'd made a convert. If only they knew!

"You should have come in with me, Kevin," he said, shaking the collecting tin along to the music on the car radio. "I'm having a rattling good time!"

The car sped away from Larkwood towards the town centre. It was nearly six. Licking his lips, Gary imagined a long, cool pint.

A pub sign came into view and he was about to pull into the car park when he spotted a light in one of the tumble-down terraced houses a hundred yards down the road.

Gary couldn't resist it. He remembered that anyone living alone was easy prey, especially if they were elderly.

It took ages for anyone to answer. Gary stamped his feet and rapped again - louder. He was about to go when the door creaked open.

"What is it? Whatya want?" a hoarse voice asked. "Who are you?"

Gary could make out the shape of an old woman. Her features were indistinct, but he took in a wispy head of silvery hair, a tatty shawl and an even tattier cat.

"Save the Elderly," he said, holding up the tin, "charity collection."

For an instant the woman looked puzzled, then she smiled. "Oh why didn't you say? Come in, come in. It's about me heating benefit, isn't it? I knew those buggers at the council were cheating me…"

Gary's mouth fell open.

"No," he started, "you don't understand. I'm just collec…

But the old woman waved him inside.

His mind raced. Should he leave or play along? Finally, he stepped inside. Old people kept their life savings under the mattress, didn't they?

The front room was like a time capsule. In the corner, a battered black and white television set huddled next to a brown, shapeless valve radio. On a table, a wind-up gramophone towered over a vase of dried-up flowers.

Everything smacked of neglect and poverty. Gary looked at the empty fire grate.

"Aren't you freezing?" he asked. "Why don't you light the fire?"

The old woman gave him a withering look. "Cos I ain't had any coal for weeks. Can't afford it."

"Oh," he answered, suddenly embarrassed. "Sorry, I wasn't thinking."

The woman told him how difficult it was to manage on her pension. Gary listened, transfixed. As she went on, he realised that she reminded him a little of his long-dead Gran.

He squirmed. Gary had always been close to his Gran.

"Can't you get help? Can't you get money off the social or something?" he asked.

She shook her head. "Naw. They just keep giving me forms. Forms - huh! I don't want to be doing with no forms at my age."

She disappeared off to make a cuppa. Gary knew he should be turning the place over, but he didn't have the heart. Instead, he followed her into the kitchen. If anything, it was colder than the front room - and shabbier.

As the old woman filled a rusty kettle, Gary gazed at the pantry. It was empty save for a small tin of baked beans and three stale rolls.

"Is that all you've got to eat?" He couldn't hide his incredulity.

"I don't need much," she answered, "besides, I like me beans on toast."

Sipping the tea, Gary remembered his Gran's kitchen, being warm in front of the huge range; the smell of fresh baking.

It made him angry to see the state of this place. He'd never have left an old woman alone like this - cold and hungry.

He looked down at the collecting tin - Save the Elderly. Suddenly, he felt guilty. Taking money off the yuppies at Larkwood hadn't seemed wrong - but this…

He'd handed over the tin before he realised it.

"Here," he said, a lump in his throat. "It's a hundred quid. Get yourself some coal and some decent grub."

The old woman looked startled, but she took it. With tear-rimmed eyes, she said: "God bless you, son. I wish there were more like you."

He left, promising to call back to check on her. He couldn't explain it, but Gary felt good about himself for the first time in his life.

* * *

Edith watched Gary drive away. Slowly, she knelt down and stroked her cat.

"What a nice man, puss," she said.

Picking up the sleepy moggie, she headed for the back of the house. Climbing the deeply-carpeted stairs, she swung open the door to her newly decorated flat, flicked on the colour telly and checked the T-bone steak grilling merrily on the electric spit.

Without pausing, she placed the collecting tin on the shelf with the three others. Not a bad week, she told herself.

"Now, kitty," she said, "which will you have tonight - salmon or venison?"

Fiddle of the Sphinx

Ramses the First stared out the palace window, surveying the vast flat desert plain in the distance where his mausoleum was going to be. The sandy site was huge, stretching as far as the eye could see. It was awe-inspiring.

He couldn't help a surge of pride and excitement. This would finally silence his critics, especially those toffee-nosed Romans. This would show he was truly divine – a living God on Earth.

The sepulchre was going to be so large, so tall, so elaborate and richly decorated that even Ra himself would be jealous.

"Tell me again," he instructed his two newly-acquired advisors. "Tell me how grand and magnificent my burial building will be."

The first stroked his beard and held up his hand, as if painting a picture in the very air. "Mighty Pharaoh, it will be the most mind-blowing, wondrous, extraordinarily extravagant sight ever beheld by Man's eyes. It will make The Hanging Gardens of Babylon look like a window box."

"Compared to its majesty the Grand Library at Alexandria will seem a mere second-hand book stall," his companion added.

"It will be so massive it will give the Colossus of Rhodes an inferiority complex and he'll rush to change his name to Titch," they elaborated.

That's wonderful, Ramses thought. Gosh, it's going to be even better than I'd dreamt. I won't be facing eternity in standard accommodation after all – I'm upgrading to an executive tomb!

"It will take an army of slaves working round the clock some thirty years to complete it," the duo pressed on expansively. "It will use up every piece of stone in the land. Extra chunks will have to be imported and shipped along the Nile."

It would, they promised, still be drawing tourists in 3,000 years' time – and reaping benefits for the hospitality and trinket trades.

"Sounds amazing, and just the sort of thing I'm looking for," the Pharaoh conceded, then suddenly frowned. "Just, isn't it going to be a bit… expensive? The Royal treasury's a tad empty at the moment what with the famines and the plagues and the compensation claims for all the flooding from that nasty business with the Red Sea parting."

The two exchanged a knowing look that Ramses couldn't quite figure out.

"We thought you might say that, oh Mighty Ruler," the lead advisor admitted, "so we've come up with a plan."

"A plan?"

"To pay for it all – a fiscal strategy," advisor number two elucidated. "A sure-fire way for you to cover the cost of all the building work and materials, and turn in a tidy profit."

A profit! Great! I need a way of raising some dosh, Ramses thought happily. I like these two!

"We launch an investment opportunity – in the Royal household's name – for ordinary Egyptians to put their cash into the construction project. We offer all investors a ten per cent return on their cash," Beardy explained.

"With interest rates like that, money will pour in," his sidekick agreed. "Before you know it, you'll be up to your regal eyeballs in gold."

Wow! Brilliant! The Pharaoh was about to congratulate the geniuses when a thought struck him. "But how do we pay the interest to the investors – when we don't have any cash to start with?"

"Ah, that's where the clever bit comes in," the wise men said, tapping the sides of their noses. "You use the cash that comes in from the second wave of investors to pay the original savers their interest. And money from the third wave to pay the second wave and so on…"

"And is that legal?" the ruler asked.

"Oh yes, quite legal. A collateralised debt package – reverse securitised in a credit default swap. Standard banking practice. And if anyone raises any questions, you can always refer them to us… in the Holy Lands, where we'll be administering the whole operation for our usual twenty-five per cent cut."

Doubts banished, Ramses the First shook on it.

"What's this investment device called?" he enquired, pouring them all a deal-sealing drink.

"Some people call it a Persian Ponzie," they told him, "but in Jerusalem we prefer to think of it as a Sumerian shuffle."

The Pharaoh breathed a sigh of relief. "That's all right then," he said, beaming. "For a moment there I thought it might be one of those dreadful pyramid schemes…"

Prophet Margin

After an hour of searching, Roderick finally found Egelbert drowning his sorrows in The Trebuchet and Duck, sitting under the garishly painted sign of a massive boulder flying over a startled serf's head.

His friend was gazing gloomily into a pint of mead, oblivious to the fistfights, giggling wenches and assorted farm animals milling around the tavern. Indeed, Egelbert appeared so immersed in dark contemplation that he hadn't even noticed infamously flatulent "windy" miller milling around the popular medieval drinking hole.

Something was definitely wrong.

"I've been looking everywhere for you," Roderick told him, thumping down on a bench and signalling for a tankard of foaming ale to come his way. "I'm dying to hear how the job interview went. Come on - spill the beans. Did you get it?"

Egelbert sighed like a drawbridge being slowly lowered, dull eyes making pained contact with his. "Take a look at my face - what do you think?" he lamented. "Is this the joyous visage of a man who's just been appointed the King's official fortune teller?"

No, it didn't - it looked more like the face of a man who'd been told that it was his turn to muck out the dragon's stall. Roderick didn't know what to say to offer consolation. His friend had been training for the job since he was a nipper - schooled in reading runes, interpreting portents, conjuring visions and all manner of esoteric seer skills. It was taken for granted that he'd be a shoo-in for the prestigious position. Flunking it was never on the tarot cards.

"My mum is going to kill me," Egelbert mumbled, taking a shuddering gulp of alcohol, the words not just a figure of speech but the only accurate prophesy he'd made in years. "You know she'd set her heart on me working at the Castle, wearing all the fancy robes of office, getting my own water closet and endless supply of turnips. How am I going to tell her I screwed up?"

Roderick grimaced. He didn't envy his friend that daunting prospect. Egelbert's mother was a fearsome foe, the only person the local witch was frightened of, quick to pick a fight and slow to forgive; the woman who'd put the feud in feudalism.

He remembered how outraged she'd been years back when Egelbert had tried to explain that he had absolutely no aptitude or appetite for prognosticating. He literally couldn't see any future in it.

The whole village had heard her bellowing: "What do you mean, you can't be a soothsayer! I've never heard such nonsense in all my long days. Your father was a soothsayer, and his father was a soothsayer and his father, grandfather and great-grandfather were all soothsayers - the eldest male in our line has always been an oracle, right back to the time when Norman was just a name and not a term of abuse!"

When she heard today's disappointing news she was liable to spontaneously combust - hitting the roof so hard it would set the thatch ablaze.

"I don't understand how you could have messed it up," Roderick puzzled. "You've got a City and Guilds in foretelling, a diploma in divination and a grade two certificate in tea leaf reading. You've got qualifications coming out of your ears!"

Egelbert looked around conspiratorially. "Not really. The truth is, I failed the exams," he confessed in a whisper. "Every single one. I'm hopeless at all that hocus pocus stuff. I bribed the tutors to give me the scrolls."

Roderick's eyebrows met in the middle at this unbelievable revelation.

"Okay, I get it that you've no talent as a clairvoyant and your credentials are fake," he said slowly, processing the new information, "but you should have still been able to bluff your way through. You know all the mystical sounding buzzwords, and we practised the interview questions; went over all the model answers. You were word perfect, unflappable."

The shame-faced lad nodded in sorry agreement: "You betcha and I was cruising it, at the beginning."

He ticked off the questions on his fingers. "Why do you want to work at the palace? Answer: I've always admired your Majesty and think I could play an important part in helping him in his wise and kind rule of the Kingdom."

He bent back a second finger: "Have you ever had to overcome a difficult situation? Answer: well if you ignore me being caught with Squire Terrell's daughter in the haystack and convincing him that I was helping her search for a lost needle, there was still that time I saved the village from the wild boars by making wolf noises to scare them off."

Roderick scratched his head in bafflement: it all sounded great, exactly what they'd rehearsed.

"Don't tell me, let me guess which question tripped you up," he speculated. "What's your biggest flaw? You didn't confess, did you?"

"No, nothing like that. I told him exactly what we'd agreed. Answer: I tend to be a workaholic and I can let my work- life balance get out of kilter. Then for good measure I threw in the reserve answer: I can be tempted towards violence when I think anyone is being treasonous towards the Crown."

These were well clever lines, guaranteed to play to the ego of their tyrannical ruler, Roderick mused. So how had it all gone pear-shaped?

"I got wrong footed, right towards the end," Egelbert explained philosophically, "The King asked one question I hadn't predicted."

"And what in heaven's name was that?"

"Where do you see yourself in five years' time?" the sullen sybil revealed, draining his glass in a single swallow.

Special Forces

There was a flash of movement and Jackson shuddered in surprise, gasping as he fell backwards into the undergrowth. Cursing, he rolled onto his stomach, glancing rapidly left and right through the darkness to see if anyone had been alerted by the commotion.

He remained stock still on the ground, pulse racing, aiming his semi-automatic rifle through the bushes into the forbidding woodland. Straining, he listened for any snapping twig, any footfall or breath; any sign that someone was near, ready to attack.

He frantically scanned the area through his night goggles. Something dark and swift-moving had crossed his path just a second ago, he was certain of it.

Locate the enemy, his inner voice screamed at him. Get the hostile before he gets you. But he couldn't see anything through the eerie green glow except trees.

Another sweep then he spotted it! Two white burning circles stared back at him, and he relaxed.

"What's the bloody racket?" the voice in his earpiece squawked.

"A cat ran out in front of me," he whispered into the microphone attached to his flak jacket lapel.

"What!" his sergeant exclaimed.

"A bloody black cat. I spooked it," Jackson replied with a relieved sigh. "Or to be more accurate, it spooked me."

Sergeant Rawlings muttered a stream of hissed swear words over the RT, pausing only to tell him what horrors lay ahead if he jeopardised the covert mission any further.

"Not another noise," the voice growled. "Don't even break wind!"

Jackson rolled his eyes but he knew the sarg was right. He'd been clumsy, letting his attention wander. He was too good a soldier for that kind of nonsense. He had to be on his top game if he was going to come out of this op in one piece.

The others in the elite team were depending on him, as were the prisoners he'd been tasked to locate and rescue. Their futures lay in his hands.

Refocusing, he remembered the crack unit's motto. The words lacked the elegance and polish of other regiments' maxims but tonight, with the incredible unknown danger they all faced, it had never seemed more chillingly apt.

"He who screws up, dies."

* * *

The briefing had only been two hours earlier, in a draughty hut next to the helicopter pad where the Chinook was already waiting, rotors spinning madly, rear loading ramp down.

Jackson and the rest of the squad had listened intently to a hurried rundown of what sketchy information regimental intelligence had been able to pull together. The ambassador's eight-year-old twins had been snatched on a nature outing from the city, kidnapped by hostiles in the woods.

"Our information is the two - boy and girl, codenamed H and G - are in the gravest danger. We haven't time to reconnoitre the area or wait for more intel so you'll be going in blind," the Captain explained, to a low chorus of groans and profanities.

"It can't be helped," he informed the unhappy commandos. "All we can be sure of is that the enemy are dangerous and well co-ordinated. The children's bodyguards never stood a chance and were immediately overwhelmed. So we take no chances. We go in mob-handed and we go in fast. Exterminate the opposition with extreme prejudice."

A hand shot up. "The hostages? The kids? Do we know if they're still alive?" The boss shook his head. "We can only pray that they are. But there's been no ransom demand or communication from their abductors." He breathed in heavily. "But whatever the case, the embassy has given strict instructions that the bodies must be retrieved."

Others shouted questions - did they know what armaments their enemy possessed, was there any idea how many opponents they faced, did the brass have an exact location on where the kidnappers were holed up.

"That's the only piece of good fortune we have," the Captain replied to the last query. "H and G were wearing standard tracking devices. The GPS signal is still working. As of five minutes ago, their location was here…" He slapped the pointer against a large scale map of the terrain. "It seems to be some sort of dwelling right in the heart of the deep, dark forest."

The squad's drop zone would be in a clearing a mile and a half to the north of their target, far enough away for the helicopter noise to be sufficiently muffled.

"I can't stress this enough," he told the troopers as they gathered their kit and headed solemnly out the door. "Stealth is our only advantage. They know we're coming. But not from what direction. Make it count."

* * *

With the cat incident pushed to the back of his mind, Jackson pressed on, venturing through the ominous mass of trees, trying hard to ignore the eerie night creature noises coming from the thick, drooping canopy. Screeches and howls echoed above while leaves fell as indeterminate shapes leapt from branch to branch keeping pace with him.

He wondered how close the other squad members were and how they were faring. The plan was to approach individually from various points of the compass. It increased the odds of catching the enemy unawares, certainly, but the isolation of working alone did nothing for his nerves.

The target couldn't be far now, he reassured himself, and glancing down frowned in puzzlement. Just by his feet, there was a line of small white shapes leading away down the crooked, twisting path. He couldn't tell what they were. Some sort of marker?

Placing his boot gingerly on the nearest he noted that it wasn't a pebble or anything else hard. The shape gave under his weight, squishy, like bread.

There wasn't time to investigate further. In the distance, a sudden light flooded the scene and he saw the tumbledown structure he'd been searching for. A doorway had opened and a strangely contoured silhouette was standing framed in the illumination.

Risking a short, murmured message, Jackson activated his RT. "I have visual on location Zulu and one of the abductors. Am moving in closer. Will update in three minutes."

He sucked in air. Keep your cool, he told himself. Approach nice and slow. No stupid heroics. Merely observe until the others turn up. Wait to strike in numbers.

Ducking down, he edged forward, hugging whatever cover was available. After a few moments the figure went back inside, closing the door, and the area went dark again.

Excellent, Jackson thought, this was his chance to get right up to the window and see inside and, balancing on tip toes, covered the remaining ground in a soundless sprint.

He collided with the building, face pressing hard against the cottage wall, and immediately did a double take. His nose twitched. There was a smell he recognised from his childhood, an aroma that shouldn't be there - not in the middle of a forest.

It could only mean…

A cackle behind broke into his fevered thoughts, and spinning he barely had a second to take in the wide-brimmed, pointed hat, the hooked nose and the wart-covered chin before she attacked. He went to fire his gun, but the wand was faster.

The pain was incredible. But so was the agony of knowing that despite all his training and experience he'd walked straight into a trap.

Other cackling figures joined her, emerging from the shadows, wands zapping his body all over, taking him into a world of torment and he knew it was over. He was a goner.

He could hear the children screaming inside the kitchen as they were plunged into the large, boiling cooking pot, but he was powerless to stop it.

And as his head drooped forward onto his chest, his last thought was how criminally stupid the unit had been to think they could go up against a foe with supernatural powers; the ultimate special forces.

He breathed in a final time, drinking in the overpowering scents of defeat and gingerbread…

A Brush With Evil

The driver's mittened fist thumped heavily on the roof of the Hansom cab causing Lord Dudley's already racing heart to jump half way out of his body.

"We've arrived, Guv'nor. This here's the Bayswater address you gave me," the Cockney bellowed down.

Forcing himself to calm, Dudley gathered his cane and top hat and, flinging open the cab's wooden front doors, immediately gasped at how impenetrable the smog had become even on this short journey from his club. It was as if a malevolent giant's breath had engulfed every yard of the city, wrapping each building, each tree and street lamp in a ghostly gauze.

The sight was eerie, and Lord Dudley scolded himself for letting its sense of menace add to his already growing nervousness. But considering his daunting destination and who he was about to encounter, he felt his skittishness was understandable. Yet, being afraid wasn't going to solve anything. He had to be brave and resolute.

He tossed the driver a shilling, informing him brusquely: "I shalln't require your services any further."

Catching the coin in a fluid motion, the cabbie touched his forelock. Dudley stood back as the driver's thin whip flicked the horse's rump and the rickety transport jerked forward, rattled away across the cobblestones and disappeared into the swirling mist.

For a few seconds Dudley stared after it, wondering if he should have simply abandoned this dangerous madness and ridden the cab straight home; wiping the night's paranoid possibilities from his mind.

Well, it was too late for that.

The invitation in his pocket was tastefully presented, the copperplate handwriting effortlessly elegant, its signature intriguing: *from Dorian Gray Esquire, Connoisseur of Life's Esoteric and Forbidden Delights.*

The words send a cold shiver through his frame. The blatant, unashamed, hedonism of the man was breath-taking. But there was more than that. Gray's description of himself hinted at appetites that went beyond the mere erotic - to pleasures tainted with the sulphur stench of Hell itself.

And this depraved dabbler in darkness and desire had summoned him this evening. It was couched in terms that might, to the uninformed, appear a polite request but Dudley knew better, His presence was demanded at the grand townhouse.

The doorknocker was forged in the shape of a voluptuous naked woman being pleasured by a leering fork-tailed demon, head back, fangs bared. He hesitated to touch it but steeling himself, lifted the metal bar and brought it banging down once, twice, three times, the noise echoing through the large hallway inside.

For long, nerve-twisting, moments nothing happened and he considered thumping the knocker again. Then, with a deliberate, pained squeal, the door opened.

"May I assist you, Sir?"

The voice was syrupy; smooth, deep and brown. And barely above a whisper.

"I am expected by your employer," he told the servant, a coffee-skinned boy of about 14, dressed in the style of a Maharaja prince with turban and colourful, silk, Paisley-print garments.

He handed over his own business card. *Lord Selwyn Dudley, MP, KCVO. Director of the National Portrait Gallery*

The young footman bowed his head. "The master has asked me to show you to the library. He will join you presently."

With that the youth turned and gestured gently for the visitor to follow into the gloom.

* * *

Dudley had used the resources of many scholarly collections across the civilised world but he had never seen anything remotely like this libertine's library.

It contained thousands of volumes on every perversion known to Mankind, titles that tantalised and titillated: digests of unbridled debauchery, and for those of an equestrian bent guides to bridled debauchery. They shared shelf space with instruction manuals to sex in tombs, sex in dunes, sex with brooms, lewdness with whips, lewdness with whippets, and all the tomes in crisp leather bindings - especially the ones about the boudoir uses of crisp leather bindings.

"Ah, I see you're admiring my humble little assortment of bedtime reading matter," his host noted with a wry smile as he entered the room. "If there's anything there that tickles your fancy, M'Lord, don't hesitate to say and I shall make a gift of it to you, with my compliments."

Dudley blinked. "But these are…."

"Corrupt? Pornographic? Blasphemous?"

"Priceless," he said, turning to make eye contact with the ridiculously handsome stranger. "They are first editions. Incredibly rare. They should be locked up in a vault, under armed guard."

Dorian Gray laughed, his ocean blue eyes twinkling. "As should I, if the gentlemen of the press are to be believed."

Gray brought a long, onyx cigarette holder to his perfect lips and took in a deep draw of perfumed smoke. From the exotic aroma, Dudley guessed the tobacco blend to be Turkish and incredibly potent. He sensed there was something else, less benign, hidden away in the mix. Hashish?

"I can tell that you have many questions," the young man observed, daintily licking his finger tip and rubbing it over an immaculately plucked eyebrow.

"Quite a few," Dudley agreed. "I am curious to know if what they say about you is true. If the reality of your hell-bent hedonistic life is as shocking as the rumours suggest."

Gray shrugged languorously, like a cat stretching. "Of course the stories are all correct," he conceded as though any other notion was ridiculous. "If anything they underplay the wicked excesses of my deliciously selfish and nihilistic existence."

"The gambling and drunkenness?"

He nodded.

"The orgies? The deflowering of innocents?"

Dorian gestured in the affirmative.

"Devil worship? Sadism?"

"All these evil acts and more," he admitted. "Not forgetting gluttony, greed, heresy, murder and lust. I have enjoyed them all."

And yet, Dudley thought in profound puzzlement, not a sign of any of these debased, shameful and narcissistic indulgences showed in his host's unblemished and unbelievably angelic countenance.

"I can tell what you are thinking. The one rumour that intrigues you most of all. The infamous necromancer's portrait? The painting of me that allegedly ages while I remain forever youthful; that is scarred and deformed with traces of every heinous, unholy, depravity I have ever committed. Does it exist?"

Dudley agreed eagerly.

The young man didn't reply but smirked, the corners of his lips twitching.

"Yes. Of course it does. And that, my dear fellow, is why I asked you here tonight. You are a connoisseur, an authority on the portrait painter's craft. You have a trained aesthetic eye and an aficionado's appreciation of the great masters' capture of likeness and form. I seek your expert opinion."

Dudley felt himself tensing. So that was it. Gray wanted an appraisal of the infernal artwork. But what good could it do?

"My opinion on its worth? There can be no doubt that it is valueless. No-one would ever want to purchase such a monstrosity," he pointed out.

Again the smirk from his host. "Oh, you misunderstand me, old chap. I don't intend to sell it. Quite the contrary. I intend to make a gift of it, a gift to the nation. I propose to donate my damned depiction to our gracious monarch Queen Victoria, for her private collection."

* * *

Dudley thought his trembling legs might give way at any moment as he was led up the staircase to the attic, Gray holding a silver twelve-branched candelabra aloft; the sickly yellowy glow lighting their way.

Inside he was in turmoil, two instincts at war. Part of him wanted to turn, to bolt, to flee this house of evil and never return. But the other part, the unrestrained intellectual curiosity, the burning urge to know, argued seductively that this was an opportunity few had ever been granted. He might even describe it as a privilege.

Dorian was clearly deranged. The idea that the mythical monstrous masterpiece could ever be displayed in Buckingham Palace was so outrageous as to be laughable. Yet the libertine was a charming and persuasive tempter.

Presently, Gray came to a halt outside a shiny black door. Dudley guessed it must be the attic entrance by the numerous locks and the six hefty bolts keeping out all inquisitive trespassers plus, of course, the sign that said; ATTIC ENTRANCE. STAY OUT.

"This is your last chance to change your mind," the young man told him menacingly. "Once we go through this cursed doorway, there is no going back. You cannot ever forget or unsee what lies hidden beyond."

Breathing in deeply, Dudley nodded. "Proceed," he replied, a slight quiver betraying his anxiety.

It took four full minutes to unlock all the security measures and venture inwards.

The air was stale, still, heavy with the smell of ancient dust and decay. In the unnatural illumination, Dudley glimpsed the imposing shape of the picture, positioned on a wrought iron tripod, a thick velvet curtain hiding the massive portrait itself. At either side, infernal goat head relics stood guard, and on the floor a large pentangle completed the tableaux of terror.

"Steel yourself," Gray instructed.

Dudley's eyes dipped for a moment as though refusing to subject him to the deep shock and dread about to be unveiled.

With one theatrical flourish Dorian gripped the curtain and, with all the aplomb of a manic matador, swept it to one side.

Lord Dudley couldn't help himself. He didn't just gasp but screamed, and staggered backwards.

Oh my God, oh Good Lord above, it was worse than anything he could ever have imagined.

His brain fought to find the right words to describe the grotesque sight - *obscene, disgusting, horrific, repellent, hideous*; none of these seemed adequate to encapsulate the freakish, inhuman, abomination.

For a moment he thought he might throw up. "Where?" he spluttered. "Where… where on earth did you get that ghastly frame!"

Dead Men's Shoes

David couldn't conceal his irritation. "Okay, okay, so I've come like you insisted. So what's so urgent that it can't wait until tomorrow?"

Tony Barton didn't reply, but fixed his twin brother with a long, burning stare.

"I needed to speak to you, darling brother," he said, eyes narrowing in the gloom, "away from flapping ears. About my future. Or rather, about our future." He waved a hand around the empty factory. "About this place."

David tensed. "What are you talking about?" he demanded angrily.

His twin shrugged. "About injustice. About how this business should be mine and not yours. About a lot of things." He looked over the catwalk rail to the factory floor fifty feet below. "But mostly about my jealousy."

David groaned. He'd heard it all before – the I'm fed up living in your shadow routine. Everyone knew that identical twins were supposed to be equal in ability, yet Tony and David disproved the rule. While David excelled, Tony found life a never-ending struggle.

When their father died and someone was needed to take over the management of the family shoe-making business, David was the obvious choice. Tony's resentment had festered for years.

"I'm jealous," Tony went on, his voice echoing, "jealous of you, my oh-so-perfect twin brother. I'm eaten up with it. I hate you for having everything I want; everything I can't have."

His face darkened. "So I've decided there is only one solution. I'm going to become you. I'm going to kill you tonight and take your place."

He waited for David to flinch; break down with fear. However, his brother merely shook his head and stared at him in a mixture of sadness and contempt.

"This is ridiculous," David replied icily. "You're off your head, and I'm not standing around to listen to any more of this crackpot nonsense. I'm going home."

Snatching his briefcase, David hurried across the catwalk towards him. "And I don't want to hear any of this nonsense again – you hear me!"

Tony shrugged. As his twin shoved past, he brought out the hammer he'd been clutching under his jacket and smashed it down on David's head. It was a small cobbler's hammer, more suited to hitting nails than skulls, but Tony liked the irony of it. The blows weren't fatal, but David was stunned. "What the hell are you doing to me?" he gasped, stumbling.

Tony hissed: "I've told you already. I'm killing you." With that, he shoved hard. David's body flipped over the balcony rail and fell.

Tony kept peering down into the darkness long after his brother's scream had faded. Tony was motionless, paralysed by the enormity of what he'd done. His brain shouted at him that he'd finally succeeded. After all these years of silent, simmering hatred, he'd finally plucked up the courage. It had been simple, too simple; laughably simple.

A low laugh formed in his throat, but Tony choked it down. Hysteria threatened to take hold of his senses, and he fought the urge to whoop with glee. This was no time for celebration, he told himself firmly. He had a body to dispose of, and a new life to start.

Rushing down the stairway, he went over the plan he'd devised to hide David's remains. There was a large forest not ten miles from the factory, and he could be there in fifteen minutes. It wouldn't take long to pack David's corpse into the boot of the car and ferry it to the secluded clearing he'd found.

It had drizzled non-stop for two days and the ground was soft. Ideal for a spot of late-night digging. On the short drive, Tony imagined the delights that awaited him in his new identity. As David Barton, CEO, no door would be closed to him. For once in his life he'd know what it was like to command respect.

Tony grinned. He'd have David's wine cellar, the rambling mansion, the yacht and complete access to his brother's considerable wealth.

Then there was Mary. Tony had lusted after his sister-in-law from the very first day he'd seen her. He'd been enthralled by her dazzling green eyes, and her shoulder-length raven's hair. He'd wanted her the second he'd heard her tinkling, cut-glass laugh.

Oh yes, he told himself, he was going to enjoy stepping into his dead brother's shoes. It was going to be a huge joke on all those who had despised him. And the great part of it was they'd never know… never suspect.

* * *

Burying David took less time than Tony had imagined, and he grabbed the opportunity to get cleaned up at the factory.

Mustn't arrive home to my wife looking like I've been hiking through the countryside, he told himself as he settled behind the padded wheel of his dead brother's Jaguar. It smelt of leather and polish inside, and Tony savoured it. It was the smell of money, of five-star luxury. It was the smell of his future.

He lit a cigar and blew out a series of smoke rings. Then, waving happily to the night watchman, he roared out of the gates and joined the evening traffic.

It didn't take long to arrive at David's house – his house – and he smiled as he noticed that the lights were on. Great, Mary was at home. Maybe we should have an early night, he thought eagerly. After all, it had been a hard day. And what better to follow than a hard night?

She stood framed in the doorway. God, she was beautiful. His breath tightened. He wanted to grab her and crush her in his arms. But he knew that would only make her suspicious. So he made do with kissing her on the cheek.

"You're late," she said coolly, "I've been waiting over an hour. Dinner's ruined."

"I got held up at the office," he replied, wondering if she suspected. "My bloody brother."

"What did he want this time?"

"The usual." Tony shook his head. "Money. He says he wants to move away, start again."

Mary made a face. "Did you give him any?"

"A couple of grand. I know I shouldn't but I can't help feeling sorry for Tony." He headed for the cocktail cabinet and poured a generous measure of whisky, making sure to choose David's favourite brand. "I think he really means it this time… about leaving. Something tells me that we won't be seeing him again."

He watched Mary for a reaction. He was expecting disappointment, anger, sadness. Instead, he saw suspicion.

"Something's bothering you, isn't it?" he challenged, fear building. His nerves twisted. Did she know?

Mary Barton looked at him in disgust. "So you were with Tony, were you?" She snorted. "With some bitch more like. The game's up, David. I know. I know all about it. I found these."

He followed her hand to the pile of mail lying on the bureau, lying above the drawer that had been forced open.

"I've suspected that you were up to something, but I could never prove it. Not till now." She let her anger flare. "Go on, you bastard, pick them up. Read them out."

Tony touched the letters gingerly. The envelopes reeked of scent; the writing unmistakably a woman's.

"Love letters. From some cheap slut. Your little bit on the side." Mary spat venom. "It's all there. Every bloody sordid detail. Go on, David, go on. Tell me you haven't been with her this evening. Deny it."

Tony gulped, confused. How could he deny it? He didn't know anything about the affair. David had never confided in him.

He licked his lips, mind racing. He'd have to play the scene as David. "It's over," he muttered. "It's been over for months. Finished. It was a mistake, a terrible, awful mistake."

He looked up pleadingly. "I couldn't go through with it, Mary. I realised I loved you too much. I couldn't… couldn't betray your trust."

Trembling, Tony studied his sister-in-law. This was going all wrong!

"Is that it, then? I'm sorry, love, it was all a mistake?" Mary's voice was low, dangerous. "Well, it won't do this time, David. I'm sick of it. And I won't stand for it anymore."

Although the gun was small, no more than a toy, Mary's aim was surprisingly good. Tony felt a jolt on the temple, and his knees buckled. The second bullet hit harder.

He didn't have time to feel pain. Coldness seeped through his body, freezing as it spread.

Mary stood over him, raising the gun for a third time. "You know, David, I always knew it was a mistake marrying you. You were too clever, too perfect, too bloody self-centred."

She sighed. "I could have loved you, really loved you. If only you'd been more caring, more human. More like Tony!"

From Bad to Norse

Face like thunder, Bede the Venerable watched the murderous mayhem raging in the village below. From his vantage point at the monastery window high on the hill, he regarded the burning thatches with alarm and very unchristian fury.

It was finally happening. What he'd warned about. Having sacked every nearby community, the devil-eyed, bearded invaders with their terrifying, horned battle helms had sailed up the coast, leaping excitedly from their longships into the lapping waves and up on to the beaches.

The bellowing, riotous gang were running amok, pillaging and despoiling. No-one was safe, nothing could stop them as they satisfied their animal lusts - seizing meat, mead, women, skins, livestock; all manner of plunder...

As raucous screams rent the air, Bede observed the flash of battleaxes in the dancing flames. This was worse than he'd dared imagine.

Turning to the room full of trembling monks, he announced: "You see! This is exactly why I said we should never cater for stag-dos. They're always rowdy, loud, messy and upset the locals. Goodness knows what the parish council is going to say. They complained that last spring's flower festival was too boisterous, and that only featured dead heading, not be-headings!"

The holy gathering looked suitably repentant. Only one cleric dared make eye contact.

"But there was a democratic vote," Brother Augustus protested. "We all decided that we needed something to boost tourism, and that a few more visitors would put Lindisfarne on the map."

Bede snorted. "Yes, but only sedate sightseers. I thought our new influx would be burgeoning not bludgeoning. This heathen horde is going to wipe us OFF the map."

Augustus flushed but Bede was only getting started. "Have you seen out there?" he demanded. "I dread to think what our insurance liability is going to be. Next year's premiums are going to go through the roof - especially as we're going to have to replace all the roofs."

Just wait, the venerable scribe warned, things were really going to kick off when the blond-haired barbarians realised the Holy Isle didn't boast paint balling, late night strip bars or health hazard kebab shops. Thor wouldn't be the only one pissed off not being able to get hammered after midnight.

And there was a very real danger that the upset outlanders would ransack the monastery in revenge, looting the gold altar pieces and silver chalices.

"The thing is," Bede berated the men cowering in their cowls, "I don't understand how this happened. I thought we had a strict rule. We were going to vet all bookings. We'd insist on references and security deposits."

They nodded.

"Plus, we'd only offer hospitality to small select groups on organised excursions, from recognised shipping lines. Pensioners and pilgrims from civilised tribes. No Visigoths, Franks, Angles, Jutes, Gauls, Saxons - and definitely no Vandals!"

They all confirmed this with a cautious mumble.

"So what went wrong? How have we ended up with a load of long-bearded louts?"

Brother Augustus swallowed hard. "Look, there was a mix up. No-one specifically banned Danes," he pointed out. "And the nice young lady at the cruise line assured me in her booking scroll that the party was a respectable group of herring fishermen, flat-pack furniture makers, meatball manufacturers and Fjord Focus salesmen."

Bede put his head in his hands and groaned. "I can see where this is going," he volunteered. "And was the company by any chance called Viking Cruising?"

Augustus blinked in surprise. "Wow! That's right!"

"And was the person who signed the scroll a Miss Val Halla?"

"Yeah! However did you know?"

Bede sniffed philosophically. There was no point turning the cock-up into an Icelandic saga.

"Just a lucky guess," he confided.

That's the Spirit

"Hands up," the female tour guide said, "all those poor misguided souls who don't believe in ghosts."

Smiling cynically, Rick raised his hand. The other ten people in the group looked at him sadly.

"Ah well," the elderly guide remarked, frowning. "There's always one Doubting Thomas. Never mind, young man, I'll do my best to win you round. You're going to hear some blood-curdling tales, I can tell you. This is a chilling tour!"

"Okay," Rick replied to the bespectacled woman whose name badge bore the words Elmelda Wright, Spirit Guide. "Have a go by all means, but don't bust a gut. I'm a professional sceptic and no amount of tales about haunted hounds, wailing nuns and floating phantoms are going to convince me of spooks and spectres."

Elmelda nodded with a knowing smile. "That's what they all say," she announced in a breathless tone, "but they soon change their minds!" She clapped her hands. "Let's get walking. It's getting dark and we have many scary places to visit."

As they moved off into the town centre Rick grinned, despite himself. The old girl was a real ham, but he couldn't help liking her. The tourist office obviously picked a winner when they'd selected her to run the new evening Ghost Tour walks around the city streets.

He'd been uncertain when the news-editor at *The Evening Sentinel* had suggested Rick go along to do an expose on the council's new haunted hi-jinks tour.

"I'm a sports reporter," he'd pointed out. "I don't know anything about ghouls and ghosts. I interview legless footballers, not headless horsemen."

But the news-editor was adamant. "You're just the right man for the job," he'd insisted. "After five years of seeing rugby players in the showers, nothing can frighten you."

The idea, the boss explained, was for Rick to go undercover – not to let on that he was a journalist. The tour brochure promised that every visitor was guaranteed to see a ghost before the evening was through, and the paper didn't want to give the tourist office the chance to rig up anything special.

"I want you to get exactly the same tour that any member of the public would get," he said. "You know what the city council is like. If they thought we'd give them a free advert they'd have the mayor running round in a white sheet rattling his civic chain!"

Rick's task was clear. If the tour was on the level, he was to say so, but if it was a rip-off he was to have no mercy.

"Any sniff of horror-movie hokum and we'll do a front page exclusive on their phoney phantom fraud," the news-editor announced happily. "We'll grab them by the doppelgangers!"

* * *

"Okay, everyone," Elmeda Wright announced after half an hour traipsing up and down the narrow alleyways.

"We've visited the terrorised tavern, the ghostly ruins of the priory and the burger bar with the strange unearthly odours. Now, this is one of my most favourite haunts."

She nodded to the roof of the town's run-down theatre. "In 1902, Cyril E. Sharpe, the famous critic, plunged to his death from that very spot. There were rumours that he had been pushed by an outraged playwright after a particularly vicious first-night review."

Her eyes went wide in a suitably theatrical way. "Nothing was ever proved but it is said that Sharpe's restless spirit still walks the corridors of the theatre. Actors claim they can hear loud knocking."

The tour group gasped, shivering, but Rick wasn't moved. "I suppose you'd expect that from a theatre critic," he volunteered. "Knocking is a way of life for them."

A couple of the others laughed politely, but the tour guide fastened him with a beady gaze. "You shouldn't mock the departed, my dear," she warned sternly. "Not all manifestations have a sense of humour. You wouldn't want to get on the wrong side of a sulking spirit."

"Sorry," he replied, with a wink. "I'll keep quiet. Not a word… as silent as the grave."

Ignoring the jibe, Elmelda led them onwards. "Now we're outside the most haunted building in town: the reference library. It's said there are as many spooks as books housed in its dusty rooms."

Her bony finger pointed upwards to a candlelit window high up in the red-brick building. "Perhaps, tonight, if we're lucky, we shall have a sighting of Annie McPherson, the town's first ever librarian who died tragically of–"

"Boredom?" Rick suggested.

"…a broken heart after she was jilted by her lover." Elmelda's voice chilled. "Her moans are terrible to behold."

At that instant a deep, hair-raising, groan rumbled through the building and swept out across the group in the street.

"See," Elmelda hissed, pointing towards the vague woman's shape that had suddenly appeared in the flickering flame light. "It's dead Annie!"

The tour group shuddered – all but Rick. He held his hand over his eyes. What a load of a baloney!

"No wonder her bloke gave her the elbow," he observed. "No-one wants a moaning girlfriend!"

The old woman spun round, furious. "Why aren't you taking this seriously? You're seeing a ghost, a phantom, an apparition, a spirit from another plane of existence – right before your very eyes."

Rick shook his head. "Sorry. Nice try, but it's not working. What I'm seeing is Lucy Smith, the council's director of tourism, dressed up in a badly-fitting Victorian frock."

He waved up to the window. "Hi, Lucy."

The fake phantom waved back, red-faced.

Elmelda looked set to explode. "Not her," she cried. "Me. Me! I'm a ghost. I'm a spectre!"

With that the old woman started to lift off the ground. Her voice became a haunting sob. "Oh why, oh why does no-one ever believe!"

For the first time in his life, Rick was lost for words. He stared, open mouthed, as Elmelda Wright screamed in annoyance, faded to nothing and vanished. An unworldly icy blast hit the group, sending them reeling, and Rick swore he heard a huge door being slamming, angrily.

* * *

"I hope you're happy now," Lucy told him, arms folded, glaring from underneath the lacy bonnet, which was now askew. "Have you any idea how long it took to find someone as qualified as Elmelda? You've ruined everything – sabotaged the whole enterprise."

"It won't be that bad," Rick promised the tourism chief. "I'm sure you'll find someone else. You've plenty of other guides from your other tours. There must be lots of people dying to do it."

"Yes," she snapped back. "But none who had actually died!"

Nodding to the still stunned walking group, she said: "I suppose you and *The Sentinel* are going to have a field day with this. What's the headline going to be: *Petulant Poltergeist Pisses Off?* Or *How I Hacked Off the Haunted Hostess?*"

Rick shook his head. "Please, nothing so crass. We're a quality newspaper. I thought something more refined…"

Remembering the ghost's outraged and bad tempered exit, he suggested teasingly: "How about *Things That Go Grump in the Night?*"

Devil's in the Detail

The saleswoman looked at High Priest Lucius as though he was stark raving mad. He could see her fingers edging towards the button that would summon the slumbering, fat security guard from his seat by the shop doorway.

"Sorry. Can you say that again?" she asked, using the calming, level, non-threatening tone she'd been taught to employ in such tricky situations.

He sighed but indulged her. "I'd like an ogre and two demons, please," he repeated. "The ogre in green and the demons in red. I'm a bit traditional that way."

She frowned. Yes, there was no mistake. She HAD heard correctly the first time.

"Whatever makes you think we'd stock things like that," she queried, with a swallow. "We're an electrical store."

Lucius gestured to the sign: MONSTER SALE THIS WEEKEND.

Her gaze flicked between his disconcertingly intense face and the garish notice.

"Ah yes, I can see where the confusion is," she explained at length, obviously deciding he was a sad simpleton who took things too literally. "It doesn't mean we sell monsters. Last month we had a GIANT SALE, but we didn't actually sell giants."

Gotcha.

Lucius whistled shrilly and Goliath appeared, ducking his head to get through the doorway, before grabbing the security man and tucking him effortlessly under his huge, hairy armpit.

"I've got a receipt," the occultist announced smugly.

If looks could kill, he'd be history. Her nostrils flared like a pair of 70s jeans.

"Okay, okay, you win," the saleswoman conceded with ill grace, reaching under the counter and producing the hissing, snarling, multi-clawed merchandise he'd requested.

"Have your bloody demons," she declared firmly, "but I'm not gift wrapping them!"

Her eyes burned into him. "Anything else… *sir*?"

"I'll need something to feed them," he answered, thinking about the appliance shop's famously confusing name. "Three vindaloos and a garlic nan bread should do the trick."

Only Fools and Camels

De'hel Boy wasn't fast enough. The words "What the Fakir!!!" escaped his lips before he had a chance to stop them. They hung in the air for a moment, as if awaiting applause, before reluctantly evaporating into the ether with a hurt sniff.

Frantically scanning his 12th century tat and trinket shop, De'hel checked that neither of his browsing customers had taken offence. Luckily, they hadn't noticed, attention fixed instead on the large, rotating, wooden crate that had magically popped into existence.

The tourist couple were taken aback, eyes wide, but not as bemused as De'hel who barely had time to curse the fact that living in enchanted Ancient Arabia presented many dangers, (ironically, mostly from curses) before realising that the whirling dervish delivery which had scared him half out of his wits wasn't scheduled.

It had come, metaphorically and metaphysically, out of thin air.

And more puzzlingly, he didn't know what it was. Not a clue. He hadn't ordered anything from his suppliers, not even the thieves that worked for that basket case Ali Baba. And even if he had, the murky merchandise his contacts provided was far too dodgy to trust to Fed-Hex to transport.

There could only be one explanation, and wafting away the smells of necromancy and singed rosewood, he bellowed to the back of the store: "Rudni, get over here, you plonker."

Nervously, De'hel's gangly, sand-for-brains brother emerged from the relative safety of the stockroom.

"Oh! Ah! Okay," Rudders began, sweaty palms going up in submission. "It's not as bad as it looks. I can explain."

Giving Rudni a glare that suggested that relative safety wasn't the same as being safe from your relatives, De'hel motioned for his shaking sibling to approach.

"What have I told you, about buying stuff without consulting me?" he hissed.

His knuckle-headed assistant gulped. "I know, bruv, but you weren't here and it was too good a deal to pass up. It was cheap as chips - whatever chips are."

"So was the water damaged mermaid you bought last Christmas!"

Frustratingly, there was no sign of a dispatch address or any name on the still rotating, smoking box. Only the stencilled message "NO REFUNDS! NO GUARANTEES! NO USE SOBBING!"

"Who'd you buy this from?" De'hel demanded. "Who's done you over this time?"

Rudni's face went redder than a Sumarian sunset.

"I got it from De'neem," he confessed, looking towards the ceiling and trying to whistle innocently.

Instantly, the boss of Al-trotter Independent Traders - branches in Persia, Palestine and Peckham - felt the world stumble and swoon. He did the same.

"De'neem! De'neem! The Jean Genie!" he gasped. "That conniving, two-faced swindler! You dipstick. how could you get mixed up with a sort like him?"

Everyone knew that in a world of wide boys, De'neem - the demonic dispenser of wishes and woes - was a legend, responsible for every rip-off, scam and bit of criminal naughtiness in Marrakech.

Notorious for selling baggy, blue trousers where shoddy stitching meant that the bottom fell out of them (and the market) with alarming regularity, he had escaped justice on numerous occasions - fittingly, by the seat of his pants.

Sadly, the same couldn't be said about his hapless associates, most of whom now had jobs in the harem and very high voices.

What the hell were you thinking of?" De'hel muttered, his mouth drying at the prospect of sharing the same falsetto fate.

"It's okay," Rudni replied. "He promised it's all good stuff. All legit. No one will miss it - it fell off the back of an ox-cart."

In his mind's eye De'hel had a frightening image of what the evil spirit could be off-loading on them. In the past it had been Camel cigarettes made from real camels. This time, he feared, it was might be Turkish Delight made from real Turks!

Ignoring Rudni's protestations that someone had to do something to rescue their failing shop from bankruptcy, he wondered how dangerous it would be to send back the consignment. It only took a second to decide that rubbing up the lamp dweller the wrong way was asking to be on the receiving end of a charm offensive. With offensive charms.

Sighing, De'hel tapped the box making it come to a halt and, hands shaking, opened it to investigate. He could hear a voice whispering in his head that there was no way this was going to be lovely jubbly.

* * *

It hadn't always been such a struggle to turn a profit, he remembered wistfully. There'd been a time, a heady past many Arabian nights ago, when the shop had enjoyed the accolade of being the most bizarre in the bazaar. Customers flocked in, (usually with their sheep) to see what novel items of useless bric-a-brac and junk were being displayed.

Perfumed princesses to wizened wizards had marvelled at the objects described by a wag on the local gossip sheet as "Mustafa Treasures" to "Shabby Sheik".

In those days the stock flew off the shelves, especially the magic carpets. Even crazy items like razor-sharp veils - *ideal for making veiled threats* - had been snapped up. De'hel couldn't print his "the Wazir was here" tee-shirts fast enough.

But then the authorities had diverted the silk road to speed up caravan traffic and De'hel saw trade desert him - quite literally vanishing into the desert! Punters were passing but so far away they had no chance to buy anything, demonstrating that calling it a buy-pass was more accurate than anyone could have foreseen.

Desperately, he'd stocked more and more outrageous and bewildering items in an effort to rekindle interest. He'd even dabbled in the exotic plant smuggling trade hoping to win favour with his catchy ditty: "Stick a peony in me pocket and I'll fetch the souk case from Iran". But none of it worked.

Worryingly, the two bemused looking travellers still gawping at the singed crate were the only ones who had crossed the threshold in days. If things didn't pick up soon, De'hel calculated, the Al-trotters were going to be - to quote Baghdad Boycie - totally Farouked.

* * *

Peering into the delivery crate De'hel instantly experienced mixed emotions - relief that there was nothing lethal or felonious inside, but despair that the contents were the kind of cast-offs and cack that gave the Kasbah a bad name.

At the top of the chest was a consignment of belly-dancer outfits complete with tassels, frills and zils - the brass finger instruments that made a tiny tinkling sound by crashing them together. Underneath were four dozen curly-toed slippers - all left feet, various tatty umbrellas - all left luggage, sixteen well-thumbed copies of The Happy Hookah, and right at the bottom a large, rather smelly wicker basket overflowing with what were labelled as "detachable goatee beards - made from genuine goat's hair."

It was a job lot that could, De'hel reckoned, easily apply for unemployment benefit.

He groaned.

"I warned you about that shyster," he chided his blushing brother. "He's responsible for so much funny business he should be headlining the panto at the Ottoman Empire."

Ah well, better find out just how bad things were.

Plucking one of the three-inch-long stick-on beards from the basket, he shoved it on to Rudni's chin. The effect wasn't inspiring. If it was supposed to make the wearer appear trendy or sophisticated, it singularly failed. On Rudni it doubly failed.

"How'd I look?" his brother prompted hopefully. "Debonair? Handsome. Irresistible?"

De'hel couldn't lie. "To be honest, bruv, you look a bit of a tw-"

"Twit?"

"That wasn't the word I had in mind."

Just then it dawned on him. These weren't goatee beards at all but something much more cheeky and near the knuckle. Merkins! Intimate follicle replacement products.

"What-kins?" Rudni asked, frowning in bafflement.

"Merkins," De'hel repeated, voice dipping so not to scare off the paltry patrons. "You know, wigs for those who require a barnet below."

Rhodders blinked, none the wiser.

"Mon Dieu. How can I put it? Certain individuals require an artificial covering for their more personal areas."

"What people?"

"You know - nudists, nomads, ne're-do-wells, those who sin bad with sailors, good time girls, bad time girls, courtesans, gents who want to cause a stir at the public baths, male strippers intending to do a very full Monty. And then there's punters who want to keep their privates private and those turned on by hirsute pursuits. The merkin market appeals to a very small but select clientele."

"Oh!"

"Exactly." De'hel agreed. "And we've got a blooming basket full of the unmentionable things to get rid of."

It was going to take real marketing genius, he told himself ruefully. He'd have to use all his street smarts and a fair amount of his cul-de-sac cleverness.

The slogan: "Let us tickle your fancy" suggested itself, but he discounted it immediately. He also discounted discounting the raucous rugs.

Suddenly it hit him. The perfect sales strategy.

"Rudni," he asked mysteriously. "Can you do a Russian accent?"

* * *

The world of commerce and high finance was full of medieval merchants who succeeded by taking their companies public. For De'hel, it turned out, the route to riches lay in taking his company pubic.

He beamed as he looked round the busy shop and heard the music of ringing tills.

Admittedly, pretending to be a Soviet salesman was rather undignified, but it brought in the cash. And so much of it. By this time next year, he predicted, the Altrotters were going to be millionaires.

In fact, *Compare The Merkin* was going so well that he'd abandoned all other trading activities and had three factories producing the tawdry toupees round the clock.

Not that it had been instant success. It was only when Rudni - in a rare flash of creativity - suggested offering a free gift with every sale that things took off.

"And what exactly do you propose we give them," De'hel had challenged.

Rhodders had been prepared and, handing over the tiny brass musical instruments from the crate, replied with aplomb and a St Petersburg's accent: "Cymbals."

Crash, Bang, Wallop

Wayne's voice cut through Tracy like a chainsaw. "You're driving like a nervous vicar. Can't you go faster? We're going to miss the start of the race!"

Cursing under her breath, Tracy pushed hard on the pedal, imagining that she was pushing her foot on her husband's face.

The van, straining under the weight of its loaded trailer, picked up speed but Wayne still wasn't satisfied.

"It's easy to see that you're used to being driven," he tutted scornfully.

"Yes," Tracy agreed sweetly, "driven to distraction." But Wayne wasn't listening. He was too busy staring worriedly at his watch.

They'd been due at the stadium half-an-hour ago and Wayne, already wound-up by the prospect of competing in the area's biggest stock car race – the Northern Counties All-comers Championship – was growing more frantic by the moment.

That's why he'd insisted that Tracy should help him load the car on to the trailer then drive the van to the racetrack. "If you drive I'll have time to mentally prepare for the race… time to relax," he'd explained.

That was the theory, but Tracy couldn't see how getting annoyed at her driving was helping him to relax!

She'd never been able to see why Wayne was so obsessed with stock car racing. Okay, so it was fun for one evening to watch two dozen bangers smash into each other as they careered around the track. But every week? And the same drivers, smashing up the same cars? It was baffling.

Almost as baffling, Tracy thought, as her acceptance of the piles of oil-stained overalls, the weekends spent watching Wayne tinkering under the bonnet of his beloved black 'Widow-maker', and the fact that the holiday money always vanished every time the awful machine needed a new part.

She'd put up with it for years. "I must be crazy or it really must be love," she'd told Zoë, her best friend. "Sometimes I think he wouldn't notice my bodywork unless I wore a pair of headlights and stuck a number 13 on my chest."

Zoë, whose husband Larry was Wayne's mechanic, had nodded knowingly. "I told Larry once that I was having an affair with the bloke from the local garage," she confided. "Do you know what he said? Does that mean you can get me a discount on a Focus fan belt?"

Well, Tracy thought, after tonight things were going to be different. Wayne didn't know it yet, but this was his last race!

* * *

The clock above the competitors' entrance read 7.13pm as they pulled up to where Larry was waiting anxiously.

"I thought you'd bottled out," Larry told Wayne as they rolled the Widow-maker off the trailer. "The others are already doing warm-ups."

Wayne punched his friend on the arm. "Don't worry. I don't need warm-ups. I'm sizzling already, remember?" He turned to Tracy. "You going to watch me from the stand?"

She shook her head. "I'm off home. The repeats of *Sex and the City* are on the telly." As she walked away, Wayne muttered: "Women!" then turned his attention to the banger.

Tracy spun the van round and headed across the gravel car park. But, instead of going through the exit, she parked up out of sight behind a line of trucks.

Zoë came running over. "Do you think this is such a good idea?" she asked, nodding to the red stock car hidden nearby. "The boys will kill us."

"Let them," Tracy replied. "By the time they find out, it'll be too late. They always call the shots but tonight we rewrite the rules."

Ignoring Zoë's worried stare, she ran her hand over the car's gleaming bodywork. She could hardly believe they'd done it. When Zoë had shown her the car two years before, it had been no more than a dented shell with a few rusted engine parts. Thousands of man hours… woman hours… had gone into rebuilding it.

The work had been hard, but it wasn't as hard as keeping it a secret. At first, it had been a sort of game – but as the wreck slowly turned into a recognisable vehicle, Tracy had dared to dream.

Wayne had finally clinched it when he cleared a space for the Northern Counties trophy and declared: "There's no-one can beat me, Tracy love. The cup's as good as mine."

She'd asked innocently: "But what if something happened? What if someone DID beat you?"

Wayne rolled his eyes at the absurdity of the suggestion. "I'd call it a day, wouldn't I? But there's no man can out-drive me."

Now, easing herself into the car's cockpit and firing up the powerful throaty engine, Tracy heard Wayne's words echo in her head.

"There may be no man who can beat you, darling," she vowed, "but here's a woman who's going to give it a really good try!"

* * *

As Tracy drove onto the track the stadium loudspeaker blared: "And here's a last-minute, mystery entry. Give a big hand everybody to number 66, The Red Devil."

The applause wasn't exactly deafening; just enough to be heard over the bedlam revving of engines. Tracy waved to the crowd and slotted into the rear of the pack.

She surveyed the opposition. They all looked so tough. The car next to her had KILLER TERRY JACKSON painted on the side. It only took one glance to see that Killer Terry was fifteen-stone of meanness, the sort of driver who could give you nightmares – and that was before he got behind the wheel!

Tracy wondered: what if he was one of the wimps? What if they were all bigger, tougher? She didn't have time to dwell on the thought. The carburettor cacophony burst into a roar as the flag went up, held for a moment, then swept down. They were off!

* * *

Within seconds the race became a metal-grinding tournament of terror. As the gasoline gladiators sped round, Tracy winced at the bone-crushing bumps and collisions.

Half the field went out within the first few laps, smashed into submission. Cars spun madly, others limped off, some wrecked motors died with a splutter.

Keeping well back, Tracy managed to manoeuvre through the growing scrap yard. She swerved to avoid a three-car sandwich, and immediately felt a shoulder-wrenching jolt at the rear. She glanced back anxiously. Terry Jackson, teeth bared, was shunting her towards the pile-up.

Tracy braked, whipping the wheel to the left. The Red Devil started to spin, but heavyweight Terry was still connected, still shunting. Tracy cursed and fought the wheel. The tangle filled her vision and she prepared for the crunch.

Just then, a black shape rocketed into Terry, side on. It was Wayne's Widow-maker! Tracy almost cheered, until she remembered that she was racing against him.

Now free, Tracy sped off as Wayne shoved Terry Jackson's car into the pile-up. She side-swiped two rivals off the track and then realised that she and Wayne were the only two cars left.

She knew he wouldn't keep his distance for long and sure enough the Widow-maker soon roared up behind her. She weaved about for half a lap, then Wayne made painful contact – once, twice, three times…

Slowing, Tracy moved over, letting Wayne pull up alongside. He grinned and made a cutting motion across his throat. She was sure he had a nasty surprise ready for her – but not as nasty as the surprise she had for him.

Pulling off her crash helmet she turned and blew him a kiss. His face became a mask of confusion and shock. His mouth fell open. It was still open as Tracy swung the wheel hard over and sent him speeding off the track and out of the race.

* * *

The crowd gasped as Tracy got out of the car, then they started to clap. The applause became rapturous. Tracy looked up into the stand and spotted Zoë jumping up and down, cheering.

Girls Just Wanna Have Fun belted out over the loudspeakers as Tracy ran up to the winner's podium.

Wayne looked ghastly pale. "It's a joke, right?" he insisted. "It couldn't have been you behind the wheel!"

"Why not?" she beamed at him. "You saw me. Ran you right off the track. It's not my fault you drive like a nervous vicar."

She waved the trophy at him. "Isn't it a beauty? It'll look great on our mantelpiece… with MY name on it."

Wayne's eyes bulged, but Tracy pressed on. "Things are going to be wonderful now you're giving up racing. You did say you'd quit if you were beaten."

"B-b-but how did you learn to drive like that?" he gasped. "You pulverised the opposition."

"Oh that?" Tracy shrugged modestly. "I thought it was going to be murder at first, then I remembered that I'd got the best demolition derby training in the world."

She motioned to the mangled cars. "Dealing with that lot was nothing compared to fighting my trolley round the supermarket on a Saturday morning!"

The Emperor's New Wall

"**H**ow much!!!"

Emperor Hi Sing Wah did a double take, rubbing his eyes to make sure they weren't playing tricks on him. It couldn't be true. The builder's estimate carved into the clay tablet was so hefty he was amazed it didn't shatter the pottery.

He'd never seen so many zeroes in the same place. They were more bountiful than the stars in the sky, which is probably why the word "astronomical" leapt straight into his mind.

"But this is hundreds of times what I thought it would cost," he gasped.

Kneeling at his imperial feet, Royal architect Chu Han swallowed hard. "I agree it will be a tad more expensive to construct than we first thought," he admitted, "but you know how it is with a building project. There are always extra overheads."

"Overheads?"

"Yes. Like the skulls of your opponents you want to mount on poles every 100 yards, as a warning to any other traitorous subjects."

For an icy moment, Emperor Wah studied his servant to check that his underling wasn't sending him up, but the man appeared totally serious.

"And you did specify that the structure had to be so big it could be seen from the very Heavens," Chu Han added cautiously.

Ah yes, that was true, the Emperor conceded.

Shuddering, Wah recalled the fateful night a few weeks earlier where, in a surge of over-enthusiasm at a Forbidden City rally, he'd got a bit carried away and promised his subjects that he was going to construct the most wondrous fortification line ever witnessed by mankind.

"We're going to build a wall, folks," he'd told the rapturous crowd, all waving their *Make Ancient China Exalted Again* hats. "Going to build a huge wall to keep out the barbarians. I guarantee it's going to be a beauty - the most fabulous, greatest, Great Wall the world has ever known. Oh yes. Bigger, better, stronger than anything my loser deadbeat ancestors ever threw up."

The pledge had been empty bluster of course, just something to gee up the doubters who'd been criticising the dynasty, but next morning as he nursed a dragon-sized hangover he realised with horror that his supporters had taken the idea seriously.

"Did I actually say all that?" he asked, swigging the foul-tasting herbal remedy his wife shoved in front of him.

The Empress nodded, not offering him quite as much sympathy and understanding as he was expecting.

"And much more," she reported with a weary sigh. "You said it didn't matter what it cost because it was our enemies who were going to pay for it."

He'd groaned at that point, but not as loudly as days later when messengers from Mongolia returned to report exactly what they thought of his plan and their proposed financial contribution to it. The gifts of medical dictionary, crispy duck and gallon of soy sauce were very welcome, not so much the suggestion of how to utilise them in a way guaranteed to ensure he'd never wok straight again.

Replies from the other neighbouring states had followed on the same culinary and self-harm theme. It was obvious that no dosh was coming. Not a Yuan. Not a bean - black or yellow.

Which left him in a right Royal bind. Either he exposed himself as a fraud or cleaned out his own treasury to finance the vainglorious scheme.

Looking pleadingly at Chu Han, he urged: "There must be something you can do to make the wall cheaper? Isn't there an element you can miss out?"

This time it was Chu Han who checked to see if he was being sent up. "What do you suggest, Your Regalness. There are only two components involved - rock and mortar. Removing either one will be, how can I put it - problematic."

He allowed himself a self-indulgent smile. "Such an approach would most certainly be a barrier to the success of the ... er... barrier."

The Emperor didn't smile. Jerking his head towards the house of the High Lord Executioner, he reminded the official darkly: "No wall, no need for an architect. Or as you might put it, we can swop an undertaking for an undertaker."

Further threats were unnecessary. Chu Han's mind whirled like a Catherine Wheel.

Confucius says that necessity is the mother of invention. What is less well known is that he also said it could be regarded as the sibling of self-preservation.

And moments later, slapping his hand to his forehead, Chu Han squeaked: "That's it!"

"That's what?"

"The answer to our predicament. I've just thought of the solution."

The Emperor looked round furtively, then leant in. "Go on. Tell me."

Sucking in a deep breath, the architect prepared his pitch. "We don't get rid of either the mortar or the rock," he said, encouragingly. "We remove BOTH!"

* * *

"It will never work," Emperor Hi Sing Wah declared after the whole barmy idea was set out to him.

It would take a lot of guile and precision, the architect conceded, eyes bright with excitement, but they might be able to pull it off.

"Pretending to build a wall but not laying a single brick?"

"Yes."

"Telling my subjects that because the wall is magic, it's also invisible?"

"Yip!"

"Explaining that only really clever people can see it?"

"Indeed."

"And relying on the idea that no-one will admit that the infernal thing doesn't actually exist lest their family and friends think them imbeciles?"

"That's the plan in a nutshell."

Emperor Wah frowned. It sounded good but there was something vaguely familiar about the scam. Something about a king who ended up the butt of derision, mostly because of his bare butt?

"Yes," Chu agreed, "that WAS unfortunate. But you don't need to fear anything similar happening to you because we'll be the ones doing the conning."

The regal frown got even deeper.

"But people aren't as stupid as you might believe," Emperor Wah warned. "This is a dodge that they could, quite literally, see through. They only have to try to touch the barricade to expose the whole swindle."

Chu Han wet his lips. This is where the whole caper could fail. "Not if we make them too scared to ever go anywhere near the *'magic'* wall," he ventured.

This Hi Sing Wah had to hear. "And how do you propose we do that?" he enquired dubiously.

The architect tapped the side of his nose. "We'll tell them it is charged with a mysterious force. Something horribly painful that will send a million bee stings through their bodies. We could call it - I don't know - how about, electrickery."

"That's ridiculous. They won't buy it."

"They will if they see someone being electrickerifed," Chu promised. "The secret's all in making the illusion as real as possible. It's quite simple - we employ actors to approach the make-believe fortification from time to time, and section to section, pretending to touch it and then roll around in feigned agony. It will fool everyone, most importantly our enemies, especially if people observe it from far away."

Snorting, the Emperor told himself the whole idea was nuts. Yet, an inner voice whispered that perhaps, just perhaps, it was crazy enough to work. And what better way of fixing the problem, it coaxed, than with an off-the-wall solution?

One thing was certain: paying a bunch of deadbeat thespians would be miles cheaper than actually building the troublesome edifice.

"I like it," he announced after a few moments' deliberation. "But there's still one thing concerning me.

Security is going to be crucial. What if the secret gets out?"

Chu Han acknowledged the objection with a nod and, digging inside his robes, produced a tattered theatre bill. The words *"Marvel to the Silent Delights of the Radiant Dawn Mime Company"* stood out clearly at the top.

"Don't worry," he promised "I know just the chaps who can be trusted to keep their mouths shut."

Twin Piques

It was no surprise that Mark Johnson was beside himself with anger. Having a faulty replica of yourself turn up on the doorstep at nine o'clock at night was guaranteed to spark that kind of reaction.

He stared at the unrecognisable figure who'd just rung his bell, and demanded: "Who are you?"

"I'm your carbon copy," the stranger replied, in a hurt tone. "Your synthetically created identical twin. As you ordered. Don't you recognise me?"

No, Mark told him frostily, he most certainly didn't.

"You can't be my facsimile. You don't look anything like me!" he snarled. "I'm six foot tall - you're five foot nine."

"It's an optic illusion," the newcomer countered. "Plus you're wearing thicker shoes."

"And I have black hair and yours is brown."

"A trick of the light."

"My eyes are a different colour, they are further apart than yours and you have a short stubby nose and mine is long and slender."

That made the unfamiliar caller pause. He frowned, chewing at the side of his mouth, frantically trying to think up a rebuttal and failing.

"All right," he conceded. "You got me. I'm not Mark Johnson mark 2. I'm actually a perfect duplicate of Fred Chapman, your neighbour from around the corner."

For a moment Mark thought he'd gone mad. "Then what the hell are you doing here?"

The inaccurate imitation swallowed hard. "There was a bit of an accident at the laboratory," he admitted. "We experienced an unfortunate power cut and your reproduction was... eradicated. The protein growing chamber went haywire and we lost all your DNA data. So I'm here as an alternative."

"An alternative!" Mark's voice went so deep it would require a submarine to retrieve it.

His dodgy doppelganger winced.

"And you thought what?" Mark suggested sarcastically. "Let's do a switch. Send the poor schmuck a mangled mirror image and he won't notice? Is that it?"

Fred version 2 blushed. "Not quite," he replied, giving an apologetic smile nothing remotely like Mark's. "It's actually in the small print of our sales brochure, just below the printer's name. In the event of any shortages the company is entitled to make a substitution of materials to the same or greater value."

Mark slapped a hand over his face. It was that or scream. He should have guessed something like this would happen.

 He'd had doubts all along about the wisdom of ordering a genetic double but he'd been snowed under with work. Running his own company meant accommodating a never-ending cavalcade of press interviews, conferences, speeches, flights, factory openings, functions, meetings and tiresome business meals. There simply weren't enough hours in the day. And being replicated seemed the obvious way to be in two places at once.

But there was a snag. Reputable bio-science enterprises charged ruinous prices, more than he could afford, so he'd reluctantly opted for a shady, low-budget approach.

Well, the cheap-skate option certainly hadn't worked, he told himself sagely as he regarded the twisted twin. So much for being promised a spitting image, this one was an image guaranteed to make him spit!

"I'm not standing for it," he declared after a moment's furious thought. "I'm simply not accepting delivery. You can take a new DNA sample and repeat the process."

"We'd have to charge you again."

"Okay, okay," he growled. "In that case I'll simply have my money back."

The newcomer sighed at Mark's naivety. "That's not going to happen, I'm afraid. It was clearly set out in the contract. No returns, no guarantees, no refunds."

It was all the businessman could do not to throttle his erroneous alter ego. "But that's robbery! You're crooks, charlatans! Rip-off merchants!"

The botched binary nodded. "Yes, that's true, and you're not the first dissatisfied customer to have pointed this out, but you have to accept some of the blame for knowingly employing a cowboy outfit."

He leant in conspiratorially. "I mean, be fair, what were you expecting from a firm called The Clone Arranger?"

Credit Crunchie

The mob surged against the factory gates, angrily buffeting into the line of security guards. For a moment the helmeted, padded men were forced backwards – but after a few swift jabs with their crackling cattle-prods, the sea of protestors reeled and retreated. Both sides glared across the narrow divide as the taunting chats began again.

"Out, out, Oompa loompas out."

"Go home, you orange-faced scabs."

"Pack yer bags, you creepy pint-sized freaks."

Young Charlie Bucket shivered, even though the interior of the limousine was uncomfortably hot. This wasn't right, he told himself. This wasn't how it was supposed to be.

As the car slowly approached the swirling mass of bodies, his nine-year-old eyes read the placards with a growing sense of unease.

British jobs for British workers.

Wonka is a Judas.

Bar this chocolate!

It was awful. Sickening. How could the town's love for Willy Wonka have evaporated so fast, he wondered sadly. It had vanished as quickly as, well, a bite of candy.

When Wonka had laid off the men who worked in his mysterious confectionery production centre, he'd sounded genuinely sad and wracked with regret. It was the economic downturn, he'd explained on the evening TV news, holding his famous top hat to his chest in contrition.

"I might be able to take a sunrise, sprinkle it with dew, cover it in chocolate and a miracle or two… but even I can't beat global market forces," he'd remarked ruefully.

And perhaps the stunned families who depended on Wonka's superlative sweetie empire for their livelihoods would have backed him in his moment of crisis and despair – had he not kept on the oompa loompas. At minimum wage. And shipped in even more of the bizarre, diminutive, ochre-skinned figures to man the remaining production lines.

The town's outrage and sense of betrayal was unconfined – and now, it seemed to Charlie, it was about to explode.

Hatred shone from every gesticulating demonstrator and he was terrified they'd attack the lemon sherbet-coloured limousine when they spotted the Wonka logo on the side and the silent, stony-faced oompa loompa driving.

He reached across, grabbing his grandfather's hand. "I'm scared," he whispered. "Can't we just forget it all and go home, Grandpa Joe. This visit is a really bad idea. I don't care about the tour. I don't care about the free samples, honest. I just want to go home."

Grandpa Joe winked reassuringly. "Don't fret yourself, Charlie. It'll be fine," he promised. "Mr

Wonka has it all arranged. We're going in the back door. No-one will know. We'll be in and out before anyone realises."

Charlie hoped his silver-haired gramps was right. It might be fine, and no-one would know, but he still felt he was being disloyal to all his friends and their now jobless fathers.

He sighed. This was supposed to be the happiest day in his life. But somehow it felt like the saddest.

* * *

Winning an exclusive, VIP, all-areas, no-doors-barred trip to Willy Wonka's chocolate factory had sounded like the ultimate dream. Months earlier when he'd first clutched The Golden Ticket – the most valuable and sought after possession in the entire world – Charlie knew he was the luckiest boy who'd ever lived; maybe even the luckiest person who'd ever lived!

But now, the ironic, cruel timing of it hurt like an insult. How could he enjoy the tour – and the lifetime's supply of free chocolate – when his neighbours were struggling to get by on thin soup and stale bread?

That thought echoed around his brain as they rumbled over cobblestones and the car came to an abrupt halt in a small courtyard at the rear of the enormous, brooding, gothic factory.

The driver didn't budge, didn't turn round or say a word. It made Charlie feel even more uneasy.

"Look, Charlie, look," Grandpa Joe exclaimed.

Gazing to where his grandfather was pointing, he could see a scrum of small tangerine-toned figures tumble through the imposing double doors, rolling a narrow red carpet out before them. It whipped across the cobbles, opening with a crack right by the passenger side of the car.

And then, suddenly, framed in the doorway like a work of art, a twinkling, glittering, ethereal presence appeared in top hat, frock coat, checked trousers and frilly blouse. It was him: the candy man, the pixy-personality purveyor of sugary dreams, the mythological master chocolatier, the king of confectionary… Willy Wonka.

Stepping forward in one fluid motion, he tapped loudly with his cane, sending up a flurry of pink sparks.

The oompa loompas surged forward and formed an honour guard. In a jaunty walk – part swagger, part tap dance – he approached the car and pulled open the door. With a sweeping bow, he took off his top hat.

"Ah, Charlie Bucket and his illustrious grandfather," he said gleefully. "Welcome, welcome. We have so much to see, so much to do, so much to taste and nibble. Come, come, my friends. Time, tide and taffy wait for no man."

Grandpa Joe grabbed Wonka's hand and pumped it up and down. "I just wanted to say what a real privilege it is to meet you. We're beside ourselves with excitement. Aren't we, Charlie?"

Charlie nodded uncertainly. "I guess…"

"And I'm so pleased to see you," the candy king replied as they headed hurriedly for the factory doors. "We so rarely have guests and here you are…" He nodded over the tall wall at the threatening chants. "…and in one piece, too."

A small dark shape arced upwards from the crowd and spun through the air, clinking off the top of the wall and landed at their feet, bursting into flames.

Charlie yelped in surprise, and his grandfather jumped.

"Ah, more Molotovs," Wonka observed, dancing neatly round the flames as they ignited the carpet. "Must be cocktail hour."

He shooed them forward, ignoring the various orange figures frantically trying to stamp out the mini inferno.

"Personally, I don't think the bombers know what they're doing," he whispered conspiratorially. "They keep forgetting the little umbrellas and those cute maraschino cherries on a stick."

A second petrol-filled bottle hurtled through the air, but the trio didn't see it land. They were already through the opening and into the famed and fabulous factory of fondant-filled fun.

* * *

Charlie had spent endless hours fantasising about what the fabled interior of Wonka's factory would look like. Sometimes he imagined it as a futuristic, gleaming, stainless steel cathedral full of robotised assembly lines, computer control panels with dancing, flashing lights, and laser guns beaming their precise prism rays through solid shimmering sheets of marzipan munchiness.

Other times, he pictured a fairytale landscape with golden fields of barley sugar, and enchanted woods where liquorice grew on lemon-drop trees and praline pigs snuffled around the ground for buried chocolate truffles.

But as he and Grandpa Joe signed their confidentially contracts and his gaze spun round, he realised with a sinking heart that none of the dreams had prepared him for the reality. Wonka's world was, well, not really that magical. Not anymore. In fact, it looked a little squalid.

"Is this it?" he muttered, before he could stop the words pouring out. "Is this all there is?"

Wonka gave him a sharp look. "I know things aren't quite what they once were, Master Bucket, but there's a credit crunch on and the banks have cut our overdraft. We've had to make a few economies."

Wow, Charlie thought, he wasn't joking. The factory was chilly – the furnace turned down to the absolute minimum. And the lights were so dim that Charlie could barely see more than a few feet ahead. But even in the gloom he could tell that there hadn't been any maintenance carried out in months.

Wind whistled in broken windows high up on the walls, and in the middle of the grand entrance hall the once majestic river of flowing, melted chocolate lay stagnant and unmoving. Against one bank, the bewitching barge that normally transported wide-eyed guests round any part of the factory at breakneck speed, lay broken and abandoned.

Nodding to it, their host shrugged and said: "I'm afraid we'll have to walk round the tour."

"But I'm nearly ninety-seven-years-old," Grandpa Joe complained. "Keeping up with my old legs will be impossible."

Wonka thought about it for a moment and patted his arm sympathetically. "Yes, true, but if you get too far in front, you can always wait and let us catch up."

Without waiting for an answer the candy man sauntered forward, signalling them to accompany him. But to what, Charlie wondered queasily as his grandfather hobbled into first gear and they followed Wonka into the semi-darkness.

* * *

Production lines lying idle; mesmerising magical machines, cold and still. Nougat bushes untended and wilting. Emaciated squirrels precariously carrying the last of a failing crop of nuts, the levitating lemonade fountain misfiring, sending erratic bursts of bubbles across their path.

For an hour they viewed saddening sight after saddening sight. The tour was heart-breaking. Every device in the place was malfunctioning for want of a little repair cash, storerooms were empty, the miserable oompa loompa packing staff worked at a snail's pace, and an air of despair wafted through every corner of the once colourful and theatrical treasury of treats.

It was as though a huge curse had infected the building and all those who toiled inside. Charlie was stunned.

And it had affected the products themselves, he noticed sadly. Every sweet tasted flat and ordinary, as though cheaper, less flavoursome, ingredients had been substituted. The hues were muted, and the wrappers seemed made from thinner, less robust paper.

The only uplifting moment came at the end as, eyes sparkling mischievously, Wonka gestured for them to join him at the one bizarre-looking contraption that seemed to still be going at full capacity.

At one side the machine was sucking in long, brittle, hard sheets of toffee; at the other, pallets of soft, sugary, Scottish tablet.

With groans, bleeps, whistles and creaks, it relentlessly forced the opposing confections into a densely packed mass of malevolently mangled molasses.

"Orders are down dramatically for both," Wonka confided, "so I've combined them."

The appliance bucked and shuddered, and a tiny compartment flew open. Reaching down, Wonka fished out a small brown square and popped it into his mouth.

"I like to think of it as a clever, creamy, caramel concoction, a wedding of wonderful wackiness," he said, dreamily chewing. "I call it my fudged compromise."

* * *

So why, Charlie puzzled, had Wonka agreed to show them around when things were so bleak, when he was obviously fighting for his business survival? Didn't he appreciate just how bad things had got?

"Profits are down, costs are up and my sales projections are now a work of fantasy fiction," Wonka admitted. "And yes, at this rate the recession could end it all. The future's looking sour for sweets."

"But isn't there anything you can do?" Grandpa Joe prompted.

The chocolatier nodded and looked hard at his fob watch. "Yes, yes, indeed, indeed I can," he said, smiling in a mysterious lopsided way that made Charlie shiver. "And that's why you're here. You're going to make it all better."

Charlie and his gramps exchanged baffled looks.

"But how can we help?" Grandpa Joe demanded, stifling a yawn. "I'm just an old man and Charlie is barely nine. We can't save an entire candy factory from disaster. I don't see how—"

The pensioner crumpled and hit the floor, fast asleep.

Charlie wanted to yell in shock but he suddenly felt too tired to even open his mouth. It must be all the walking.

"Snoozeberry chews," Wonka explained, as Charlie lost the sensation in his body. "You sampled some earlier on. Guaranteed to send you off to the land of nod. Sweet dreams, Charlie Bucket."

That's the last thing I'll have, Charlie told himself in terror, as the darkness opened up and he fell headlong into the beckoning slumber.

* * *

Through his thumping headache, Charlie worked out that he'd woken up in Australia. Everything was upside down.

"Wha… wha… what's going on?" he mumbled, his lips still thick and numb.

"Ah, you're back with us; splendiferous," Wonka's voice said far out of his eye line. "I was worried for a moment that you'd miss all the fun."

Fun? Charlie's fuzzy brain struggled to take in what the candy man was saying.

"Why am I upside down and where's my grandpa?" he asked, woozily comprehending that he wasn't in Oz after all but was hanging by his feet from a pulley.

An oompa loompa grabbed Charlie's legs roughly and spun him round through 45 degrees. He could see

Grandpa Joe, hanging upside down on another pulley nearby.

"You all right, Charlie?" the old man yelled. "You okay? Have they hurt you?"

Charlie tried to shout back that he was fine, but Wonka's amused high-pitched voice cut him off in mid-sentence.

"Of course we haven't hurt him. What would be the point of that? We need you both intact, unblemished, in perfect condition. You might say, ha-ha, in mint condition."

Charlie's blood chilled. "In mint condition for what?" he asked, afraid of the answer.

"For the ceremony, of course."

That didn't sound good. He may only be nine but he knew when a cackling megalomaniac drugged you and hung you upside down, a ceremony was the last thing you wanted to be part of.

"It's all very simple," Wonka said, turning his head upside down and staring unblinking into Charlie's eyes. "You've seen how awful things are. We're desperate. So there's nothing for it but to appease the angry Gods of Commerce; to win back their favour…"

He paused thoughtfully.

"…by killing you both."

The candy man's face – once thought by millions to be kindly, elf-like and eccentric – darkened; a ruthless sneer replacing the wild and wacky grin.

"I know, I know. It's not exactly the way to treat guests, but times are hard and we all have to make sacrifices."

With a merry clap, Wonka signalled to the oompa loompas to lower the two dangling Buckets. Charlie shook uncontrollably, but his fear only multiplied when he was on his feet and could see what lay ahead.

"You can't," he gasped, his voice strangled and pitiful. "Not you… you wouldn't… you couldn't."

"Ah, but I would and I could. Sorry to have tricked you, Charlie, but you just have to kick the bucket!"

Dozens of tiny oompa loompa hands began forcing Charlie and his now shrieking, writhing, grandfather towards the two distinct figures in the gloom… the two distant giant figures… the two giant cane figures.

Charlie felt his mind lurching as he screamed and screamed, his glass-shattering wails merging with his grandfather's sobs and mutters.

"I did think about drowning you in a vast vat of mocha, but it lacked a certain dramatic flair," Wonka explained conversationally, as they were thrown into the basket figures and padlocked in. "Besides, it would have taken ages to clean out the vat and the health inspectors are such sticklers.

"Then it came to me. It was the Molotov cocktails that gave me the idea. That, and the fact that the oompa loompas love watching *The Wicker Man*. This is going to be so perfect; a perfectly petrifying pagan solution to all my woes."

Grabbing in panic at the wicker door, Charlie yanked and struggled; willing every ounce of power to come to his trembling hands. But it was no good. The door wouldn't budge. There was no escape. He was going to die! Grandpa Joe was going to die!

He heard a whoosh and saw a sea of burning torches hurtle toward them. The flames took hold immediately, and the oompa loompas watched in rapt fascination, orange faces captivated by orange tongues of fire. Then they started singing, and clapping, and dancing in sheer glee.

The pain lapped around Charlie, whips of burning agony flailing at his skin. He heard Grandpa Joe screech in a long unbroken cry of tortured torment and knew this was it.

He glanced desperately over as the top-hatted, frilly bloused, mad-eyed master of ceremonies beamed in delight, brought out a bag of assorted small chocolates, and declared: "Let the Revels begin..."

Turning the Tables

Spiros strode manfully across the taverna floor, flicked his waiter's towel with aplomb, and breathed heavily as he bent over Maureen Grimthorpe's table.

"Is there anything else you desire, Maurrreen? Something to nibble. Something sweet and Greek for afters?"

Maureen's eyes widened. Spiros didn't need to be a mind-reader to see she wanted something else – something not on the menu.

He smiled – a wolf's smile. He always had this effect on women, especially English women.

Hands fumbling, Maureen knocked the empty retsina bottle to the floor. Spiros tutted, bent and picked it up. As he straightened, he gazed into her eyes. Maureen melted.

"N-n-no thanks," she stammered. "Just a coffee, please. A Greek coffee."

"Okey dokey," he grinned. "For you, Maurrreen, a special coffee. Very nice, very strong, very potent."

With a suggestive swing of his hips, Spiros headed for the kitchen. Over his shoulder he could see the English woman staring after him in confusion.

This one would be easy, he told himself happily. A lonely woman tourist looking for a Greek god. And she had money. He could tell.

Filling the cup, he allowed himself a glance in the mirror. He was, without doubt, the most handsome man on the island. Spiros was sexual dynamite. And he knew it.

He put the cup on the table slowly. Huskily, he offered to walk her back to her hotel at the end of the evening.

For an instant, he thought she was going to swoon. "Oh, yes, please," she simpered, blushing.

"Then we have a date." Spiros made it crackle with promise. He hummed to himself softly as he wandered away.

Despite being a lover of life's finer things, like rich women, Spiros would never have called himself a gigolo. He preferred the term 'professional romeo'.

He'd long ago found that his olive skin, twinkling eyes and wide grin melted the wariest female heart. He'd also found English girls so easy to charm. They'd all been brainwashed by that Shirley Valentine film and came to Greece looking for romance.

Spiros never charged for fulfilling their fantasy, but he always mentioned the business schemes that needed investment. Then there were the Greek tragedy hard-luck stories.

He glanced at the waves lapping the beach as he locked up. Sure enough, the English woman was there, gazing at the moon.

"Now, pretty lady, we have a night to remember, yes?"

Maureen gulped and nodded. He put his arm around her and she trembled like a small trapped bird.

Back in her hotel room, Maureen had another drink, then another. Spiros' handsome face drifted before her eyes.

"You are a very beautiful woman," he murmured, nibbling her ear. "Why you on your own?"

Maureen thought of telling him about the boring husband, dead-end job and unfulfilled suburban life, but she had a feeling he'd heard it all before. Instead, she said: "It's a long story. We've better things to talk about."

They kissed. He moved her towards the bed, but she protested. "You're going too fast," she gasped. "I need time, romance, wooing."

Spiros blinked, baffled. "But we are in love, no?"

"No – I mean, yes. But I'm shy. You undress first, it will help me overcome my nerves."

The waiter frowned, but started unbuttoning his shirt. Then he took off his trousers. His hands moved to his underpants – but never reached them. The door opened and a huge man burst in.

"What the Hell is going on here?" the stranger bellowed. The same thought raced across Spiros' mind. He didn't have time for an answer.

"My wife!" yelled the towering figure.

"My husband!" yelled Maureen.

"My God!" yelled Spiros, and he dived through the open window head-first.

Maureen shook her head. She never ceased to be amazed at how gullible Mediterranean types were.

"See that?" she asked the grinning intruder. "We're two storeys up. I hope he's all right."

George, Maureen's long-time partner in crime, leaned out of the window. "He's okay. He's running full-pelt. He's even faster than that flamenco dancer in Benidorm."

Chuckling, they picked up Spiros' trousers and emptied the pockets. Chequebook, mobile phone, credit-cards, bank notes and coins. Not a bad night's work.

As George rang a cab, Maureen found a snapshot with Spiros cuddling his children.

"Oh Spiros, you're such a naughty boy – and what a pretty wife," she murmured as she found his home number and dialled.

The woman who answered didn't understand at first, but Maureen knew she'd soon figure it out.

"I have a message for Spiros," she said. "Tell him to stick to tending tables. They're less likely to turn on him. My name? Oh, say Shirley rang… Shirley Valentine!"

Judgment Day

The Dark Lord's hellish features were crimson, anger making them even redder than the hissing, swirling flames on his infernal throne.

The remaining Three Horsemen of the Apocalypse all gulped and trembled, trying to avoid his withering, scorching, searching stare. Looking down at their feet, they felt like naughty schoolboys summoned to the headmaster's study.

"I set you one simple task," the Feared One snapped, from his elevated position hundreds of feet above. "Bring about the destruction of mankind. End the world. Make the biblical prophecies come true. But somehow you numbskulls managed to screw it all up."

He looked down at the paranormal parchment, smoke spiralling up from its edges, and growled in disbelief.

"It's a bloody farce. A total defeat. Nothing destroyed. No terror and anguish. No gnashing of teeth and suicidal despair. Mankind happily untroubled. You might as well have not bothered. The holy men call this gospel Revelations, and I'm beginning to see why. Believe me, your crap performance has been a revelation to me."

Sighing wearily, he listened intently as one of the two flanking demons whispered into his ear.

"And that's another thing. You clueless clowns even succeeded in getting one of your bloody team annihilated. How'd that happen?"

Pushed forward by his fellow allegorical purveyors of woe and wretchedness, Famine coughed apologetically. "Oh, Mighty Lord, it was the archangels."

"Archangels?"

"Michael, Gabriel, Peter. They were waiting for us. They jumped Death before he was ready. He never stood a chance. It was metaphysical murder."

The Dark Lord's brow furrowed. "Rather ironic, isn't it? Killing Death? Who says God doesn't have a sense of humour? But blaming your opponents isn't going to get you off the hook."

"It wasn't fair," Pestilence volunteered, rushing to the defence of his colleague. "They had wings. They could fly out of danger. But we were saddled with horses!"

"And the odds were stacked in their favour. Have you read the Bible? They had more prophets than us," War added.

As the Infernal Emperor's mighty fist came down with the force of a thousand thunderclaps and the churning heavens shook to their core, the cowering equestrian trio realised that emphasising their lack of prophets wasn't the trump card they'd hoped for.

"I just don't understand it," the grizzled, wrinkled, ancient master of mayhem said, half to himself. "You are supposed to be the best. The famed Horsemen of the Apocalypse, the legendary A-team. And you turn out to be a bunch of lacklustre losers."

Slowly, determinedly, inscrutably, he studied Famine, Pestilence and War in turn.

"It's a tough one," he said finally, his voice icy. "You all sound like you've messed up. But I've come to a decision."

His finger jabbed down from the clouds. "Pestilence – you're fired!"

The Gospel Truth

Mrs Jonah always knew when her two-faced sleazy husband was lying - and he was definitely telling a whopper now. She gazed deep into his weasel eyes searching for any clue that he was about to crack and tell her what had really happened.

He'd been missing for 72 hours, probably shacked up with some floozy from Sodom and Gomorrah or out getting smashed with the sozzled Samaritans. Last time he'd vanished for that long he'd been giving it large with Goliath, and running up a damages bill of biblical proportions.

What he hadn't been - then or now - was trapped in the stomach of a piscatorial predator; of that Mrs Jonah was certain. If that tall turbot tale was true, then she was the Queen of Sheba!

"So let me get this straight," she said, dripping sarcasm. "You're telling me that you spent three days and three nights in the belly of a huge fish? It just swallowed you up, did it?"

He agreed, face deadpan. "I can't tell you how frightened I was. It was dark and horrible and smelly. I thought I'd never get out. It was a miracle."

"And you were rescued when passing sailors heard you indulging in some choir practice?"

He nodded. "I was reciting hymns - you know, to HIM, the big boss. The acoustics were amazing, just like a cathedral."

"Not scales then? You weren't practising scales? I'd have thought would that made more sense with you being gobbled up by a giant haddock."

"I didn't call it a haddock," he reminded her. "I said it was a leviathan."

"Oh yes, I remember," she agreed with a chillingly reasonable smile. "But didn't these sailors think it was a bit odd you warbling away inside your *leviathan*?"

Jonah hesitated, wondering whether he'd over-egged the ambitious alibi and should come clean and admit the last thing he remembered was passing out in a Jerusalem belly dancing club.

"Not really," he said, with sudden divine inspiration. "I told them, it's true what you've heard, boyos... everyone sings in whales."

Sting in the Tail

Miriam Hodges screwed up the letter and threw it across the room.

"What does he mean, they're not good enough! How dare he! Doesn't he know who he's dealing with?"

She hugged the pile of stories to her chest. To Miriam, a writer of thirty years' experience, her stories were her babies. They were her whole life, and she wouldn't tolerate them being attacked, especially not by a publisher who was still wet behind the ears!

For six months since she'd come back out of retirement, Miriam had been trying to get Mark Dixon to accept them. She knew Mark, the son of her old publisher, was putting together a horror tales collection for the Christmas market, and she'd knocked out a handful of ghoulish chillers for it.

She'd expected a four-figure advance. What she hadn't expected was Mark's reaction; he'd thrown them back at her!

Miriam's brow furrowed, remembering their last meeting. Mark had shaken his head, saying: "Times have changed, tastes have changed. You can't just waltz back from retirement and churn out the same old material, expecting it to sell."

Showing her the firm's interactive website, Facebook forum, and author podcasts, he'd continued: "The world's moved on since Dad's day. The industry's moved on. Your brand of twee, comfortable stories haven't. They're dated, old fashioned. Face it, Miriam, these stories are practically antiques. They belong in a museum, not a bookshop."

Antiques! Belong in a museum! Miriam had hardly been able to contain her anger. "But my books still sell!"

"Yeah. Old aunties buy them. Libraries take them, but that's it. No-one regards you as a modern writer and no sane publisher is going to take the risk of putting you into paperback."

Miriam had bitten the back of her knuckle in frustration. "So I might as well give up and die, is that what you're telling me?"

"What I'm saying is you've earned your retirement. Just enjoy it. Travel. Sit in the sun. Spend the royalties. Bask in your well-deserved reputation. Just don't write anything."

"But I'm a writer!"

A strange expression crossed Mark's face. "No, Miriam. Not anymore."

* * *

Miriam had almost given up after that. It took several stiff gins to bolster her battered ego. She knew Mark was wrong. She still had hundreds of marvellous stories inside her – gripping stories, exciting stories, scary stories.

"I'm as sharp as I ever was and I'll prove it," she'd hissed. "I'll get my stuff into that bloody anthology without that young fool knowing it."

The answer, she'd reckoned, was simple. She'd submit her work under a pseudonym. Then, when it was safely in print, she'd reveal her true identity and watch gleefully as Mark ate his words.

That thought had buzzed in her brain as she churned out a string of sure-fire sellers – *Logan's Rune*, a tale of ancient witchcraft in a creepy isolated New England village; *Caught in the Act*, a chiller about a maniacal, murdering thespian; and *Soul Survivor*, a story about a woman passenger on the Titanic saved from a watery grave by making a pact with the Devil.

But, despite weeks of effort, her spine-tingling tales – written in the name Edith Allen Poe – all came back. Rejected.

True, Mark wrote notes saying her work showed maturity and a pleasing style, but the word 'dated' kept cropping up.

Miriam was determined. She was going to appear in that horror anthology even if it killed her! Arthritic fingers aching, she fed a sheet of paper into her trusty fifty-year-old typewriter.

"Okay," she muttered. "I'll change the style, liven up the characters and tighten the writing. I'm not going to be beaten."

This time she put her whole heart into it. *For the Chop* was a classic macabre masterpiece. Diners disappeared from a steak restaurant which never seemed to have any meat deliveries.

She was pleased with the yarn which cleverly blended cannibalism, shock and terror. Mark wasn't.

His rejection note was short: "The idea of *For the Chop* is intriguing, but the story is predictable. The ending is telegraphed from about the half-way point.

"Such a story would have worked some twenty-five years ago, but today's reader expects a yarn with a clever sting in the tail."

Miriam's rage would have put a volcano to shame.

"Predictable! Telegraphed to the reader! You stupid, arrogant, spotted-faced little twerp. My tales were scaring people half to death when you were still soiling your nappies!"

She was consigning the letter to the bin when a thought struck her – an unusually fiendish thought. Sting in the tail, eh? You want a surprise ending? Okay, sonny boy, I'll make sure you get one!

Smiling grimly, she reached for her pile of envelopes.

* * *

Not many came to the funeral. The weather was atrocious and, besides, most of his former colleagues were away at the big book fair in Frankfurt, but Miriam preferred to see the poor turnout as a sign of Mark's unpopularity.

A few employees turned up, a couple of long-faced friends, but that was all. Only Diane, Mark's PA, seemed upset.

"It's just not fair," she sobbed. "Mark was so young. He had his whole life ahead of him. No-one deserves to die like that."

Miriam, watching the coffin being lowered into the ground, nodded absent-mindedly. "No. I suppose not."

"I just can't believe it. Who could be so cruel, so cold-blooded?" Diane blew her nose noisily.

"I mean, who could have hated him enough to post him a live scorpion?"

Ram-a-Lama Ding Dong

"Holy sh–"

His Most Exulted and Celestial Reverence the Dalai Lama slapped his hand across his mouth just in time to prevent a string of obscenities turning the Tibetan air blue.

Blinking, he rubbed his eyes unable to accept what he was seeing. Instead of a benign, portly man with bulging stomach and holy aura, the statue that had just been unveiled was an animal – a towering twenty-foot woolly vision with horns.

He gazed darkly at the beaming young monk leaning proudly against the plinth of his creation, clearly delighted at the results of his six-month labour.

"Whaddya think, Chief?" he urged. "Isn't it great? Isn't it just what we need to bring in the punters?"

The Dalai Lama wanted to answer: "I can't believe it's not Buddha" but had an eerie feeling he'd heard the phrase somewhere before. Instead, he spluttered: "But it's a… a… sheep!"

The monk made a face. "Technically, yes. But actually it's a ram. Much more impressive."

His Most Holiness' various lives flashed through his mind as he tried to recall what he'd ever done to deserve this. The orders he'd issued had been clear – build a new religious edifice to boost the dwindling numbers of pilgrims making the arduous climb to the temple high in the Himalayas. Create something traditional; demonstrating that this was a place to seek enlightenment, inner knowledge and spiritual peace. He hadn't mentioned anything about livestock.

"It's in your honour," the monk explained. "I researched your Heavenly Highness' birth chart and discovered you are an Aries. Hence the ram."

For someone who was supposed to be at one with everything, the Dalai Lama found himself at sixes and sevens. It was all too much. He couldn't be totally sure – all the monks looked identical with their shaven heads, bare feet and orange robes – but he had a horrible feeling it was the same initiate who'd suggested a range of Buddhist t-shirts emblazoned with slogans like:

Reincarnation: in my next life I'm coming back as evaporated milk!

Keep Karma and Carry on Meditating!

When you get angry, stop and count to Zen!

Nirvana – you've heard the music, now try the state of mind.

He knew he should be furious, but reminded himself forcefully that the demented disciple had meant well. Besides, he suddenly had an idea of how he could rescue something from the mess.

"Fetch me some paint," he instructed. "And rollers, lots of rollers."

Several hours later, His Most Exulted and Celestial Reverence smiled serenely as he surveyed pilgrims making their way upwards – hundreds of them – all attracted by the dazzling sunlight reflecting off the top of the newly glistening statue.

The yellow hued ram was gaudy, admittedly, but he knew once word spread the curious would be – he allowed himself an inner chuckle – flocking to see it.

It just went to prove the golden rule of all faiths, he mused wisely. If you gild it, they will come…

What the Dickens!

Bob Cratchit groaned loudly, loudly enough to be heard over the buzz of the counting house computers. "But, Mr Scrooge, it's just not fair! You do this to us every Christmas. We just want to go home and be with our families!"

Ebenezer Scrooge swayed on the ladder in surprise and let the highly-coloured tinfoil streamers drift downwards like snowflakes. His light-up Santa Claus hat slid perilously over one eye.

"But we always have a Christmas party," he told his senior clerk. "It's a company tradition. You know – egg-nog, mince pies and a good old sing-song? The big binge. Furtive flings behind the filing cabinet. Secretaries faxing photocopies of their backsides to our Birmingham office. Punch-ups in the car park. It's a great night."

Bob Crachit sighed. "For you maybe, but not for the rest of us. We appreciate the thought, and don't think we're not grateful. But none of us likes Christmas any more. We think it's a terrific waste of time."

Ebenezer's mouth fell open. "But everyone loves the Chrissy party blowout. It's the highlight of the year!"

Bob silently waved a hand around the high-tech trading floor of Scrooge and Marley International Investments PLC. There wasn't a Christmas card, a clump of mistletoe or an advent calendar in sight. Even the usual dog-eared artificial tree had gone – manhandled earlier through the office shredder.

"Sorry, Mr Scrooge," he said, "but we're sick of it. You're the only person left in Canary Wharf who looks upon Christmas as anything more than a pain in the wallet. This year we're all giving it a miss."

Blinking in surprise, Scrooge held up his sprig of holly. "But what do I do with this?"

Bob Crachit bit his lip and shrugged, resisting the overwhelming temptation to reply with the obvious, painful answer.

* * *

That night, as he enjoyed a televised carol service, Ebenezer couldn't help feeling sorry for his trusty staff. Getting them into the festive spirit was going to be a problem and no mistake, he told himself, but he was determined not to be beaten.

He was about to ring Bob and invite him over for a drink, when the TV picture unexpectedly vanished – replaced by a snowstorm of interference.

Tutting, Ebenezer fiddled with the controls, but couldn't get the picture back. Instead, as he watched, a face formed in the swirling dots… a face he knew well – his old partner Jacob Marley.

Ebenezer thought he was going to faint. "I-I-I don't believe it," he gasped. "You're dead. Buried. Gone. It can't be!"

Jacob grinned. "No-one dies on television, you know that. There are always reruns." The phantom winked. "Think of it this way. I've been sent to give you a message."

"A message? What message?"

"A message from our sponsor. Mend your ways, Ebenezer Scrooge. You must abandon all this Christmas nonsense before it is too late!"

Ebenezer was baffled. Christmas nonsense? When Jacob was alive, he'd enjoyed the annual knees-up more than anyone.

"Ah, but I was a fool, an empty-headed fool," the spirit told him, reading his thoughts. "Like you, I savoured the delights of plum pudding and crackers. I, too, watched the Queen's Speech and bought over-priced wrapping paper. But I was wrong – oh so wrong. Christmas was my undoing and it shall be the end of you, Ebenezer!"

Shaking his head, Ebenezer told himself that he was having a hallucination. Snatching the TV remote, he flicked to another station, but Jacob's features continued to stare at him. Anxiously, he clicked through the channels but the ghost image remained chillingly the same.

"Learn by my mistake," his dead partner pleaded. "Remember my festive fate. I died at the office Christmas party, choking on a mince pie while groping Mavis from Accounts. That nibble did for me. Don't let it happen to you!"

Ebenezer was terrified, yet stood his ground. "You've got metaphysical sour grapes," he said. "Just because your Christmas didn't work out, there's no reason why I shouldn't enjoy mine."

At that Jacob wailed, almost knocking Ebenezer off his feet. "You're a fool, Ebenezer, completely Christmas crackers. I see there is no alternative but to show you the error of your ways." His voice dipped low and menacing. "Tonight you shall be visited by three spirits…"

"Spirits? Oh goody, I love a nice spirit at Christmas. Especially that one with whisky and cream. What's it called?"

"DO NOT MOCK!" the screen boomed. "These spirits will show you things that will chill your blood. Things that will touch your very soul. Fear their coming, Ebenezer Scrooge, fear them…"

With that, the television switched back to the carol service.

* * *

After several drinks, including the one with whisky and cream, Ebenezer convinced himself that he'd been the victim of one of Bob Crachit's famous practical jokes – like the exploding toilet seat in the executive loo during the wages dispute.

I'll have to think up some prank of my own to play on him, he thought happily, as he fell asleep clutching his copy of Delia Smith's Yuletide Yummies.

He was dreaming about revenge when a hand fell on his shoulder and a deep, rasping voice whispered: "Wake up, Ebenezer. It's a spook at bedtime!"

Blinking, he sat up groggily and gazed in shock. In an instant he was wide awake, shaking. There, floating above him, towering above him, swirling above him, were three incredible visions from Hell.

The first nightmarish figure was decked out in flashing Christmas tree lights. The second wore a garish orange sweater, several sizes too big, and sported a necklace made up of bottles of cheap aftershave. The third wore only a black hooded shroud. Together they looked like a Stephen King version of The Three Stooges.

"W-w-who are you?" Ebenezer demanded.

"I am the ghost of Christmas Past," said the twinkling apparition, "and this…" He pointed to his nearest companion. "…is the ghost of Christmas Present."

The second phantom gave a little wave.

"And the character on the end is the ghost of Christmas to Come. He doesn't speak much."

The shrouded figure on the end nodded slowly – like a coffin lid being lowered.

Ebenezer grasped the duvet tightly. "Wha-what do you want with me?" he stammered. "I've done nothing wrong. You've got the wrong bloke. I love Christmas. I can't get enough of it."

"That," said the first ghost, "is the problem. You've got it bad. You're suffering from acute tinselitis!"

* * *

"Let me get this straight," Ebenezer repeated after the apparitions had spent half-an-hour explained things to him, "you're here to make me despise Christmas?"

"That's the idea," the spirit of Christmas Past agreed. "We've only one night to save you from yourself so we're keen to get cracking. Haunting's not cheap and we charge double time after midnight."

Ebenezer shrugged. "Sounds a bit bizarre if you ask me, but go ahead. But you won't find anything in the past to upset me. I remember the Christmases of my childhood, and they were wonderful. Lovely times, warm, friendly times… joyous times."

The phantom made a face. "Joyous times? I've never heard such sentimental clap-trap in all my life." It soared over to Scrooge's side. "Memory plays tricks, my schmaltzy old friend, and it's done a whole Paul Daniels routine on you."

With that, it snapped its fingers and Ebenezer felt himself lifting, being sucked towards the grandfather clock. Swirling round and round, he gazed as the clock's hands whizzed backwards and he was transported back through time – back to December 25th 1964.

The twirling stopped abruptly. He gasped, watching himself at the age of six, sitting by the Christmas tree, sobbing.

"You don't remember this, do you?" the spirit whispered in his ear. "You don't remember getting a smack because you wouldn't kiss your Great Auntie Enid. Remember her horrible moustache and how sick it made you feel?"

Ebenezer swallowed hard. He had forgotten that. The ghost pressed on. "And what about the nauseatingly cutesy pixie suit your mother made you wear. Remember what a fool you felt in it, and how the other boys used to jeer?"

Scrooge shivered in recollection. "And what about the Christmas party piece you had to sing for all the adults. Little Boy Blue. Yuck!"

Suddenly, Ebenezer felt hot. The ghost's promoting brought back a tidal wave of bad memories. How could he have forgotten all those awful family parties with his hateful cousins and grandmother complaining all the way through lunch that the sprouts were too hard for her false teeth?

"Okay," he conceded. "Perhaps it wasn't all that great back then, but I've had some fantastic Christmases as an adult."

Sighing, Christmas Past brought them back from Scrooge's childhood. The apparition patted his colleague on the back. "Over to you, Present old lad. Tell it like it is."

"I am the ghost of Christmas Present," the second spirit announced, "or rather, I am the ghost of Christmas Presents. The spirit of all those naff, totally tasteless, useless gifts people give you at Christmas."

He clapped his hands, and the flat began to fill with a treasure-trove of tat.

"Behold," he said, "the flotsam and jetsam of Christmas consumerism. The over-priced, tweely packaged, cringe-making stuff no-one would ever buy at any other time of the year."

Gazing at the mountain of packages, Ebenezer gasped. There were space-age silver Christmas trees, tablemats with Dickensian street scenes, a plastic nativity scene with light-up baby Jesus, a Mr and Mrs Snowman cruet set, a Santa Claus jewellery box that played Rudolf the Red-Nosed Reindeer, ceramic cherubs, artificial candlesticks, a family-sized tin of Monarch of the Glen shortbread – enough Yuletide yuckiness to fill a dozen mail-order catalogues.

"And that doesn't include socks, hankies, individually packaged Olde Worlde English Marmalades or…" The phantom pointed sadly to his jumper and aftershave bottles. "…the old favourites."

Stunned, Ebenezer realised the ghost was right. Most Christmas gifts were over-priced rubbish – useless items even a junk shop wouldn't handle. He had cupboards full of the stuff he'd never even opened!

Confused and suddenly depressed, he looked across at the third ghost. "Of all the spirits, you are the one I truly fear the most," he said, with a gulp. "Show me what horrors are to come."

Silently, the shrouded figure pointed a bony finger towards the television set and it flared into life. On the screen Ebenezer could see the Crachit family.

The scene in their front room was bedlam. Bob and his wife knelt on the floor, hands over their ears. All around them chaos reigned as the kids re-enacted the sacking of Carthage.

Electronic toys beeped and whirled, computer games screamed, a karaoke machine boomed out '*so here it is – merry Christmas*' and the kids yelled at the tops of their lungs, trying to be heard over the ear-splitting din.

The children berated their parents for not buying enough batteries, while Bob tried to explain that the shops were shut. The kids were in no mood to listen! Even saintly Tiny Tim jumped up and down in a tantrum, snapping his walking stick.

"Is this the future then?" Ebenezer asked, shuddering. The ghost didn't answer, but Ebenezer needed no reply. He gazed hollow-eyed at the three spirits.

So this was the true face of Christmas. The face he'd been too naive and blind to see. Childhood misery, cheap shoddy gifts and an electronic nightmare to look forward to. It was awful. Now he knew why everyone groaned at the very mention of the word Christmas.

"Okay," he told the rapidly fading phantoms. "You win. I'm convinced."

* * *

First thing next morning, Ebenezer leapt out of bed and phoned his secretary in a panic. Glenda sounded surprised: "A flight? Today? But where?"

"Anywhere," Ebenezer replied, "Timbuktu, Outer Mongolia, the South Pole. I just want to escape this Yuletide lunacy. Away from crowded shops, turkey leftovers, family quarrels, department store Santas, piped carols and the hundredth rerun of *The Sound of Music!*"

Although Glenda was convinced that her boss had flipped, she promised to do her best. She rang back after an hour.

"I've got you booked one-way on an Air China flight to Shanghai," she announced. "It wasn't easy at this time of year, but I pulled a few strings."

He hung up before she had a chance to wish him Merry Christmas, and began packing. Somehow he managed to block the idiotic festivities from his brain, even getting the taxi driver to stop humming *I Wish It Could Be Christmas Everyday* with the promise of a large tip.

At last, Ebenezer was safely on the plane. He settled back in his seat, relaxing, letting every thought of Christmas drain away. As the engines roared into life, he allowed himself a satisfied smile. He'd done it! He'd escaped the Boxing Day blues. He was leaving the mistletoe madness behind!

"Boiled sweet?" the stewardess asked, thrusting a small basket at him. Gratefully, he popped one into his mouth. The sweet's musty flavour took a moment to burst on his taste buds, but when it did he started to gag.

"Bah," he spluttered in disgust, "humbug!"

Brought to Book

The voice was thin, pale and weedy. When Emma looked up from the enquiries desk, she found its owner was thin, pale and weedy too.

"Excuse me," the man said sheepishly, "I was wondering if you had any books on... bodybuilding."

Emma regarded his lanky, ungainly, beanpole figure and, smothering her laugh with a diplomatic cough, pointed to the back of the library.

"Non-fiction section. Physical culture," she informed him. "They're quite heavy, so give me a shout if you need a hand lifting them."

The young man, wearing a misshapen scarf that looked as though his mother had knitted it, blinked a couple of times. "Err... um... I will," he answered, the joke totally lost on him.

For the next half hour, Emma watched the puny-looking man, transfixed by his clumsiness. He looked so fragile that a gust of wind might snap him in two.

Finally, he staggered over and thumped a heavy hardback down on the counter, handing over his library card. Emma read the name on the plastic strip: Colin Crabtree.

"Don't strain yourself," she said mischievously, as she stamped the book with its return date. "Remember, if you feel any discomfort while reading stop and take a rest."

Colin Crabtree grinned awkwardly. "Oh... no, I won't. I'll be careful," he promised. "Only one chapter at a time."

As he left, Colin struggled to open the stiff door. Luckily, a passing pensioner helped him.

Two weeks later, Colin returned the muscleman manual. Emma didn't see any difference in his physique but at least, she noticed, he didn't seem to have as much trouble carrying the book.

He took out a slightly heavier volume. Two weeks after that, he borrowed another – this one even thicker. By the time he'd worked through the whole exercise section, Emma was beginning to see an improvement.

"That's the last fitness book we've got," she said. "What are you going to do now?"

Colin gave an uncertain smile. "I thought I might have a look at this." He held up a slim book with a jazzy cover. It was entitled: *Improving Your Image*.

"Wise choice," Emma agreed solemnly.

* * *

Her shifts meant that Emma didn't see Colin for more than a month. When she did, it was amazing. She hardly recognised him.

The pudding bowl haircut was gone, replaced by a smart, modern spiky styling. The dandruff had gone too; so had the mail-order clothes.

The man standing in front of her was wearing a sharply tailored designer suit, and fashionable black leather coat. The owl-like thick spectacles had vanished, replaced with discrete contact lens.

"What happened to you?" she asked, stunned. "What a difference!"

Colin blushed and looked shyly at his new Italian shoes. "I just followed the advice in the books," he confided, fidgeting with his button down collar. "I'm not really sure it's me. Do you really like it?"

"Like it?" Emma repeated. "Like it? I love it. It's fabulous. It makes you look almost normal."

Colin beamed. "In that case, I'll stick with it," he said, then frowned. "If you think I should?"

Nodding, Emma stamped the book he was borrowing. It was: *A Beginner's Guide to Being Assertive.*

"Are you sure you want to take this out?" she asked teasingly.

"I think so," he answered, chewing his bottom lip for a moment. "But I could always be wrong…"

* * *

Colin was confident he wanted the second assertiveness book and downright insistent that he had the third.

Returning it days later, his body language signalled that the self-help handbook had been a let-down.

"It was okay as far as it went, but I wanted something more dynamic, more definite," he declared, dropping it on the counter with an impatient sigh. "It was a bit wishy-washy. A bit lame!"

Emma could hardly believe her ears. "It's a very useful volume," she told him. "It's helped lots of people learn how to stand up for themselves."

"Well, I don't know how," he replied, with a dismissive wave. "It was far too apologetic. Haven't you got anything better; stronger?"

Sniffing, Emma clicked on the central library's computer database, replying that it would take her a while to find it. Colin sat down on her chair without being invited and told her: "Fine by me. I can wait."

His manner suggested he'd sit there all day if needed. Feeling a little bewildered, Emma suddenly had an idea. She went into the storeroom and brought back: *Getting Your Own Way – A Winner's Guide to Success.*

"Now that," Colin said firmly, "is more like it."

* * *

Emma was busy stocking the shelves when Colin came up to her and tapped her on the arm.

"Hi," he grinned, "I haven't been in for months. Missed me?"

"Every day without you has been heartbreak," she replied dryly. "Where have you been, big head?"

Colin shrugged expansively. "France, Spain, Italy. Since my last promotion, I've hardly been in the country for two minutes." He sighed contentedly. "Still, all that time in the sun has given me a chance to work on my tan."

Emma looked slowly down Colin's well-proportioned torso and shook her head. Was this good-looking, confident man really the shy, insecure weed of a year ago?

"I suppose this is goodbye," she said. "You've read it all. There's nothing left for you here."

"Oh, I wouldn't say that," Colin answered, producing a single red rose. "There's still one section I haven't mastered."

Before she realised he'd grabbed her tightly and they were kissing. Emma was going to struggle, but she was enjoying it too much.

She didn't remember much about what happened next. Colin mentioned dinner and a weekend in Paris, and she nodded mutely.

As he swept her out to the waiting taxi, Emma glanced at the sign they'd been standing under. It said: *Romance...*

Animal Crackers

Noah was getting one of his headaches. He could sense the tension tightening behind his eyes. It was always the same at these debrief meetings - the petty arguments and point scoring, the accusations and blame dodging were doing his head in.

I'm 600 years old, he told himself, I shouldn't have to put up with these hassles. It's been 18 months since the flood waters abated, for Heaven's sake. Surely by now my three knucklehead sons should have tied up all the loose ends and put the whole nautical episode to bed.

But no. Shem, Ham and Japheth couldn't sign off on the project. They kept going on about doing a proper statistical analysis, seeing what lessons could be learnt, implementing new strategies, tightening up on procedures. As if there would be another watery apocalypse anytime soon.

"You know," Noah told them wearily. "I'm beginning to regret sending you all to business college." And looking down at the agenda for that afternoon's meeting, asked: "What's this rubbish about health and safety?"

Shem flashed him an irritated look: "It's not rubbish, Father. Do you realise that we crammed two of every creature in creation into a rickety wooden tub only 450 feet long, 75 feet wide and 45 feet high; a boat held together with pegs and tar! It's a wonder that there wasn't a disaster."

Noah was going to point out that the drowning of virtually everyone on the planet could be considered a disaster, or at least a major mishap, but he was still trying to figure out what the ark's dimensions came to in good old-fashioned cubits. Why did people have to keep changing the measuring systems?

"I did say to Shem at the time that we needed a proper risk assessment but he wouldn't listen," Ham interjected. "We had lions lying down with lambs, cats and dogs in the same section and made spiders and flies bunk mates. It's a miracle we still had any animals left at the end."

Japheth nodded in agreement, adding: "And there were no inflatable vests or lifeboat drills. It was all very amateurish. I dread to think what our insurers would have said."

Probably, help, help, it's getting very wet, can I climb on your boat, Noah thought wryly. He ran his eyes down to the next item: future uses for the vessel.

"Okay, who wants to kick off on this one," he enquired.

Ham coughed modestly and walked over to the flip chart. He quickly drew three pie charts.

"Having carried out extensive market research and put it to focus groups, the overwhelming public response was that the ark remains a wonderful community resource and should be put to some sort of heritage use. Perhaps a flood museum. These diagrams show the breakdown of ideas based on various socio-economic demographics."

Focus groups? Public response?

"We asked our wives," Japheth explained.

"And who is going to visit this museum?" Noah asked, despairingly.

"Our wives," Shem replied. "And of course there are the four of us, plus Mother."

Noah couldn't help himself. Rubbing his forehead he asked whether ArkWorld would generate a profit, which immediately brought the room to an embarrassed silence. The boys admitted shame-faced that they hadn't quite got round to doing long-term earnings projections. Although, there might, the sons suggested, be the chance of a stock market floatation.

"And don't you feel that our star attraction being stuck half way up a mountain is going to pose some accessibly problems?" he suggested.

"We've got that covered. We're going to build a funicular," Shem explained, to an encouraging nod from the other two chuckle brothers. "The Ararat Adventure Railway."

Gazing up at the heavens, Noah mouthed: "C'mon, Lord. What did I ever do to you? Give me a break."

The rest of the afternoon passed in a similar crazy fashion. Noah listened gobsmacked, wondering whether his wife had dropped all three sons on their heads as babies and hadn't told him.

"So that's agreed," he said, trying to bring the meeting back on track. "We've still got 800 tons of animal… er … waste products to dispose of but, on the positive side, it should give us a record-breaking crop of rhubarb. Just proving the old saying: where there's muck there's boracic…"

The boys smiled dutifully.

He glanced at the agenda. They'd covered everything. Well, almost everything - there was one thorny issue that the group had studiously avoided discussing; had been ducking for months. No-one was going to admit messing up the most vital task in the entire messianic rescue mission.

Noah prompted: "Any other business?" and waited expectantly. But no. The trio all shuffled up their papers and filed out, Japheth muttering to his siblings: "I told you the funicular was a crazy idea. We should go with a chairlift instead then we can get into the ski holiday business."

For a moment, their father thought about calling the numbskulls back, insisting that they dealt with the unspoken problem that overshadowed them for months - that someone had made a mistake counting off the disembarking animals.

But he decided it could wait for a more diplomatically appropriate occasion. In the meantime, he reached into his desk drawer, and pulled out a sticky bun.

Sighing, he tossed it to the bulky shape in the corner saying: "You know, Nellie. It's true what they say in the business world. No-one ever dares mention the elephant in the room."

Bang on Time

I'm gasping for breath, forcing my aching legs to keep pumping. Although my quarry isn't far off in the night, it's a struggle to make up the distance. He's fit, motivated, and surging with adrenalin.

I've almost killed myself keeping up since he bolted from the van intercepted at our roadblock miles back, but my discomfort doesn't matter. I have to stop him or hundreds – maybe thousands – will die.

He's hoping to disappear into the darkness, black boiler suit and balaclava letting him melt away. He's been taught how to evade capture at the training camp, and is quick thinking and resourceful.

But I'm a professional too, Special Forces – and it's my job to stop him, whatever it takes, no matter how bloody it gets. He's carrying a medium-sized bomb in a backpack and that's slowing him down, just enough for me to keep him in my line of sight.

I fire off a shot but it misses, ricocheting off the ground at his feet. Without breaking stride, he turns left, rushes up to a chain fence and clambers over. I fire again and the bullet whines off the metal.

I follow, leaping the fence with a curse, and fall awkwardly. Then I'm up – and he's off again, diving through a side doorway into a factory unit.

I chide myself for letting my radio drop early on in the chase. I could have called back-up, got a chopper overhead. But I'm on my own.

The inside of the factory is even darker than the street outside. I pull out my night-sight goggles and watch as the chilling blackness turns an eerie unnatural green and I can see. My luck has changed. He's trapped. There's only one doorway and I'm standing in it.

"It's no use," I yell. "You're cornered. There's nowhere left to run. Give it up."

The terrorist shouts back a dismissive, angry reply but it's in a language I can't understand.

Then I hear the distinctive ticking and tense up. He's activated the bomb – its timer is going full pelt. I've just seconds to act.

My carbine rattles off several bullets. He dances jerkily like a puppet as they hit and, as he falls, he tosses the bomb into the lines of shelving nearby. It knocks over several crates and the crash echoes as they burst open.

I'm dashing over, the last of my energy set on getting to the device before it explodes. The ticking is louder… tick, tock, tick, tock.

But as I reach for it I notice there are more ticks, more tocks. Dozens and dozens. What's going on?

And then I see what has happened. The floor is covered with piles of ticking boxes. The bomb is lost somewhere underneath.

Sweeping my gaze round I see the sign and realise my troubles are only beginning. I'm not in just any factory – I'm in O'Grady and Company, Clockmakers.

And I'm running out of time…

Road Hogs

Charlie Wolf growled in fury at the TV. On the flickering screen, an army of unwashed hippies struggled with an equally large army of yellow-jacketed security guards.

Screams and threats issued from the set but Wolf – C.E.O. of Wolf Construction PLC – didn't have to watch the melee to know what was happening. Those fools at the site had bungled and let the dungaree and lentils brigade interfere with the tree-felling operation.

He couldn't believe it! His site staff had allowed the rag-tag collection of malcontent misfits to stop any attempts at cutting down the oaks.

Angrily, he punched the buttons on his intercom and told his cowering secretary: "Get me that clown Jenkins on the line – NOW!"

He glared at the set. An excited female reporter gushed: "Thirteen people had to be taken to hospital following renewed violence at the motorway site deep in the big dark forest today as anti-road protestors clashed with construction workers and bailiffs.

"Friends of the Earth have claimed that bailiffs used excessive force and have demanded an inqui–"

Wolf muted her with a flick of the remote control, studying the battle's progress in eerie silence. After a second the phone rang and he snatched it from its receiver. The site manager's voice was a mixture of awe and terror but there wasn't enough terror in it for Wolf's liking.

"I'm coming down there to sort this out personally," he thundered down the line to his quivering employee. "I'll show you how it's done. I'll get those yobs off the land in no time. They'll wish they'd never put their Jesus-sandaled little tootsies on my site!"

* * *

The helicopter pilot signalled that they'd be arriving in ten minutes. Wolf nodded curtly and went back to his troubled thoughts.

He'd always known the Forestway project would be controversial, but he hadn't been prepared for the tidal wave of protest it unleashed. Before he'd known it there were questions in Parliament, newspaper leaders, online petitions, demos, and damning TV documentaries.

"Sir, this is only the beginning," Derek Jenkins had warned him. "The whole forest community is united in opposition and they have press backing. We're going to be made out to be the bad guys. Perhaps we should think again."

Wolf, who took great delight in being big and bad, had snarled: "This road is progress, and nothing gets in the way of progress… especially when it's linked to my profits!"

At first, it looked as though Wolf would triumph. To demonstrate that he meant business, he'd taken out court injunctions against the protestors – including the Bruin family, whose thatched cottage had been the first threatened by the bulldozers.

The family – father, mother, baby and blonde au pair – had defied the courts; refusing to budge. They'd been carted off to jail – to endure an apt diet of porridge. But their plight had galvanised opposition, and now months of work were being held up by an ill-assorted bunch of welfare bums, lefty pinkos and nature nuts.

It was beyond comprehension. It was also, he told himself, beyond a joke. Every day of delay cost the company £200,000 and the shareholders were already becoming restless. And restless shareholders were the one thing on earth that frightened Charlie Wolf.

The company chopper circled the site 300 feet up. Below, he could see the two groups skirmishing like soldiers in an ancient war.

"We can't land round here," the pilot told him. "I'll have to find a field. There are too many trees."

Wolf gave one of his famous predatory grins. "Not for much longer," he promised.

* * *

"Okay," he declared. "Tell me what the Hell is going on. Why aren't those men working? I want those oaks down now!"

Derek Jenkins swallowed hard and nodded to the rickety structures high above their heads, his hardhat bobbing comically.

"It's the tree houses," he explained. "A group of fanatics have barricaded themselves inside. We can't get them out. It's dangerous to take the hydraulic platforms too close."

Wolf glared up at the shanty town of stick sheds balanced precariously amongst the spreading branches. The shacks looked as though one gust would blow them away.

"What goes up, must come down… especially with a little help," he muttered darkly to himself.

Snapping his fingers, he demanded: "Who's the ringleader?"

"I suppose it's a bloke named Trotter," the site manager replied nervously. "He and his two brothers seem to be the most vocal."

"Where are they now?" Wolf asked.

The manager pointed high into the forest canopy. "Up there."

Taking off his jacket, Wolf Construction's boss threw it to Jenkins.

"Hold on to this for me," he said, climbing into a hydraulic lift, "I'm going up there to talk to them."

* * *

It only took one look at the piggy-faced brothers to know that Trotter was an ideal name for the tree-loving trio. They were plump, unwashed and had rings through their noses – the complete porcine picture.

"We're not shifting, you fascist git, not by the hairs on our chinny chin chins, so save your breath," Ziggie Trotter – the eldest brother – declared, folding his arms defiantly. "None of us is moving till you give up murdering the environment. You can huff and you can puff but you won't blow this tree house down."

Charlie Wolf puffed – on his cigar – and leant against the swaying platform, 25 feet up.

"That's more or less what I thought your attitude would be," he replied with a shrug. "Don't worry, I wouldn't dream of blowing your house down."

He paused, savouring the look of bemused surprise that crossed the three porky faces. They didn't appear to have a brain cell between them. They were obviously Media Studies students.

"I'm not going to blow your tree house down. Heaven forbid." He fished into his pocket. "No, I'm going to blow it up."

Chuckling deeply, he produced a stick of construction dynamite and lit the fuse from his Havana.

The platform descended rapidly. As it plunged, he lobbed the explosive tube in through the tree house window. The bang, he noted with extreme satisfaction, was very loud.

* * *

The TV news-crews recorded the falling confetti of leaves, sticks, squirrels and newly-extinct eco-warriors, and transmitted the pictures in their lunchtime bulletins. There was also a shot of Charlie Wolf looking distressed. He loved pretending to be distressed.

Voice trembling, he told reporters: "What has happened here is a tragedy. A terrible, terrible accident. We are all stunned by this senseless waste of human life. I personally want to pass on my sincere condolences to the families of these poor unfortunate young people, so cruelly cut down in their prime."

Suppressing a snigger, he added that Wolf Construction would be planting a tree in their memory! Charlie loved irony – almost as much as he loved pretending to be distressed.

He was back in the office examining plans for the next phase of the roadway when the phone rang again. It was Jenkins.

"Don't tell me there's more trouble on site, because if you do I may just have to torture you," he growled.

Jenkins gulped, his voice a strangled sob. "I'm afraid there is, sir. I'm so sorry… so sorry!"

"You will be," Wolf snapped back. "You're fired!"

* * *

Wolf didn't know which irritated him more – the fact that there was a line of protestors linked arm in arm across the path of the bulldozers or the fact that they were singing *We Shall Overcome* out of key!

"All right! All right! Enough with the singing," he snarled at the demonstrators, who'd been joined by assorted dwarves, gingerbread-eating children and placard-carrying witches. "Shuddup and send out your spokesman."

The group parted and a young girl walked forward, a slight figure in a crimson hooded cape.

"Are you responsible for this rabble?" he demanded.

She nodded determinedly. "I am the elected spokesperson but we have no hierarchical structure. We are all equals: all brothers and sisters united in our environmental struggle. We are a band of like-minded activists joined in our burning sense of outrage at your–"

"Save it for the cameras," Wolf hissed, cutting her off. "I don't need self-righteous speeches. I don't need lectures in conservation, sisterhood or class struggle.

What I need is to know what you tree-hugging weirdos intend to do."

The girl jerked her head towards the red-brick woodman's cottage lying in the way of the demolition machinery.

"We intend to save my grandmother's home," she replied. "We're holding a mass sit-in. You can't knock it down if we're all inside. Even you wouldn't do that."

"Don't count on it, doll," he yelled, climbing up into the cab of a gigantic yellow tractor. "You're about to find out that the property market is crashing. There's no such thing as safe as houses!"

The engine bellowed like an angry bull awoken from a deep sleep. The tractor shook with mechanical rage; Wolf revving the motor violently.

"Oh, what a big digger you've got," the girl gulped.

"All the better to crush you with," Wolf replied.

"Oh, what a big ball and chain you've got."

"All the better to smash down your walls," he chuckled and let out the clutch.

The bulldozer charged forward, sending bushes, protestors and barricades flying.

The girl flung herself across his path, arms outstretched – red hood billowing out in the whirlwind.

"Stop! Stop!" she yelled. "This is immoral, insane, criminal. You can't get away with this. Don't you know that the wolf is always beaten? Look at any fairy story. The wolf always comes to a sticky end. You can't fly in the face of narrative convention."

Charlie Wolf, the fabled big bad-ass of Wolf Construction PLC, thought about this for a moment then shrugged.

There was a soggy, squidgy sound as he ran over the girl, followed by a deafening crash as the first bricks tumbled. With a dozen mechanical snorts, the rest of the demolition fleet moved in.

"There's another narrative convention. Much more important," he said, howling triumphantly. "Fairy tales are always grim!"

An Ugly Way to Go

Barry squinted cross-eyed in the searing midday sun, grinning both at the eight rifles levelled straight at him and at the large crowd of peasants who'd turned up to watch his impending demise.

He knew smiling wasn't the normal reaction of victims facing a firing squad, but he had the advantage over most condemned men – he actually wanted to be there.

True, he'd have preferred not having to die if there'd been any other way to achieve his desired goal, but it was a small price to pay. You didn't become a legendary revolutionary by playing safe and keeping out of harm's way, he told himself. Troubadours didn't sing rousing and tearful ballads about your deeds if you lived to cash in your annuity and tend your rose garden.

And while he'd have preferred meeting his end anywhere else but this fly-blown, God-forsaken, barren, dust hole of a town, he knew you had to go where the work was. And there currently wasn't much call for dashing iconic rebel leaders to battle the jackbooted forces of evil in Milton Keynes. Well, not in the part where he hailed from…

No, this was what he wanted – a death that would make him famous, revered, loved; a glorious heroic end that would make men envy his devil-may-care bravery and women swoon at his memory and curse the Gods that they hadn't thrown themselves at his feet and begged to be swept away to his bed.

This was the end that would finally make people see him for what he was – not how he looked.

Okay, he admitted to himself – as a line of sweat trickled from his forehead down the side of his squat, misshapen nose – ending his days in a gunfight would have been more courageous; and better for the legend of Barry the brazen bandito. But bullets were bullets after all, he reasoned, and they'd kill him just as certainly whether it was here tied up in the town square or free in the cactus covered foothills in an ill-fated ambush on the Federales' payroll convoy.

At least this way the common people – his beloved people – would see him fall for their cause.

"You wish a last cigarette, Senor?" the mustachioed Captain asked him, interrupting his reverie.

"I don't smoke," Barry replied, adding with a wonky wink: "Besides, they can kill you and I wouldn't want to take the risk."

If the officer got the joke, he gave no sign of being amused. But he did nod slightly, acknowledging the bravado of a fearless hombre who laughed at death.

"Well, maybe some other request… a last wish."

That was a tricky one. Barry frowned, pondering, huge bushy eyebrows meshing into one hairy caterpillar. A fabulous meal would be nice, maybe a glass of a decent chardonnay and an after dinner mint. But considering the rancid beef he'd been served up and the beer that tasted as though it had already been through one pistolero's body, he knew it was unlikely he'd find anything in this depressing dump that was remotely palatable.

"I tell you what," he said, after a few moments deliberation. "It would be good for my image if my last request was a long, lingering, sexy embrace from the prettiest girl in the village."

At this the Captain did a double take. "You want a girl to kiss you?" he said, obviously surprised.

Barry sighed. He'd half expected this comeback. It was the same reaction he got whenever he suggested that he'd like to enjoy the company of a gorgeous woman.

"Okay, I know I'm not the most attractive man in the world," he began defensively. "In fact, I know I'm downright ugly…"

"Repulsive is the word I would have used, Senor."

"But that's why I got into this whole South American freedom fighter lark. It didn't matter that Che Guevara had a face like the back end of a bus or that Fidel Castro was no oil painting. The chicks digged them. Rough-hewn liberators with beards and guns give off this hunky, sexy vibe – they're babe magnets. That's what I wanted a slice of."

"And did it work?" the officer enquired.

"Not really," Barry admitted regretfully, with a crooked, buck-teethed grimace. "But I thought the poetic firing squad death would at least make some women fancy me after I was gone."

A look of pity touched the Captain's stern countenance. "That is sad, so sad, my friend. I promise I will do my best to get the prettiest girl in the village to kiss you. You deserve at least one moment of happiness."

Barry nodded his thanks to the man. For a vile, swaggering, mad-dog lackey of a corrupt, oppressive, fascist regime hell-bent on trampling the long-suffering peasant population to dust, he seemed quite a decent sort.

128

So this was it. Only moments to go. Only a few seconds before he would meet his maker. Goodbye hideous Barry – hello the swashbuckling fable of *fanciable* El Barry.

He watched the Captain approach a ravishing beauty who was dressed in a flowing gypsy gown – an almond-eyed girl with wild raven-black locks, red full lips, and bare sensuous shoulders.

In a silent mime the Captain spoke to the smouldering senorita and jerked his head towards the post where Barry was tied. The girl looked stunned and threw up both hands.

Enticingly, the officer produced a roll of banknotes and began peeling them off. With each note, the girl hesitated, but it was no good. Even being offered the equivalent of a year's wages wouldn't sway her.

Barry cursed his repellent Quasimodo features as the Captain turned and shrugged helplessly. Well, at least the chap tried.

"I have let you down," the army man said on his return, voice heavy. "I was convinced… even with the way you look… that I could persuade her. But I failed. I am sorry."

Don't worry about it, Barry told him. It was a stupid request anyway. "Let's just get on with it, shall we?"

Nodding, the officer signalled for the drum roll to begin and held up the customary rough canvas bag.

"But I don't want a hood," Barry exclaimed. "I want to see the faces of my executioners."

"Yes, Senor – but they don't want to have to see yours. They're having lunch just after, and the boys are already complaining of feeling a bit nauseous. It would be a great favour if you would just…"

Dejected, Barry agreed. It was the final insult, the last of many. What a ridiculous way to go, what a stupid idea the desperate Che Guevara thing had been, he suddenly understood. Even the reward offered for his capture hadn't been handsome!

As the Captain put the hood over his head, Barry heard a whisper. "I have one question, my friend. Something that has been troubling me. Whatever made you think that becoming a radical rebel would make you attractive?"

"It was the last girl who turned me down," Barry replied as the firing squad's guns cocked. "She gave me the idea…"

The drum roll ended abruptly and the square rang out with eight deadly whip-crack bangs.

"She told me I had a face like a guerilla," he gasped as he slumped.

Sale of the Centuries

Blinking in disbelief, I read the incident report. It didn't make any sense. Why would anyone want to steal three hundred 40kg sacks of out-of-date, sub-standard, condemned cement powder?

And more to the point, how the Dickens did they smuggle it off the base? They'd have needed two lorries and a forklift truck. And that's the kind of thing the MoD guards at the main gates would have noticed – even on an off day.

I rubbed my eyes. Unfortunately, as chief of security at The Institute, the sticky conundrum had landed in my in-tray. And I hadn't a clue what to do. No-one was going to miss the stuff, but the fact that someone could just wander into one of the country's most top secret and militarily sensitive research establishments didn't say much for security, or the longevity of my job.

I could just hear my boss's stinging words: "Ah, I see we're now operating an open door policy, Jack. God knows who is going to turn up next. Today a builder on the make, tomorrow a fanatical terrorist. Perhaps we should just open up the place to tourists."

Ouch! I had to solve the puzzle – and fast.

Gloomily I reread the six-paragraph document. It had to be an inside job… but who?

The door opening broke my train of thought. That and the lights suddenly going out.

"Oh, bloody hell," a voice growled from the darkness, "I've stubbed my bloody toe. I can't see a damn thing!"

131

Reaching into my top drawer, I took out the torch and shone it over at Frank Peters. My deputy was hopping on one foot, rubbing the other through his shoe.

"That's the third time this week," he complained. "They keep knocking the power off. It's buggering up my Sky Plus box. Can't you do something about it?"

"What?" I asked deadpan. "Fixing your Sky Plus box?"

He made a sour face. "You know what I mean. Stopping the geeks in Y lab causing chaos every time they play with their science projects. I swear it's worse when they watch Star Trek. I bet they're trying to invent warp drive."

I told him I couldn't intervene. I had no authority over the scientists based at The Institute and that went double for the pizza-munching, t-shirt and bearded skateboarding weirdoes who worked on the highly classified Dark Matter Project.

No-one had a clue what they were working on. Maybe it WAS warp drive! All we knew was that they were running up equipment bills big enough to fund an entire shoe collection for a dictator's mistress. Usually people gave the long-haired, unwashed nerds a wide berth, which was probably a good idea as the geeks were responsible for at least half of the explosions that kept the builders permanently mixing concrete to repair the base.

"I'll have a quiet word," I promised. "I don't know what the problem is. They have their own nuclear generator. They shouldn't be tapping into the main base supply."

The lights flickered back on.

"That's better," I sighed, putting the torch back for the next time. "Now, Frank, what did you want to see me about?"

My number two frowned. That was bad. When Frank's brow creased it always meant trouble.

"It's Doc Mitchells," he said, referring to the facility's longest serving egghead. "I'm worried about him. He's acting screwy."

That was hardly news. "He's always acting wacky," I pointed out. "He's the original mad professor."

"Yes," Frank replied. "But this time I think he's really flipped."

I opened my arms in an expansive 'go on, amaze me' shrug.

"He's blabbering on about us all being in deadly danger from quantum paradoxes and alternative timelines and inverse space feedback loops…"

I gazed back, unimpressed.

"…and he keeps raving about some missing cement."

Ah! Now I was impressed.

＊ ＊ ＊

"Thank God you're here, Jack," Doc Mitchells yelled as we strode into his laboratory. "There isn't a moment to lose. The whole of reality could unravel at any second. Something amazingly unbelievable is happening."

I could see why Frank was so concerned. The Doc was frantically scrambling around the floor, madly throwing papers around, snatching up one after another and peering at them through a large magnifying glass.

133

"Yes, yes," he cried. "Here's another one. It's incredible. Absolutely impossible. It defies all logic. History is literally rewriting itself as we speak."

I didn't care if history was rewriting itself, or scribbling its own laundry list, all I was concerned about was the location of my missing masonry mix.

"Look, Doc," I began, "I can see you're busy on… *something* …and I don't want to interrupt the end of the universe or whatever but I need to ask you about–"

"Anomalies," he gasped, grabbing first me then Frank by the lapels. "Anomalies in the sequential framework of time and space. See? Look, look…"

Eyes popping, and white coat flapping wildly, he snatched a grainy black and white photograph from the pile and thrust it eagerly into my hand. Sighing, I glanced at the image. It showed a group of First World War soldiers, relaxing in a trench between bombardments.

"Very nice," I told him, "but unless they happen to have a stash of pilfered pollyfilla hidden up their sleeves I don't get the relevance. What am I supposed to be looking at?"

His finger jabbed at the left hand side of the snap. "There," he said, "the third man in from the right. Don't you see it. Don't you notice anything unusual!"

I peered at the figure. He looked much like the rest of his comrades, apart from some wires coming down from his ears.

"A radio operator of some sort?" I ventured.

Mitchells didn't answer but threw down another photo. This time the scene was Victorian. Three young girls not older than eight, each pretty and delicate… and each balanced precariously on a space hopper.

I grabbed the snapshot and stared at it through his magnifying lens. "But that's not possible. It can't be…"

Frank picked up the WWI scene, and stared in disbelief at the man with the wire. "Not a radio operator. It's not a radio – it's a Walkman. A bloody Sony Walkman. He's sitting in Flanders Field in 1917 listening to a personal stereo."

My mind spun. Today was getting too weird, even by Institute standards.

"They're fakes," I told him and the Doc. "They've got to be. You can do wonders with computer trickery. They are good, I'll grant you that, but they're doctored images. Just a wind-up."

Frank didn't seem convinced. "They look like the real deal to me. You can't do touch up work that detailed on Photoshop."

"They ARE real," the Doc yelled. "That's what I'm trying to tell you. Something is altering the course of history. Consumer items, household appliances, gadgets are popping up years, centuries, before they were invented."

He gathered up more pictures; flashed them at us. "A portrait of Sir Walter Raleigh in the National Portrait Gallery – introducing tobacco to Good Queen Bess." He paused for effect. "He's holding a packet of 20 filter tipped!"

Another picture.

"And this: a period wood carving of William Shakespeare at the height of his fame… sitting at his laptop keyboard!"

And another.

"Alexander Graham Bell. Snapped after inventing the telephone… the mobile telephone!!!"

I held up my hand. "Enough," I said. "I get the idea. But I still say they're all fakes. This is one huge practical joke."

Mitchells gave me an old fashioned look. "Well, how to you explain the conference call I got not thirty minutes ago from my colleagues at the British Museum."

My stomach lurched. There was something about his tone that told me I was about to drop down the rabbit hole.

"They've just unwrapped an Egyptian mummy that's lain undisturbed for three thousand years. They know he was a high ranking official – from the artefacts in his tomb. And the quality of his sarcophagus… and the Rolex wristwatch he was wearing!"

* * *

There had to be a logical explanation for all of this. Just like there had to be for the vanished consignment of cement. And I suspected the answer to both mysteries lay in the same place.

"I'm starting to have dark thoughts," I confided.

"Dark Matter thoughts?" Frank enquired as the lab's lights flickered and dimmed on cue.

"Yip, I think it's time we had a little chat with our secretive friends about the power cut problems and exactly what the Hell it is they're doing in there," I said grimly.

"I'm glad to hear it," a female voice behind me muttered dryly, "because I've got quite a few questions of my own."

136

I didn't need to turn round. I'd recognise the sarcastic edge of Karen Turner's tongue anywhere. How long had she been standing there? What had she heard?

"I have a baffling illogical puzzle on my hands," the Chief Inspector informed us. "Something completely irrational. And whenever that happens, I always know where to come… and who to blame."

Giving me her best withering stare, the local police force's Disaster Containment Officer reached into her uniform jacket and brought out a medieval religious miniature.

"This turned up in a local antique shop. It is, I'm told, totally authentic. The craftsmanship is unmistakeable and the artist's signature is genuine. It's been verified as being one hundred per cent correct in every detail. The canvas and paints are all typical of the period."

I spotted Frank and Doc Mitchells exchanging an anxious glance. I knew where this was going and I didn't like it.

"It is supposed to come from around about 1340 AD," she explained, looking at me accusingly. "At least that's what one of your scruffy young scientists told the shopkeeper when he sold it to him. So would you like to explain, Jack, why it looks so new?"

"Restoration?" I volunteered innocently.

"And why, when it was forensically tested, the results said it had undoubtedly been painted by the 14th century artist… sometime around 4.30pm last Tuesday afternoon."

* * *

"Whatya want?" the spotty face demanded, head sticking round the fortified security door.

"To string you and your mates up from the nearest lamp-post, Billy, but right now I'll settle for some answers," I said frostily.

I shoved at the door, but he wouldn't budge.

"You can't come in, it's top secret. Can't you see the sign?"

"What? Buffy Fan Club HQ – no vampires by order?"

"No," he said, blushing. "The other one – Dark Matter Project. Highly Classified. Authorised Personnel Only."

"But I'm the head of security," I snarled. "I'm the one who authorises people!"

I'm sure the force of my argument would have won, however Chief Inspector Turner wasn't waiting. She grabbed poor Billy by the hair and hissed: "Open up, sonny, before you make me really angry."

He gulped and the door swung open.

"See, Jack," she said marching in. "Authority. Works every time."

Our small group – me, Turner, Frank and Doc Mitchells – stood in awe at what we saw before us.

Towering sixty feet to the ceiling a spider's web of tangled wiring, electric coils, computer innards and heavy duty condensers were draped haphazardly over a framework of metal tubing and glass panels. In the centre was a swirling, churning, dancing storm of multi-coloured particles. As it twirled and spun, electric flashes arced across the front and a deafening roar echoed from deep within its core.

And next to it was what had us really stunned – enough Lord of the Rings action figures, Doctor Who memorabilia and Spiderman comics to stock an entire geeks' convention. And that didn't include the dozens of Star Wars models littering the rest of the room.

"That junk must have cost a fortune," I muttered. "Like to tell me where the cash came from, Billy?"

He looked at me then Chief Inspector Turner and his shoulders sagged. "I told the others we'd get rumbled eventually," he said sadly. "But they wouldn't listen."

He waved half-hearted at the bellowing, growling mega machine crackling and spitting in technological fury. "All the cash has come from Gandalf."

"Gandalf?" Frank asked, incredulously.

"Our pet name for the trans-mutational inter-epoch spatial manipulation device."

The what?

Seeing our bemused expressions, Billy simplified his explanation. "It's what you'd call a time machine…"

* * *

"I should arrest the whole bunch of you," Karen Turner told Billy after he'd confessed to the whole caper. "And I will as soon as your time-tripping mates step back through that vortex."

"But it's not illegal," he said indignantly. "All we've done is a bit of trading, a bit of commerce, hopping back a few centuries and swapping some modern toys for antiques and trinkets to sell in the present day. We haven't broken any laws."

Only the laws of physics, Doc Mitchells pointed out. "It's stupidity beyond words. What if you'd done real damage to the timelines, you could have irreparably changed the course of world history."

They'd been very careful, Billy insisted. They hadn't taken back anything that could be used as a weapon, hadn't given anyone in the past any idea of what major events or wars were coming.

It was mind-bogglingly reckless, but I had to admit it was damn impressive too. If activating the machine hadn't sucked up every ounce of juice on the base they might have got away with it.

"How'd you come up with the idea for Gandalf?" I asked, genuinely intrigued.

Billy beamed with pride. "Well, it was an idea from Star Trek…"

I could hear Frank choke nearby.

"…you know? The time portal in The City on the Edge of Forever? We just copied it."

But it must have taken huge amounts of time and effort, Doc Mitchells argued.

"It's surprising what you can achieve when you don't have any distractions," Billy confided glumly. "Like a social life… or girlfriends."

I spun round to Karen Turner. "Your shout," I told her. "What do you intend to do?"

But she already had the handcuffs out.

"I'm arresting the entire Dark Matter Project team," she announced. "For the theft of three hundred sacks of cement mix."

The cement! How could I have forgotten that?

"And think yourself lucky," she told Billy, "that I can't do you for criminal negligence and knowingly selling substandard building materials."

I was baffled. What was she wittering on about?

The police chief tutted at me. "Do keep up, Jack. It's obvious where your duff cement has gone." She pointed to the powder trail that led towards the towering temporal transporter.

"It's gone back in time. Back into antiquity. I'm only guessing, and it wouldn't hold up in a court of law, but I reckon even now an army of cowboy builders are slaving away with it to construct the walls of Jericho!"

Medium Rare

"Is there anyone there," the old woman moaned. "Spirits are you with us tonight?"

Across the oak table, Teresa Williams struggled to suppress a giggle. She risked a glance at her companion. Gary held a hand in front of his face, hiding a snigger.

The woman's moan became louder. "Oh spirits, come to me. Don't be afraid, my children. Come to the light. Speak to me… speak to me."

Rolling her head, she flickered her eyes madly.

Teresa wriggled, worried that the medium would spot her amusement and end the séance.

It had taken three long weeks of pleading to convince Madam Luzardi to agree to put them in touch with the other side and Teresa didn't want to blow it now. Yet the whole performance was so hammy that she couldn't help herself.

How, she thought, could anyone take this farce seriously? How could they pay to sit through this old biddy's terrible amateur dramatics?

The set-up was straight out of some creaking low-budget 1950s movie – the dusty room with the faded velvet curtains, the grey-haired eccentric with gypsy scarf and the obligatory black cat asleep on a cushion embroidered with the stars of the zodiac.

When she'd greeted Teresa and Gary at the doorway, Madam Luzardi (or Gladys Peabody as the local trading standards department knew her) had summoned them into the darkened interior with a beckoning finger.

"The heavens are charged with electricity tonight," she announced breathlessly, "the long departed are restless to make contact. I think we'll have an illuminating session."

"I do hope so," Teresa whispered to Gary as they were led through the creepy looking hallway, "otherwise we don't have any evidence."

Gary tapped the small concealed video camera. "Don't worry. We'll get every word."

Teresa had her fingers crossed. Exposing fake clairvoyants was her first assignment for Ghost Watch and she dearly wanted it to work. She just hoped she could keep up the pretence long enough to trap Madam Luzardi. Teresa had told the medium she desperately wanted to contact a fictitious relative – her Uncle George, who'd been run over by a bus.

A cold, icy breeze blew across Teresa's face, snapping her to attention. She looked across at the window where the curtain was billowing.

Music – strange, unworldly music – drifted through the air. Immediately the table rose on its own and thumped up and down several times in quick succession.

Although Teresa wanted to yell out, a hiss stopped her. It came from Madam Luzardi's lips. Leaning forward Teresa could hear the words: "My fellow braves, gather round the campfire and we shall tell stories of the days when the buffalo roamed free."

"You what?" she exclaimed.

"The spirits of the Prairie cry out, my brothers. They demand vengeance against the marauding paleface devils who defile our scared burial grounds and slaughter our children."

Gary leant forward and clicked his fingers in front of Madam Luzardi's face. There was no response. She was in a trance.

"Who are you?" Teresa asked, wondering how the sherry-sodden old dear had managed to put on such a deep, booming male voice.

"I am Flaming Arrow," the woman replied, "chief of the Chiciwatta. Guardian of the ancient land of the netherworld. I am your spirit guide."

Gary tapped the side of his head to signal that the medium was either mad or putting it on.

"A spirit guide? That's handy," he said. "It'll save having to use the sat-nav."

Kicking him sharply under the table, Teresa took a deep breath. "Flaming Arrow," she said, "I need to speak to my uncle, my late Uncle George. Can you see him?"

The Chief hissed slowly. "He is here, on the cusp between this world and that spectral land beyond. He wishes to speak to you."

Teresa relaxed. The old girl had taken the bait! All they had to do now was reel her in.

"Hello, my child," the woman said, changing her voice to that of a kindly old man. "I've been lonely up here. I wondered when you'd get in touch."

"Is that really you?" Teresa asked, feigning amazement. "Really Uncle George?"

"Of course," the medium replied. "Don't you recognise me?"

"Yes, yes," Teresa said, "I'm just surprised. I thought when the bus ran over your throat that your vocal chords would have been damaged. But you sound fine."

Gary suddenly choked, tears of mirth rolling down his cheek.

"I'm in Heaven now, dearest Teresa. In Heaven all our pains and injuries are taken away."

"And can you still speak fluent Mandarin? Has the accident damaged your memory?"

Teresa could have sworn that Madam Luzardi opened one eye and glared at her.

"Please," Teresa urged, "give me a verse of that Chinese song you always sang to me when I was little."

Madam Luzardi began to shake as though an earthquake was erupting under her seat. The old man's voice said: "I'm sorry, my dear, but everything is growing dark. I can't stay. I must return."

"But surely you've time to sing a line or two," Teresa pleaded. "Please, Uncle George, you can't go now. Not when–"

"Quiet, paleface," the word hissed at her from the medium's lips. "A growing storm sweeps towards us. I must return to the campfire. Leave me now. Leave!"

With that Madam Luzardi woke up and smiled sweetly at them. "Have I been under? I never know. When I'm in touch with the spirit world, it's like I'm in a dream, completely cut off from reality."

"You can say that again, Gladys," Teresa replied, nodding for Gary to bring out his hidden camera. "The game's up. You've been rumbled."

Madam Luzardi's expression was a mixture of shock and outrage. "I don't know what you mean," she spluttered, but Teresa held up her hand.

"You're a fraud," she told the medium, "a swindler. You don't have a link to the spirit world. It's all an elaborate con designed to part poor deluded fools from their cash."

She pointed to the underside of the table where the wiring for the hydraulic lift now clearly showed. Gary pulled back the curtain to reveal the wind-machine.

Gladys Peabody slumped, defeated. "How did you know?"

Teresa shrugged expansively. "Lots of things gave you away," she said, "but there was one thing that clinched it."

"Let me guess. You don't have an Uncle George?"

"Worse than that," Teresa replied as she and Gary produced their death certificates and began to turn an unearthly white.

"We're from Ghost Watch and believe us, no self-respecting spook we know would be seen dead talking to you!"

Once Upon a Crime

Cursing, Gretchen tugged the hood free as the overhanging branches snatched greedily at her. Stumbling back to the uneven bramble-lined path, she pushed on deeper between the menacing, gnarled oaks – a freshening wind hissing through the leaves.

She hated the forest. It had always terrified her. And if her dark mission today hadn't been so important she'd never have dared venture into its foreboding interior.

Trembling, she forced herself to concentrate on the watery sun settling low over her grandmother's cottage.

"Not long now," she muttered softly. "Soon it will all be over."

The words didn't calm her. Instead they made her focus on the enormity of what she had to do. Even the thought of the woodman, waiting nearby with his specially sharpened axe, did little for her confidence.

There was a distant figure framed in the doorway. Her grandmother had obviously heard her crashing through the malicious undergrowth. For an older person, her hearing was remarkably keen.

The woman's body language immediately told Gretchen she wasn't welcome; the folded arms and fierce animal stare uncompromising. This was going to be much more difficult than she'd imagined.

"Well, well, well. If it isn't my favourite grand-daughter." The voice was sharp-edged, flinty. "Finally decided to pay me a visit… after all this time. That's heart-warming. So very *caring* of you. What's wrong, come to see if I've been behaving myself?"

Gretchen took a deep breath, glanced again anxiously at the setting sun. "It wasn't my idea. Father sent me. He thinks we need to talk."

A sly smile crept across her nan's lips. "Do we have anything to talk about?"

God, why was she making this so awkward! Gretchen felt anger displacing her fears.

"Your health... your *condition*."

She held up the wicker basket, its contents covered with a green gingham cloth. "Please, Gran. Can I come in? I've got something for you."

Shrugging, the woman moved to one side, the movement surprisingly fast and supple.

"Might as well hear what you've got to say," she muttered. "But you're going to need a whole lot more than a basket of goodies if you and your scheming father are going to get your way."

The interior of the cottage was sparsely furnished. Gretchen remembered it being more ordered, cosier, cleaner. But that, she told herself sadly, was only one of the many things that had inevitably changed.

A stew bubbled in a cauldron suspended over an open fire. It smelt enticing, meaty but unfamiliar. Her stomach rumbled.

"Have some," Grandmother offered and, seeing her hesitate, added tauntingly: "Don't worry. You won't catch anything."

Gretchen shook her head. No matter how hungry she might be, she couldn't afford to stay a second longer than necessary.

"You don't need to be so on edge, you know."

"I'm not," the girl insisted. Despite that, she could see the old woman's nose twitch, smelling the fear.

"Let's get this over with," Grandmother commanded. "Give me the message. Make your pitch."

Pulling back the cloth, Gretchen slid the basket across the table. The coins clinked enticingly. She blinked in surprise. There were so many – nearly the family's entire fortune.

The crone started to reach into the treasure then abruptly stopped, suddenly wary.

"It's gold," Gretchen promised. "Just gold. Nothing else... no silver."

Reassured, the woman began kneading the coins, making them run through her fingers like water.

Oh what big eyes you've got, Gretchen thought with loathing as the woman's predatory pupils dilated with delight. *And what a big mouth you've got... to need such a huge bribe to keep silent.*

Slowing turning a coin in her claw-like fingers, the woman asked: "What's the deal?"

"You leave the forest, leave the territory, leave the country and never return. You sever all links with us. And you never say a word to anyone about what happened, about how you ended up like this."

"To protect the family name?"

"To protect you from fear and prejudice," Gretchen corrected. "From hotheads who'd view you as a dangerous abomination that must be chased out at the point of a pitchfork."

Yellowy eyes burning with suspicion, the older woman thought about that possibility for a moment. She rubbed a hand slowly over her neck, over the traces of healing scratches and bites.

The girl swallowed hard under her gran's hot, unrelenting, hypnotic gaze.

"Okay," Gretchen admitted, dry mouthed, "Father is concerned about it harming the business. There'll be repercussions. A backlash. When people find out about you – what you're capable of – they won't understand. We'll all suffer."

"So I just disappear?" The bitterness in the statement hit Gretchen like a slap.

"Yes," she replied. "There are already rumours. People have started noticing the way your body is altering…"

And that senseless incident with the shepherd boy didn't help. It was lucky no-one believed him… that he'd made accusations before…

…but what about next time? If Gran got her teeth into him he'd lose more than his innocence.

"And what if I refuse to go?" Grandmother asked, padding over to the window to watch the night creep in. "What if I simply take the bribe and stay? Has your father thought about that?"

Shining through the glass, the menacing moon rose high – big and round and urgent.

"Then Father says I'll have to take direct action," Gretchen whispered, feeling her nerves tingle, her heart squeezing tightly. "A more permanent solution."

Grandmother considered the homicidal threat. If it worried her, she gave no sign.

"I'm growing bigger by the minute," she growled. "And it'll take more than just you to get rid of me. You don't have a moment to lose."

"I know," Gretchen agreed. "That's why I've arranged some help."

Although the whistle was low, it did the job. The door smashed open, flying off its hinges, the woodman rushing in, silvery axe raised.

Her nan laughed savagely; a roaring, guttural, chortle. "Ah, my darling girl, how treacherous you truly are. Now I understand why you wore that…" She gestured to Gretchen's cape.

"I always said dressing in red made you look like a cheap tramp. I suppose it's a very practical colour… for hiding bloodstains."

Gretchen refused to feel guilty. The biddy had brought this upon herself by her wild, reckless, animal behaviour. If only she hadn't surrendered to her brutish hungers; overwhelmed by her most basic primeval instincts.

"Don't bother telling me we won't get away with it," she told the abhorrent *unnatural* creature. "It's all worked out. The cover story is foolproof. It was a full moon, I turned up with my usual delivery of provisions for my saintly grey-haired granny but you changed into a werewolf and attacked me."

She nodded to the woodman. "Johann was working nearby and burst in to save me. As soon as he cut your head off with his trusty axe your corpse changed back to its human form."

Gran's expression was both mocking and pitying. "And you think people will buy that load of baloney? That ridiculous, hackneyed, lycan myth?"

"The locals are *very* superstitious."

"But there are no such things as werewolves. Everyone knows that. It's a metaphor – an allegorical way of explaining why normally passive, respectable people give in to their inner beast, to their wildest temptations and desires."

Grandma patted the pronounced four-month pregnant bump in her stomach.

"Like a pensioner suddenly rediscovering her passion for rampant sex!"

Gretchen frowned, both angry and unnerved. For a simple murder this was suddenly becoming very complicated, and far too intellectually challenging.

"Look, the bumpkins round here don't have doctorates in literary allusion or psychology," she snapped. "They're just numbskulls who love all that crap about witches, magic potions, goblins and creatures of the night. They think it's real. They'll go mad for any freaky fairytale Father and I feed them."

Possibly, Grandmother conceded, however the alibi argument was academic – on a number of levels. Mostly because it was, in fact, Gretchen who was about to die.

"I'm afraid," the old woman said, giving the woodcutter a lecherous wink, "that Johann has already used his chopper on me. He's the daddy of junior here. You picked the wrong accomplice."

Mouth falling open, Gretchen spun round just in time to see the deadly blade descend… on her.

"He's got a thing for older women. Especially older women with a basket of gold."

The pain was so intense Gretchen almost blacked out straight away. She kept conscious just long enough to see the axe man take the promiscuous pensioner in his arms, asking: "Did she bring enough? Do we have enough to live happily ever after?"

"Who knows, lover," Grandma replied. "It's a grim fiscal time to be bringing a nipper into the world."

Staring directly into her murderous grand-daughter's rapidly dimming eyes, she added thoughtfully: "It's amazing how much you need these days just to keep the wolf from the door…"

Extended Run

Joan Prentice couldn't believe it. "Eight hundred dollars a jar and the goddam stuff doesn't work!"

Slamming down the bottle, she peered anxiously in the mirror. The anti-wrinkle cream had been a silly extravagance, a vain attempt to cover up the problem.

It only took one look at her reflection to make Joan shiver. She was still attractive – alluring enough to guarantee the undivided attention of every man when she walked into a room – but the critics had stopped describing her as devastatingly beautiful. And it was easy to see why.

Early middle age had arrived uninvited. The laughter lines which had once given her a mischievous, impish appeal were now etching into crow's feet; her green eyes were losing their twinkle and there was a hint of scrawniness around the neck. Brunette Joan could still set men's motors revving, but she knew that it would soon be time for the first of many nips and tucks.

"I know time marches on," she sighed, "but why does it pick a route right across my face?"

As a movie star, Joan had always had make-up men, hair stylists, and costumiers to make her look stunning. And Nature had been kind. Even as a teenager, Joan had a unique fresh-faced prettiness.

"You'll break a few hearts when you grow up," her mother had told her, and during the next twenty years, the cinema's most sought-after leading lady had broken hearts by the million. Now Joan knew all that was going to change.

At first, she'd been in denial – determinedly refusing to accept that fewer scripts arrived each day, or that she wasn't being cast so often in romantic roles. What had finally made it impossible to ignore had been the offer of a part in Spielberg's latest adventure epic.

The film's central character was a fiery girl leading an expedition up the Amazon to find a fabled lost city. Joan had been desperate for the role. But when the script arrived from Larry, her agent, she'd been cast as the girl's mother!

"Don't take it to heart," he'd told her. "The mother's part is a peach – great lines and some of the film's best scenes. You'll steal the show."

Joan had argued for the lead, but Larry wouldn't listen. "It calls for a bimbo to flounce around half naked. I wouldn't insult you with it. Not an actress of your reputation."

Larry was a dear, but what he'd really meant was an actress of her age, Joan told herself. And, as she'd reluctantly signed the contract, she knew she'd reached a watershed in her career.

"Old actresses never die," she told the reflection, "they only get more lines."

* * *

Brad's party was tedious, but Joan kept her smile firmly in place as she circulated. She knew most of the other guests, of course, mostly actors and small-time directors. But it was out-of-town producer Tom Hartmann she'd really come to meet. He was casting a new rom-com, and she was prepared to endure any amount of boredom for the chance to button-hole him.

It took nearly an hour of inane chatter and insincere hugs before she cornered the balding producer, stuffing his face at the trendy microbiotic vegan buffet.

Hartmann recognised her instantly. "You know, I'm a big fan of yours," he said, waving a piece of celery perilously close to her face, "have been for years, and there aren't many actors I'd say that to."

Joan turned on her famous smile. "Why, Tom, I'm flattered. That's praise indeed." Taking his arm, she guided him away. "I'm glad we bumped into each other because I've been meaning to have a word with your people about the new Bradley Cooper film. I believe you still haven't cast the female lead."

Joan made her prepared sales pitch, telling him she'd do anything for the part, yet as she outlined why she was the only possible choice, she sensed Hartmann's embarrassment.

He sighed. "What can I say, Joan? You're a fabulous actress and a big box office draw, but I was looking for someone… mmm… younger."

Joan thought she was going to keel over. Didn't Hartmann know that the mere mention of her name would guarantee a hit!

She struggled to keep calm. "Someone younger? Well, thanks a bunch, Tom. That makes me feel great. You may not have noticed but I'm not quite over the hill yet!"

The producer's mouth fell open, and Joan snatched the celery stick from his grasp and stuck it in his glass.

As she stomped off, she became aware of someone watching her. She glanced straight into the eyes of a tall, young man. He was dressed in the carelessly casual look that took a small fortune to achieve, and was sipping a bourbon on the rocks.

Joan took in his features in an instant. He was tanned, dark-haired and devilishly good looking. Under normal circumstances, Joan would have been attracted. Instead, she was annoyed.

"Get it all, did you?" Her voice was clipped. "Enjoy the show? What are you, just nosy or a gossip columnist?"

The young man broke into a bemused grin. "Gossip columnist? No, nothing like that. Actually, I'm just a businessman. I wasn't deliberately listening. I just happened to be nearby." He stared deep into her eyes and Joan suddenly felt hot – hotter than she could ever remember.

"Sounds like you'd have sold your soul for that part," he teased.

Joan made a face. "In this business the last thing you need is a soul."

The man nodded thoughtfully and fished a card from his pocket. Joan gave it a cursory glance. 'CHARLES PHOENIX, marketing director, FOUNTAIN OF YOUTH INC – A New You Is Just A Day Away'.

"Sounded like you might need our assistance," he suggested, draining his glass. "It's a very confidential service."

Joan tried to give the card back. "Thanks, but I don't like being hustled by salesmen. Especially not for plastic surgery or monkey glands or whatever it is you're offering."

The young man's eyes twinkled. "Nothing so crude. We offer a… total body… enhancement. Guaranteed for years."

Despite Joan wanting to tell him to go take a jump, there was something in his manner that held her captive. Did he say it would last for years?

"Look," she said, finally breaking free from his gaze. "I'm sure it's great, but I can't afford it. Okay?"

The salesman shrugged. "I understand. Keep the card anyway. You might change your mind."

He started to walk away, then turned round. "Tell you what. Forget the money. How about paying with something you'll never miss?"

* * *

Hollywood was stunned by Joan's tragic death. No-one could understand why her sports car had mysteriously plunged over the cliff. Although suicide rumours circulated for a while, no-one really believed that an actress who loved life as much as Joan would kill herself.

The intense fire had made identification of the corpse impossible. A few of the more sensational tabloids even ran a line that it wasn't Joan who'd died in the crash, but some poor unsuspecting substitute. But if people believed that rubbish, they'd have had to believe the other tabloid 'exclusive' – that Elvis was alive and had been snatched by aliens.

Eventually, the story became as dead as poor Joan and the gossip columnists turned their eye to the sudden appearance of youthful newcomer Jenny Prentice.

Only months after her aunt's demise, the unknown actress had taken Tinsel Town by storm. 'An overnight star', *Variety* wrote, 'a screen sensation'.

Her performance as the female lead in Spielberg's lost city movie was breath-taking.

'She takes a clichéd, uninspired role and makes it come alive', the *Los Angeles Post* gushed. 'Miss Prentice brings a maturity of performance, quite stunning for a newcomer'.

Wary of the hype, Jenny was cautious, shrugging modestly at the interviewers.

"I'm very flattered, of course, though it was hardly Shakespeare. I'd like to prove what I can really do when I get a more demanding role."

They all nodded. No-one doubted that Jenny was going to be a huge name; as big as Joan had been – maybe even bigger. She had it all: talent, style, poise, plus dazzling emerald eyes, soft, shiny auburn hair and the sexiest way of laughing.

"People are already calling you the next Queen of Hollywood," one tabloid reporter told her. "That's a scary prospect for an actress just making her debut. Can you promise us that you're not just a one-hit wonder?"

Jenny turned on a smile that was disarmingly familiar. "Oh, I think so. Haven't you heard, I made a pact with the devil. He gets my soul, I get the Oscars."

The reporters chuckled dutifully.

"Seriously, though. There are so many wonderful parts to play that I intend to be around for a very long time." Jenny fingered the card in her pocket. "A very long time, indeed."

Crowning Glory

Sarah froze, terrified. The footsteps behind her stopped. In the uneasy silence she imagined she heard breathing – heavy male breathing.

Peering into the gloom of the alley, she anxiously scanned the darkness for a face. Was someone there? Was someone following her? She couldn't be sure, but the hairs on her neck were taut, standing rigid.

Swallowing hard, she forced herself not to panic. The only way she was going to get out of this was by keeping her nerve and thinking clearly.

The footsteps had started not long after she'd left the sports hall. She hadn't thought much about it then, but when she'd cut through the underpass she'd noticed the steady rat-tat-tat beat was still there. It had followed her for the last ten minutes.

"Is there anyone there?" she called out. "I know there's someone there. Show yourself."

Silence. Nothing but the faint sound of breathing, slow, regular and even.

She cursed herself for turning down the offers of lifts. She'd been too hyped up, too excited after the competition and had felt she needed the walk to give her time to wind down. Now she wished she'd let one of the others at the karate club drive her to her door. It would have been so easy, so safe.

Listening intently, Sarah began to edge down the lane again. For a second there was nothing, then the following footfalls took up their menacing tattoo. It sounded like he was about 50 yards behind her.

Quickening her pace, she moved her heavy hold-all over to the other shoulder. If she had to make a run for it, Sarah knew it would slow her down but its contents were too valuable to abandon. She'd worked too hard, sweated too many hours, gone through too much pain simply to lose it all.

Up ahead she could see the blazing neon sign of a Chinese takeaway. If I can just get there, I'll be safe, she told herself. No-one will try anything with witnesses around.

For a moment her spirits lifted. It was going to be okay. She was going to be safe, but then the steps quickened. Whoever it was behind her had spotted the takeaway sign and determined she wouldn't reach it. He was running! He was going to attack her!

For an instant Sarah thought about bolting, but a sudden flush of anger surged through her. Why should she run? Why should she be afraid? She hadn't done anything wrong.

She dropped the bag and spun round. Taking up a classic defence stance she faced her attacker. She trembled, frightened but excited too. Now it was time to find out if all those years of karate training had been worth it.

The man's shape burst out of the darkness and Sarah got a fleeting glimpse of surprise in his eyes. He hadn't expected her to stand her ground.

Roaring, he charged at her. She judged the rapidly diminishing distance between them and made her move. She just hoped it was the right one. She knew her life depended on it.

* * *

Sarah had been sceptical when Wendy had suggested they attend women's self-defence classes.

"It'll be a laugh," Wendy suggested, pointing to the advert in the local paper. "It'll keep us fit. Besides, you're always hearing terrible things about women being attacked at night."

"Yes," Sarah agreed, "but I hardly think a few weeks of you and me doing judo are going to scare off some crazed knife maniac."

Wendy had been insistent, and they'd gone along to the classes in a dusty, cold church hall just off the city centre. At first Sarah hadn't been able to take it seriously, but after a couple of sessions she found she actually enjoyed the holds, the throws and the general rough and tumble.

"You're a natural," the instructor told her. "Have you ever thought about taking up one of the more robust martial arts? Karate's supposed to be really good."

So when the sessions ended and Wendy went back to pottery classes and step aerobics, Sarah joined the local karate club.

Although it had been tough at first fighting against a lot of big, hairy, sweaty, muscle-bound men, she gave as good as she got and the class adopted her as a mascot. The men were secretly proud that she could kick and punch as hard as any of them.

That was three years ago and she'd gone religiously twice a week, gaining in strength, skill and confidence. It was a matter of great pride to her that she'd worked her way up through all the grades to black belt.

Now tonight, she'd had her crowning glory – she'd faced other black belts in the southern regional competition. It had been testing but she'd fought hard.

Earlier, as she'd collected her prize she'd thought it was the best night of her life.

But now, she understood how wrong she was. It was the worst – most terrifying – night of her life.

* * *

The policeman sucked on his pencil before scribbling in his notepad.

"So let me get this straight," he said, obviously puzzled. "You're telling me you did this all on your own."

He nodded down to the ground where the would-be attacker was out cold. Her assailant looked like he'd been hit by a truck.

"I'm sorry," Sarah told the PC. "I was frightened. He came running at me. I hit him harder than I intended."

The constable looked unconvinced. Then he spotted the karate club badges on her hold-all.

"You any good?" he asked.

"Black belt," she said proudly. "I'm not someone to mess with."

That, the PC agreed, was fairly obvious.

The ambulance arrived and the attacker, now softly moaning, was loaded onto a stretcher.

Sarah watched him being carted off. She supposed she should feel sorry for the man, but she reckoned he'd asked for it.

The PC had one last question for her. "For my report. I need to know what karate move you used."

Sarah suddenly laughed, the tension flowing out of her. "Oh, I didn't use karate. At least, not in the way you think."

She showed him the trophy inscribed with the words: *Karate Regional Champion.*

It was an impressive looking piece of hardware and would look good on her mantelpiece.

She just hoped she could get the head-shaped dent out of it...

Interview with the Vampire

The room was stark, airless, all windows blocked so no hint of daylight peeked through – just perfect for what was about to happen, Lestat told himself.

"What do you want to know?" he asked the pale, nervous looking man across the table.

"Everything," his companion replied, whipping out his notepad and pen. "I want to know everything about your background. How you became a vampire, how many people you've killed, what motivates you, whether you have any regrets."

Lestat smiled, revealing perfect, even, white predator's teeth. "Regrets? Do I have regrets? Of course not. What would be the point? I am a hunter. Mankind is my prey. I do what I have to do."

He laughed – a chilling, brittle, tauntingly callous snarl. "Besides, I enjoy it. It is intensely pleasurable. Why deny it?"

The man's hand raced across the page, the lines a mere scribble in his haste to capture every word, every heinous utterance, of New Orleans' most notorious bloodsucker.

"So you aren't bothered that people think of you as a parasite, of the fear and loathing you engender? You don't care that you are shunned by all except those who would wish to destroy you?"

Tapping a finger against his thin, cruel, lips, Lestat mused. "Why should I mind? It is only natural that I am feared. With fear comes power, and power is the most exquisite aphrodisiac."

He leant forward, suddenly, coming so close that the human was momentarily hypnotised by the stare of the deep, dark, soulless eyes.

"I know what you are thinking," the undead noble hissed, heavy with menace. "Are all the stories about my kind true? All the awful, terrifying, nightmare legends? Well, my trembling friend, I can assure you that they are."

His inquisitor gulped, muttering: "So you're telling me that you could end a man's life without a moment's hesitation, drain every last drop of life force from his body until only a hollow husk was left behind?"

"Of course."

"You would show no mercy, no compassion. You wouldn't stop until you'd bled him dry?"

"I wouldn't stop until he had been driven beyond all hope of salvation," Lestat agreed. "Inflicting despair is all part of the fun."

Putting his pen down, the man sighed. "There's no point carrying on with this…"

Lestat frowned, surprised that the encounter was being brought to an unexpectedly rapid conclusion.

"…because I can see you're perfect for the job," the man announced. "You've got just the qualities and attitudes we're looking for."

He beamed. "I think you're going to fit in really well here at the Internal Revenue Service."

Lestat found himself blushing. It was so rare to be appreciated these days.

"Just before I bring the interview to an end, do you have any questions for me?" the official asked.

Thinking about it for a moment, Lestat ran his tongue over his razor-edged fangs.

"The remuneration packet," he enquired, "does it include dental?"

Artful Dodger

The reporter regarded Josie with an expression half sneering and half pitying. She knew what he thought. He was convinced she was either a self deluding fool or a scheming fraud.

"Let me get this straight," he said, his voice heavy with irony. "You're telling me you expect someone to pay £500,000 for a load of old house bricks?"

"That's right," she told him, ignoring the sarcasm. "They'll buy one of the greatest art works of the year and get it at a bargain price."

He coughed theatrically, rolling his eyeballs. Josie flushed with anger. This was the typical reaction from the tabloids. What did they know about it, she thought angrily. What did those philistines know about modern art? The nearest thing they recognised to culture were £5 posters of girl tennis players scratching their backsides.

She'd been expecting some press scepticism. There had been more than a few raised eyebrows over her last three pieces – a goat cut in half and preserved in formaldehyde, a collage assembled from discarded Kleenex tissues and the old tent (a snip at just £400,000 including soiled sleeping bag). But she'd proved everyone wrong when the pieces sold within weeks.

Normally, she'd shrug off the teasing headlines and mocking opinion columns, but there was something about this reporter's rudeness that got to her. He seemed determined to ridicule her, right to her face. It was maddening.

She could visualise how her studio looked to his jaundiced eyes. All he could see was a junk-yard stacked high with haphazard piles of old metal, half dismantled toilet cisterns, crusty paint pots and giant ripped canvases. He couldn't perceive the creative energy, the artistic potential in the crude materials…

And she had a good idea how she appeared to him. She considered her unkempt hair and carefully mismatched clothes gave her a Bohemian air, but he probably reckoned she looked more like a student who'd been pulled through a hedge backwards.

The reporter grinned, savouring his attack: "So you don't subscribe to the view of most *serious* art critics that it's just a load of over-hyped rubble and people could get better bricks at a DIY store?"

A murderous thought crossed Josie's mind. It was lucky for him that she didn't have one of the bricks to hand, she told herself darkly.

"This work is my masterpiece. It has depth of vision, a technical virtuosity. There is a modernity and immediacy in the execution of–"

"The cementing?" the man suggested mischievously.

That was it. I don't have to put up with this, she decided.

"I think it's time you left," she said frostily. "I have to get to the gallery for the unveiling." She put on her coat and herded him to the door. "It's an invitation-only do. Only for those with taste, culture and refinement."

She flashed him her nastiest look. "No press, naturally."

* * *

Traffic was heavy as she crossed town. Flicking on the car radio she caught the one o'clock news. An African president had been shot and the City was in a tizzy about dwindling gold reserves. The report said things hadn't been helped by a multi-million pound bullion robbery three weeks before. The announcer switched subjects – to her exhibition opening.

Josie listened grim-faced as her brick sculpture was described in turn as 'daring', 'controversial' and 'the biggest con trick ever perpetrated on a gullible public'. Annoyed, she snapped the dial to off and pulled into the kerb.

A knot of photographers crowded round her as she bounded up the steps to the Carlton Gallery.

Forcing her way through the ornate carved doors, she rushed into the white-walled viewing room. The gallery was filled to capacity. A host of celebrities, artists and glittering, pretty people in designer outfits nibbled thimble-sized bites of prawn and swigged champagne.

"Josie dear. This is a triumph. Quite the most prestigious event yet," Tristram, her pony-tailed agent gushed, grabbing her arm. "You're a star."

She barely had a chance to grab a drink and mingle with the VIP guests before it was time for the unveiling. The lights dimmed – all but one small intense spotlight which beamed straight down on the bright red tarpaulin.

Feeling suddenly self conscious Josie took one corner of the plastic sheet and whipped it away in one fluid movement. The crowd broke into spontaneous applause.

The fifty clay bricks lay – almost blinking – in the limelight. Josie gasped. She'd forgotten just how powerful the sculpture was, how dangerously potent, how raw and impressive.

"Thank you, ladies and gentlemen. I'm truly humbled by your generosity and warmth," she said, basking for a moment in the adulation. She held up a hand for quiet. "If you'll bear with me for a moment, I have one announcement to make. I'm afraid it's an announcement which may upset a few people."

She took a deep breath. "I'm sorry to disappoint you but the sale due later this evening is being cancelled. The piece has already been sold."

Around the room a hundred art lovers gasped and swooned.

"An overseas collector rang me this morning. Quite unexpectedly. He offered a large amount of money. Said he simply must have the piece. It's being shipped out tonight."

Tristram hugged her. "Well, Josie. What can I say? You always had faith in this piece. You told me it was more valuable than I'd ever realise – and it seems you were right."

Josie smiled, imagining the next day's stunned headlines. She couldn't wait for the press backlash. Their indignant attack on her sale would generate more art world interest and bigger success. This latest controversy would be the making of her.

Of course, the secret payment from a certain underworld gang into her numbered Swiss bank account helped make the future look very rosy too.

* * *

She listened to the late news on the drive home – this time with pleasure. There were two main topics. The presenter interviewed a security expert on how difficult it would be for the robbery gang to smuggle fifty bars of gold bullion out of the country when every airport and sea crossing was crawling with police.

The expert speculated that the bars would have to be very cleverly disguised.

Next there was a discussion about the amazing sale of Josie's sculpture. One thing in particular seemed to puzzle the panel of pundits. Why had she called the piece: *Follow the Yellow Brick Road?*

They'd asked her of course, but a true artist never explains her work…

A Rum Tale

A sudden lewd cackle made him jump. Scanning the teeming twilight-bathed dockside, Sly Jake immediate saw the source of the licentious laughter and broke into an envious smile. A drunken sailor was clumsily groping a giggling harlot, both swaying like square riggers in a gale, narrowly avoiding being mown down by a thundering cart speeding over the cobbles.

Spinning round, Jake saw the whole noisy waterfront was packed with similar scenes. Mariners and trollops; all inebriated beyond reason, all barely able to stand. Three ships of the line had moored that afternoon and their crews – deprived for months of grog, girls and decent grub – were making up for lost time.

Grinning, he scratched his unshaven cheek with the iron hook where his right hand used to be. He knew sozzled sailors were a soft touch, always ready to stand a drink for a friendly, ingratiating stranger. And Jake hadn't tasted spirits in days. Not since he'd gambled away his last piece-of-eight at poker – discovering that it was possible for your opponent to win with five aces; if he had a unique interpretation of the rules, a loaded blunderbuss and the meanest accomplices in the Caribbean.

Jake swallowed hard at the memory and at the dryness in his throat. He desperately needed a drop of rum. So, there was only one solution – find a gullible audience.

But which inn? Musing momentarily, he remembered that he hadn't been thrown out of The

Admiral Jericho for a while. It was just around the corner.

The sawdust-floored tavern was so packed Jake had to shove his way through the heaving, hedonistic humanity. The smells of roast pork, stale ale, pipe smoke and piss assailed his nostrils. Jack Tars from HMS Respite had taken over the place. They filled every corner, every nook, lounging on upturned barrels where there were no chairs; laughing, singing, cursing and arguing. The racket was deafening.

Looking over to the bar-top he spotted the ship's bosun, uniform askew, balding head buried deep in barmaid Betsy's generous cleavage. The three pink domes bobbed up and down like buoys, making it difficult to tell where bosun ended and bosoms began.

"Hey, me lads, listen up," Jake said, fighting to be heard over the din. "This be yer lucky night."

No-one paid any attention.

"Boys, be quiet and lend me your ear," he said, speaking louder. "I've got a rollockin' delight in store for ye."

The reaction was the same. If anyone heard, they gave no sign. This was no good, Jake thought irritably, and grabbed an empty pewter flagon from a nearby table.

He brought it crashing down as hard as he could.

Once.

Twice.

Three times.

That did the trick. The place went instantly quiet, all eyes swivelling to stare, curious at who had disturbed the revels and doing little to hide their seething annoyance.

He cleared his throat.

"Shipmates, good friends, fellow seadogs. Let me introduce myself. I be Captain Jake Pritheroe – former privateer and pirate – known to most as Sly Jake. At your service."

He bowed theatrically.

"For twenty and five long years I've sailed these here high seas, voyaged to exotic lands, survived hair-raising adventures and seen ungodly sights ye'd not believe in your wildest nightmares. And for a small libation, I'll recount one of my most terrifying adventures – a story to chill your vitals; a cautionary tale of fiendish forces, dark doings and drooling hell-fire creatures of the night. What ye say, lads?"

A grizzled man in an eye patch leant forward and spat noisily. "I'd say we should cut out your tongue and be done with it," he hissed. "We've all heard your fancy fools' tales before, Lying Jake."

"That's right," a voice rang out. "Like the one where you had a night of passion with a mermaid…"

The revellers sniggered.

"Or the time you sailed to the land where the inhabitants were just eight inches high."

"Yeah, and let's not forget the unforgettable occasion when you were turned into a goat by a sea witch."

The teasing mirth had a nasty undertone. Drawing in his breath, Jake studied the room. It could go either way.

"All righty, all righty, mates. Maybe, perchance, I have… *sometimes*… let me imagination run a little wild before the trade winds," he conceded. "I may have exaggerated a teensy detail here and there but I ain't never set out to deceive. And tonight, I promise ye I'll be telling this esteemed gathering the God's honest truth."

He looked beseechingly at the barmaid. "All I ask is a flagon of ale and a tot of rum to wash it down and I'll tell ye how I lost this…" He waved his hook above his head, "…to a monstrous, howling demon from the bowels of Hades itself!"

The balding bosun groaned wearily, but Jake knew he'd succeeded. The audience was curious. They leant forwards, aghast.

Gesturing to Betsy to give the storytelling seadog what he'd asked for, Eye Patch told Jake gruffly to get on with it.

"But this better be good, you old twister," he warned, "or I promise you'll lose the other hand."

Slurping down the welcome beer and letting it slosh coolingly against his throat, Jake made his voice soft and deep, with just the right edge of menace.

"It all happened on an eerie evening just like this," he began slowly, motioning them to draw close. "There was a ghostly galleon moon high in the heavens, and we'd been at sea for five, interminable, tormented, soul-sapping months…"

* * *

Five…

Interminable…

Tormented…

Soul-sapping…

Hours…

Jake was surprised it had taken The Crooked Contessa's hapless pirate band that long to start grumbling and demand to go home.

A ragbag collection of old men, rejects from other ships, wide-eyed shop boys, simpletons, braggarts and drunks, the Contessa's crew were, he conceded, not so much a complement as a calculated insult. Only two factors united them – their seasickness and their cowardice, an alliance of yellow spines and churning stomachs.

"C'mon lads, we can't turn back now," Jake told them, when they assembled outside his cabin. "The ship is barely out of sight of port. Where's ye sense of adventure?"

"Back on the dockside," Tom, the cabin boy replied, to nods from the rest of the bedraggled delegation.

"And we wants to make its acquaintance again as soon as possible," the ship's one-legged cook agreed, leaning on the wooden crutch that kept him vertical. "Turn around, Captain. Take us home. No good can come of this foolishness."

Foolishness? Getting their filthy hands on enough booty to last a lifetime? Plundering and carousing their way into the history books? Staying up past midnight and singing shanties with rude words?

"We're pleading with ye," young Tom added, with an apologetic shrug.

Jake curled his lip. They were a load of pleaders, all right. He promised himself that one day he'd make them walk the plank – if he ever got round to buying one.

For now, however, he had an idea. "Tell you what, boys. I can tell yer obviously not up for a cruise, so why don't we head back to land…"

The company cheered.

"…and see if we can slip past Mad Morgan's hound and pinch all his loot."

The company groaned.

They stepped back one pace, shaking their heads in trembling protest.

Every man had heard the stories – that Morgan, the most feared privateer on the entire Spanish Main had a dog, even more barking than him, even more bloodcurdling, aggressive and ugly than his crossed-eyed, tobacco-chewing, cannon-fisted wife. It was said to guard the caves at the foot of Smashed Skull Cliffs; caves that were used as the depository for Morgan's trove of tantalising treasure.

Many had tried to steal the riches. None had succeeded. Chillingly, not a single man had ever returned to say why.

"Look, it's just a dog," Jake said, bringing both hands closer together to help conjure an image of a small, endearing terrier.

The crew wasn't having it. They spread their hands at arm's length, conjuring up a picture of a large, snarling, entrails-ripping terror.

Jake sighed. There was nothing for it. He'd have to rely on his charisma and charm to win them round.

Two minutes later, his charisma had predictably failed, but the charm proved a winner. It should be, he reminded himself, it was the most powerful and expensive hex he'd ever stolen.

Swigging from a bottle of brandy, and noting that he was keeling over alarmingly from its brain-numbing effects, he beamed at the spell-bound crew and waved the yellowing parchment that revealed the location of the swag.

"I have a map and a list," he enthused, woozily. "What can possibly go wrong?"

* * *

The oars clattered wildly, sending up volley after volley of splashes as the longboat made its haphazard way through the swirling, spectral mist. With each chaotic stroke the boat threatened to tip over, going round in dizzying circles, and Jake despaired at how inept his sidekicks could be at even this simple seafaring task.

"Pull together," he hissed, miming the action the clueless cut-throats should be taking. "Both paddles going the same way!"

Then, with a sudden crunch and a collective yelp of surprise, they made contact with terra firma, scrapping the jagged rocks guarding the beach. Jake found himself flying through the air before making landfall with a jarring thud.

"Everyone all right?" he asked the tangled mass of arms and legs sprawled across the wet sand.

Groans, curses, a cry of "I want my mum" and three vehemently expressed offers of resignation came hurtling back.

"Any broken bones?" he enquired.

"Not yet," a deep, murderous voice replied.

Sighing, Jake got to his feet, dusted himself off and signalled his crumpled companions to follow.

"C'mon, shipmates. Don't be down at heart. It'll be a doddle from here on in. Look, up yonder – Smashed Skulls Caves. And the treasure. Just waiting for us."

At that very moment a howl – a nerve-jangling, primal, bowel-loosening roar – rent through the night air. The crew immediately came to the conclusion that a hoard of doubloons wasn't the only thing waiting for them.

For injured men they got to their feet in an impressive surge of motion, sprinting back towards the longboat.

It was an ironic switch of events. Normally a gunshot begins a race. On this occasion, it stopped one dead in its tracks.

"And I've still got another flintlock," Jake informed his minions as they froze and looked round, warily.

He waved the musket towards their destination. "Come about, me gutless gang. The caves are that-a-way."

* * *

One after another each man's mouth fell open revealing their surprise and the fact that the noble science of dentistry hadn't yet made it to the spice isles. They leant forward as one, curiosity overcoming their natural fearfulness.

Yards away, silhouetted against the dancing flames of the tar-dipped torches at the mountain entrance, a sight greeted them that left all trembling and bewildered.

"Yon cannae be a dog," cabin boy Tom murmured in awe. "It's too large."

"And too tall," the beer-bellied buccaneer next to him agreed.

As if sensing that it was being talked about, the giant feral vision turned blazing crimson eyes towards them and snarled, sniffing the air hungrily.

Jake gulped. The lads were right. This was no mere mutt. The burly beast wasn't covered in hair, but gleaming fur. It was a wolf – and a particular mean looking specimen. He'd seen plenty of the deadly predators before and this one easily dwarfed any of those.

Staring transfixed at the drooling, rumbling creature, two questions nagged at him.

What was a wolf doing in these alien, tropical parts? He'd only ever encountered them on voyages to the chilly lands up north – and only then in deep woodland.

And more puzzlingly – why was it standing on two legs instead of being on all fours?

For a full minute Jake's brain refused to accept the obvious then he let his gaze rise up to the dazzling white orb hanging high in the night sky, the wide full disc.

Not just a wolf then…

…but something much worse. An abomination that shouldn't exist outside of legend.

He frowned. This put a whole new complexion on things. Part of his brain warned that trying to seize Mad Morgan's pension pot was suicide. Yet, the other part, where greed lurked, whispered seductive words about how the pirates outnumbered the monster twenty to one.

"Okay, boys. On the count of three we're going to charge it," he whispered down the line.

He couldn't tell which scurvy cur replied cheekily: "How much?" and didn't have the opportunity to find out. For at that instant, the beast took matters into his own paws and, bellowing loud enough to shake the trees, surged forward, covering the ground in supernaturally long strides. There wasn't time to flee before it was upon them.

It should have been a battle to go down in the annals of bandit lore, a derring-do action guaranteed to inspire a dozen rousing boozy ballads, but as the creature easily tore its way through the sobbing sabre-waving rabble, the muddled melee quickly descended into a rout.

Savage snarls mixed with screams as the men went down one by one. It ripped through them like rag dolls, crunching bones, tearing out throats and hurling lifeless bodies over its shoulder.

Jake had often been asked if he had a pirate's chest and at this moment his madly thumping heart was trying to burst clean through it.

He tried to run but his legs were paralysed in fear. Instead, he raised the flintlock and took careful aim. The gun thundered, firing the musket ball with deadly velocity. The searing metal sphere spun through the air with a sizzle, seeking its target with murderous intent and made solid contact.

But, to Jake's astonishment, it bounced harmlessly off the wolf-man's rock-hard pelt. At that instant he knew it was over. He was booked on a one-way trip to Davy Jones' locker.

He'd heard that when facing death a person's whole life flashed in front of their eyes. Yet not much of the blurry, double vision pictures racing across his pupils seemed familiar. Especially not the episode with the harem girls, the whipped cream and the penguin.

A split second later, he felt sticky fetid breath upon his face and his arm jerked violently as his hand, still holding the weapon, disappeared between the beast's jagged yellow teeth. The jaws snapped shut in one brutal movement, and he felt everything below the wrist detach – bone, flesh and nerves parting from the rest of his body in a burst of bloody agony.

Looking up in dismay he watched the monster gobble down its meaty prize in one gulp, and lick its strangely human lips at the tangy taste.

Steeling himself for the inevitable, Jake prayed death would be mercifully quick. However, it wasn't the creature that acted next but a bizarre hopping dervish.

Out of nowhere, the Contessa's one legged pot-stirrer bounded unsteadily into the fray and, swinging his crutch like a mighty cudgel, walloped the nightmare animal squarely across the skull.

Although Jake had no idea how the cook has survived the slaughter, he wasn't complaining about the help or the distraction.

"Whack it in the goolies," he urged, sharing the experience of a score of bar room brawls.

The man obliged and the werewolf bellowed in pain and fury as its privates suddenly blazed – suffering almost as much nether region torment as those who'd sampled the cook's incendiary asparagus and chili wine.

There was no third blow. This time as cookie went to swing the oak prop the towering brute leapt upon him.

Jake guessed it was a desire for symmetry that made it yank off the chef's remaining leg. The poor soul's doomed shriek reverberated so loudly that Jake went to put his hands over his ears, before remembering that his bloody pumping stump wasn't likely to block out any sound.

Then, without warning, the beast froze in mid gorge, startled. Dropping the mangled leg half eaten, it gave a strangled bark, clawing madly at its throat. And lurching forward, the monster crashed to the ground, lifeless.

* * *

Jake grinned to himself, letting his sly eyes scan the totally enthralled tavern audience, each listener perched on the edge of his seat in excitement and suspense.

"The werewolf was deceased, defunct, departed. Slain in a heartbeat," he whispered dramatically.

"But how?" Eye Patch demanded.

"What killed it?" Betsy asked, agog.

Jake took a final swig of his ale. Not a drop remained. Time to divulge the punch line.

"It were poisoned, having ingested a most deadly substance, the one toxin that could destroy its hellish being," he reported. "For what the unholy fiend didn't realise was that our cook was no other than Long…"

He paused for maximum effect.

"John…"

And held out his arms wide.

"SILVER!"

* * *

Lying amongst the fragments of shattered glass moments later, Jake mused that it hadn't gone too badly. At least they hadn't beaten him up before they threw him through the window.

Glancing up at the full moon, he thought it a shame that no-one ever believed his shaggy dog stories.

Still, that would soon be rectified, he knew. The monthly transformation was already tingling through his veins, the bestial change taking grip. Admiring the fur starting to sprout from his hook, he calculated that in a few moments he'd banish all doubts.

The rowdy sailors had watered him but soon it would be time for them to quell his hunger too. And bosun boy would make such an appetising starter…

Future Tense

Douglas Jennings swallowed, mouth parched. He looked longingly at the water fountain across the control centre but knew he daren't leave his post – not now; not when the telemetry from the probe was due any moment.

"Excited?" a voice behind him asked.

He flashed a thin smile to his female assistant.

"Terrified, more like. I can't stop shaking," he confessed. "I keep thinking of all the hundreds of things that could go wrong."

"It'll be fine," Marie insisted, motioning to the rows and rows of terminals, all manned by intense-looking boffins. "The best brains in the country have worked day and night on this for two years. We've had enough funds to run a banana republic and unlimited access to the latest mathematical and engineering breakthroughs. It'll work, trust me."

Douglas hoped so. It was more than just their jobs and scientific reputations on the line. If the project failed, their angry critics would use it to attack NASA; arguing that the Space Agency had lost its senses and should be wound up.

He shivered, remembering the *Washington Post* headline three months before 'TIME TO END THE MADNESS!' and the thunderous attack: *"Professor Jennings is deluded if he thinks his hare-brained rocket scheme will succeed. It is not just impossible, but is an irresponsible waste of taxpayer dollars at a time when our nation is crippled by recession."*

Yes, it was expensive, Douglas told the various Senate committees, but the possible rewards were incalculable. It would alter everything – how the human race lived, how they viewed the future, whether they should strike out to colonise the stars.

"I cannot deny that the research is theoretical and hugely controversial," he'd conceded. "But it could be the most significant breakthrough in history."

That had won the philosophical debate, but there still remained doubts over the cutting-edge technology.

Staring at the terminal, he ticked off every worrying variable. Success depended on the hyper drive performing perfectly, on the probe surviving the immense acceleration forces, and on the returning info stream cutting through the swirling solar interference.

And then there was the almost mystical science… accurately interpreting radiation decay, ion disturbances, gravity fluctuations, planet drift, the expansion of matter, radio wave distortion and numerous other factors. All to calculate one thing – the rate of entropy gripping the cosmos.

A beep interrupted his troubled thoughts. The telemetry was coming in! He yelped in relief as bursts of numbers and algebraic symbols raced across the screens.

Marie grinned.

Then almost instantly, she frowned.

"This can't be right," she hissed, fingers clicking across her keyboard.

"What's the matter?" he asked, elation evaporating.

"It's the prediction figure for the collapse of the universe. The data says it will end in twelve billion–"

"What? Millennia?"

"No…"

"Centuries? Years?"

"No," she gulped. "Nano-seconds."

Twelve billion nano-seconds! That was ridiculous, he told himself. It was only a fifth of a minute, for Heaven's sake!

"Let me have a look," he snapped, pushing her out of the way. "It's simply not possi—"

Christopher Robin Went Down
- With Malice!

The siren grew louder – its eeyore, eeyore, eeyore screech coming nearer and nearer as Winifred gazed ruefully at the body by her feet…

* * *

In the interview room the piglet faces of the policemen were inscrutable. Winifred had expected them to be angry, or disgusted or wary – anything but flat and expressionless.

Sure enough, they were curious. Who wouldn't be? They wanted to ask her why she'd done it, to get some sort of explanation, to find out why she'd bludgeoned Chris to death with the book.

But they were clever interrogators. They were waiting for her to open up voluntarily. That way would be so much simpler.

And, after two long nerve-racking hours of tension, she cracked.

"It was a copy of *Tales from the 100-Acre Wood*," she said, finally unable to stand the overwhelmingly oppressive silence. "That's what I hit him with. It was a really heavy hardback."

"*Tales from the 100-Acre Wood*? A.A. Milne? Now, I wouldn't have expected that," the first officer remarked in surprise.

"No," his colleague agreed. "It's not exactly the kind of murder weapon we normally come across."

It was simply the first object to hand when she'd snapped, Winifred told them. "Besides," she added, "it seemed appropriate in the circumstances."

After that first admission she couldn't shut up, the words – the chilling confession – just spilled out.

"He had it coming," she began. "Every day – nagging, finding fault, treating me like a slave. Winnie fix this, Winnie clean that. Winnie wash my socks, Winnie iron my shirt."

She let all the bile pour out. The policemen, nodding understandingly, offered grunts of sympathy, looking occasionally at the tape machine to make sure every detail of this bizarre domestic homicide was being captured.

"So what caused it? What was the final spark?" the senior officer prompted. "There must have been a tigger point – I mean, *trigger* point?"

Winifred closed her eyes, reliving the moments leading up to her husband's bloody literature-themed demise.

"He wouldn't stop. All day it was. All day, Winnie the dishes need drying. Winnie – the hoovering. Winnie – the lawn needs cutting."

She shuddered, remembering the total, mad, enveloping rage that had engulfed her. "But that would have been all right if it hadn't been for the dog."

"The dog?" the interrogators chorused, bemused.

"Yeah, the dog. The dog mess. On the front door step. Chris spotted it. Could have cleaned it up himself, but oh no – he wanted me to scoop up the filth."

Winifred leant in menacingly close to the detectives.

"And that's when I let him have it – right across the skull with the A.A. Milne."

The two coppers blinked, still perplexed, still not getting it.

"It was the way he told me," she explained. "He stood there like Lord Muck, handed me the dustpan, snapped his finger and said: Winnie – the poo!"

Open Sesame

"**D**on't do this. For pity's sake, Elaine. Let me in. Please, please let me in."

Terry pounded, meaty fists making the reinforced shelter door shudder in its titanium frame.

"I can hear them. Oh God, they're breaking in. I'm begging. You've got to save me!"

Inside the concrete refuge, Elaine regarded the CCTV monitor with detachment, watching her husband's face whiten as a crash echoed from the back of the house. His thumping trebled, but she kept her hand away from the switch that would unlock the deadbolts.

"Sorry, darling, but it would be a bit crowded in here with two and you know how I hate being uncomfortable," she taunted over the loudspeaker. "Don't make such a fuss. It will all be over in seconds. A few bites, a little pain, and then you won't care…"

For a moment, he stopped hammering, stunned. His wet eyes blinked, appalled by her scorn and cruelty.

"For God's sake, Elaine. This is no time for games," he hissed. "Okay, okay, you've made your point. You haven't forgiven me for the affair. I get it. You win. I'm humiliated. I'm grovelling. I'll grovel forever, just open the bloody door."

She leant into the microphone. "It's not about your pathetic fling. I got over that ages ago. No, Terry, this is about everything else. How you look down on me, the contempt you show for my ideas, the way you keep reminding everyone how gormless and scatterbrain I am. Well, this is payback. Now you're the one who's looking stupid."

Terry mouthed a frantic reply, but she couldn't make it out, the words drowned by an inhuman screeching just behind him.

Elaine mused how chillingly amusing it was that real-life zombies should look so much like their horror movie counterparts. Terry, sadly, didn't have time to notice, too busy trying to fend them off with a kitchen chair, stabbing desperately at one yellow-faced attacker, then another.

For moments Elaine was transfixed, then had to look away as Terry disappeared under the grasping, groaning, biting horde.

Shivering, she double checked the time lock clock. Terry had told her it was complicated, too damn technical for her simple mind to comprehend, but it had proved remarkably easy to program. A few pushes of the buttons and she'd been able to set it so the shelter door would remain closed well into 2030. By then, she reckoned contentedly, the plague-ravished humans would have perished, starved of fresh meat.

For her part, she had plenty of supplies – food, water, generator oil. Even little luxuries like ultra soft toilet paper and a ten thousand strong DVD collection to stave off boredom. Which made her feel pretty damn clever.

Terry appeared on the screen again, eyes vacant, mouth twisted and drooling, moaning, hands outstretched in a parody of his earlier pleading.

She was just thinking how fitting he looked as a zombie, when the shelter door bolts abruptly clicked open.

Instantly, she realised she'd made a fatally brainless mistake. Terry was right. She was a dumbo.

And at 20.30 – half past eight precisely – her husband and his ravenous new companions lurched inside.

The Babel Fable

A tremendous cheer went round our spotter plane – Central control had found Bert Higgins! In my relief, I cheered too; yelling until my lungs ached and tears coursed down my cheeks.

Three weeks of scouring every country and nation state had finally paid off. We'd located the Preston bus driver who was the only man alive who could save the human race.

It was incredible. Just when we'd given up hope and resigned ourselves to a global nuclear confrontation, this sudden ray of salvation shone through.

Twenty thousand volunteers had joined in the frantic quest to find Bert's hideaway. An army of idealists pledged to saving mankind had worked night and day, hour after unbearable hour. Now it was down to me to fly to Bert's mountain retreat in Tibet and beg him to help stop the impending carnage.

I'd been picked because I knew this towering legend. As his former boss, I was the only one that Higgins – the most important single figure of the 21st century – would listen to. In the last decade, since nuclear bombs had become so plentiful that any crackpot could pick one off the supermarket shelf, our world had become a frighteningly unstable place. Neighbour threatened neighbour, race turned against race.

The seeds were sown for global conflict and desperately we'd organised a peace conference in Geneva. But it wasn't working. There was too much mistrust and hatred. We needed a neutral, honest broker to chair the summit. Only one man was acceptable – Bert Higgins, a man who'd escaped into obscurity, taking his miraculous conciliatory talents with him.

The greatest diplomat ever known, Bert was a strange character. Blessed with a complex personality, a faith in basic truths and a childlike simplicity of purpose, he was the most enigmatic man I'd ever encountered. He said what he thought without fear or favour, and his judgments were renowned for their wisdom.

But if his character was a riddle, it was nothing compared to the paradoxical accident that shot him to international fame. He'd been driving his double decker bus through Preston's rush hour when a runaway pram careered in front of him. Instinctively, he'd jammed on the brakes and the front of the bus dipped violently.

Bert went flying through the windscreen and landed in intensive care. Fractured skull. Deep coma. Little hope of recovery.

Only Doris, his wife of fifteen years, kept faith that he would wake again. Undaunted, she kept a lonely bedside vigil. The doctors looked at her and tutted sadly.

Months passed. Bert showed no signs of stirring. Then a friend told Doris about a young girl who'd awoken from a coma after her parents played her CDs of her favourite pop songs.

Bert hated pop music – "That bloomin' racket!" was the kindest thing he ever said about it – but Doris thought the principle might work. She went out to buy a selection of Bert's favourite show tunes.

Now, no-one knows who mixed up the disks – perhaps it was divine intervention – but when she opened the box it didn't contain the hits from Cats, Evita and Les Miserables. Instead, there was an enormous selection of language CDs, covering everything from Egyptian to Eskimo.

Doris couldn't believe it. She wept bitterly. Later, after she'd pulled herself together, she decided to play them anyway. What the hell, she thought, a CD was a CD and she had paid for them. So began Bert's unconscious exposure to the voices of the world.

Three years passed. Bert's condition didn't improve in the slightest. Every day Doris made her audio pilgrimage. Every night she'd go home, slightly more drawn and stooped. Then, as the first autumn gusts stirred the fallen leaves, Bert stirred too. It was hardly noticeable at first, but within minutes he was struggling to sit up.

Doris had rehearsed what she would do on this day. I'll tell him I love him and I'll kiss the sleep from his eyes, she'd told herself.

But, as Bert rose from the dead and scratched his backside, Doris did what any normal, caring person would do… she fainted.

Bert seemed to be a bit put out by all the attention. "Aw, quit fussin'," he told his doctors. "There's nowt wrong with me that a good pint of ale won't put right."

And there it would have ended had there not been an international medical convention in town. News of Bert's recovery reached the delegates and they hot-footed it to the hospital.

By teatime, the ward overflowed with babbling doctors, all jostling to have a few words. It was an incredible din as dozens of national tongues clashed.

Doris put her hands over her ears, and Bert was about to do the same when he made a startling discovery. He realised he could understand every person in the room. Swedes, Spaniards, Russians, Romanians, Germans, Belgians, Poles, Chinese, Nigerians – he could converse with them like a true native. It was a linguistic miracle!

Of course, word soon leaked out and the world's press had him on the front page of every newspaper. And that's where I came in.

As the chief crisis negotiator with the peace charity World in Peril, I was trying to arrange a cease-fire between the Afghans and the Uzbekistanis in a bloody dispute over border infringements, but I couldn't find translators acceptable to both sides. Then I heard about Bert.

My bosses thought I was ready for the funny farm, but they pressed Bert into action. We locked the two opposing ambassadors in a room with Bert, as a mediator-cum-referee. When they emerged two hours later, the ambassadors weren't just talking – they were engaged to be married!

I tried Bert on other thorny international disputes. The results were always the same – agreement, concord, mutual understanding.

There was no doubt about it, Bert was a born diplomat. It wasn't just that he spoke everyone's language. It went beyond mere linguistic skills. He seemed to understand all points of view. Bitter rifts were healed, age-old feuds settled and a new spirit of friendship and co-operation flourished. No chasm was too wide for Bert's patient conciliatory skills to bridge.

There were some who argued that he was a messenger from God. New Age cults sprang up, worshipping Bert as the new Messiah. They'd hold torch-light ceremonies, chanting under huge glowing pictures of Bert's kindly face.

He always laughed at the suggestion that he was an icon, telling the chat show hosts: "'ee, lad, I'm nowt more than a humble bus driver. I do my bit to help but this talk about me being some sort of angel is a load of old codswallop."

Sadly, Doris, the woman who had made this modern-day miracle come true, didn't take to their new lifestyle. She was a simple lass who couldn't adjust to Bert's high profile, high tension role. She high-tailed it.

Bert never really got over it, and from that day his enthusiasm seemed to fade. Church leaders begged, Presidents pleaded, Royalty commanded but Bert's heart just wasn't in it any more. He'd lost his vocation, his messianic mission was over.

I wasn't surprised when he decided to give it all up and hide from the world. Thankfully, the world was prepared to let him escape the limelight.

Until this moment, that is.

Now we needed his old multi-lingual magic again, and I prayed I'd be able to convince him to come out of retirement.

That worrying thought ricocheted around my mind as our plane landed at Beijing International and I raced towards a long-haul jet helicopter waiting on the tarmac, rotors already spinning madly.

Chen Lee, station chief from our Hong Kong office, was strapped into one of the two passenger seats. I leapt in beside him and we were off towards Tibet.

"Any word from Geneva?" I asked anxiously, as we sped towards the border.

He nodded. "The peace conference is hanging by a thread. The Irish and Israelis are refusing to sit beside each other in the cocktail bar, the Australians are accusing the New Zealanders of imperial expansionism and Luxembourg has threatened to annihilate any country that refuses to import its prime-time soap operas."

I gulped. Things could come apart at any moment.

In the old days Bert would have solved this tidal wave of international disputes in a few hours. He'd have had every delegate playing five-a-side football and swopping baking tips. Now, I wondered how he'd cope. Would he still have the magic? Would he still have that baffling instinct to instil compromise and companionship in everyone he met?

It had been years – long, hard, years. Years when Bert hadn't seen a conference table, hadn't touched a peace treaty. The thought that he might be rusty made me shiver. I couldn't admit it – even to myself. We needed Bert Higgins as sharp as he'd ever been. He HAD to be the saviour we so badly needed. The future of civilisation depended on it!

"Can't this contraption go any faster," I snapped. "Every second counts. Even now it may be too late!"

Chen put his hand on my arm. "We're going as fast as humanly possible," he said. "We'll get to Bert in time. I promise."

I wanted to argue – to scream my frustration – but he was right, of course. Everyone involved in the mission had pulled out all the stops. It was unfair to take out my nerves on him. Apologising, I closed my eyes, willing myself to relax.

I fell asleep to a troubled blurred nightmare of mushroom clouds and wailing women. Everywhere I looked there was death, destruction, the smell of defeat and despair. Apocalyptic images bled into each other.

Bert's famous quote spun round and round, echoing. "I'm nowt more than a humble bus driver… nowt more than a humble bus driver… nowt more than a—"

I awoke in a sweat with Chen Lee gently shaking me. He nodded towards the aircraft window. The majestic snow-topped Himalayas sat ahead of us – eerie, silent, mountains of ancient stone. We were on the roof of the world. We'd arrived.

Although our intelligence reports were sketchy, I told Chen not to worry, I had an idea how to find Bert. Leaving the helicopter, we trudged through the wind towards a village, silhouetted against the last rays of the dying sun.

Wary eyes watched us as we marched down the alleyways between the crude, stone-built houses. A yak-skin curtain twitched and a door slammed, but no-one spoke to us. The villagers were obviously deeply suspicious of strangers.

No wonder, I thought, that Bert had found this God-forsaken spot such an ideal hiding place.

Sure enough, half an hour later, we'd found him. We were huddled in an evil-smelling shelter with an assortment of Tibetans as his number 17 bus rolled up.

"Hello, Bert," I said.

"How do," he replied wearily. "I reckoned you'd come along sooner or later. I suppose it's about this peace conference lark?"

I nodded.

He sniffed non-committally and nodded to the destination board. "How far are you going?"

I handed over my handful of coins. "All the way," I said.

201

We rode with the other passengers – six villagers, three monks and a goat – until we arrived at the garage where Bert kept his buses.

Once inside, I explained the situation. Bert listened attentively while he brewed tea in a clay pot suspended over an open fire. He stirred the leaves silently, listening with his head cocked to one side, smiling sadly at the mess we'd made of things. When I finished he looked deeply into my eyes.

"It's a shame that you've gone to all this trouble, lad," he said with a sigh, "because I can't help you."

My brain did a mental somersault. Surely, I'd heard wrongly.

"Didn't you just hear what I've been telling you? The world is about to end and you're the only man who can stop it."

Bert shrugged. "I heard you, and I'd like to help, but I can't. Not anymore."

I was devastated. "But you can't reject us," I yelled, "the fate of mankind rests on your shoulders."

Bert looked sad, and then sheepish. Something was very wrong – very wrong.

Realisation came to me in a blinding light. "Oh, my God," I said. "You've lost the gift. You can't talk in tongues anymore!"

Head bowed, he nodded. "That's right, lad. It's amazing how quickly you forget languages when you're not using them every day."

Chen Lee's eyes went wide in disbelief. "But you can still remember something?" he asked.

"Oh aye. I can recall some cooking recipes in Mandarin, a few nursery rhymes in Swahili, a smidgen of Czech swear words, and I can still count to ten in Serbo-Croat."

I nearly screamed!

"In fact," he added, "there's only one phrase that I can still say in all languages."

My heart thumped. "What is it?" I demanded. "Tell me, man. All our lives may depend on it."

He was silent for a moment, then grinned apologetically.

"Fares please," he said.

That's Why the Lady is a Vamp

Ivana snorted impatiently, snapping her fingers at the liveried flunky.

"C'mon man, get a move on. I haven't got all night."

Apologising profusely, the doorman bowed and held out his hand to help Ivana struggle from the back of the limousine. Her figure-hugging designer dress was so restrictive that it would have choked the life out of any normal mortal. But she was, she thought wryly, neither normal nor mortal.

She paused in mid manoeuvre to make sure the posse of waiting cameramen caught a teasing shot of her beautiful bare upper thigh before stepping onto the Manhattan sidewalk.

Turning her million-dollar smile on them, she revealed perfect, white, sharp supermodel's teeth. The smile didn't travel up to her eyes – not just because she felt little warmth or empathy but because she was desperately avoiding the painful explosions of brilliance. Damn the flashbulbs – they were as strong as daylight!

"Ivana! Ivana! Is there any truth in the rumours? Are you engaged? Has he proposed yet?" a voice yelled.

"Are you going to be wife number six?" another added.

Tapping the side of her nose mischievously, she turned from the reporters and the flood of questions. Let them wait, let them stew.

The press were parasites, and she hated them with a cold, burning loathing, but she also respected the fact that they were incredibly powerful and deadly to cross.

Ruthless – just like herself. Merciless – just like all of her kindred. And just as determined when they scented blood.

Striding so fast that the sapphire necklace around her porcelain-pale throat bounced, she entered the towering glass and chrome corporate office block.

She was late for her assignation, but she doubted that Donald would notice. He'd be too busy on the phones turning his modest 3-billion fortune into a more respectable 4-billion fortune.

As the reception desk staff signed her in, she let her gaze rise to the various balconies and upper floors; to the stern-faced men in dark suits and crew cuts, men sporting crackling earpieces and high-velocity rifles. All of them watching her – watching like hawks – waiting for any sudden move, any excuse to open fire.

Let them dare, she thought with amusement. It was unlikely they'd bring her down with their first volley, and she'd rip out their windpipes before they had time to fire off a second. Even though the diamante encrusted four–inch heels might slow her up just a little…

She sighed. The overblown security was all so silly, so pointless, but since they'd started dating she'd learnt to put up with Donald's paranoia; ignoring the tiny crucifix around his neck, the strange aftershave that smelt vaguely of garlic and the new ultra-violet lighting system installed at both his luxury apartment and his office complex. Plus, the sudden arrival of all these ex-special forces bodyguards.

"Anyone would think you don't feel safe around me," she'd pouted at their last public appearance, a glitzy charity fundraiser for underprivileged families in her native Carpathian region.

"I do," he'd answered, with a dry chuckle, "but it never does any harm to have a little insurance. We wouldn't want any misunderstandings, any little playful accidents to spoil things, now would we?"

The private elevator dispatched from the penthouse level pinged open and, waving teasingly to the stony-faced assassins, she got in and pressed the button.

Goons and guns aside, it was a perfect relationship, she mused as the glass lift rose smoothly floor by floor. A super-rich sugar daddy passionate for Eastern European beauties with bodies to die for, and a woman who never got a day older – or wanted to hang around until morning.

So were the reporters right, she asked herself. Was tonight the night? Was he finally going to pop the question? Was it going to be 'til death us do part?

"Ivana, my darling, you look even more radiant than usual," Donald said, getting up from the long table and pushing back his unruly hair.

She brushed his mahogany-tanned cheek with her lips, giving him a tiny nip – a promise of things to come.

"You don't look so bad yourself," she purred. "For someone who has the constant headache of having to sack so many incompetent trainees."

He gestured her to sit, a momentary frown making his bushy brows dip. "I'm glad you could come over, because I've being doing some reflecting…" he began.

"Not something I can claim," she joked, tilting her head coquettishly.

"…and I think it's time to put our relationship on a more serious, more permanent basis."

She felt butterflies in her stomach – little crimson butterflies. At last!

"And I'd like to ask you if you'd make me the happiest man in the world by consenting to… consenting to…"

Oh yes, oh yes!

"…meeting a business associate of mine."

Ivana did a double take, stunned. Her hearing was super sensitive, the stuff of legend, but she was sure her ears were playing tricks. Business associate? What business associate? Where was the proposal? The grand romantic gesture? The engagement ring sporting a diamond so big it could power a death ray?

"I think you may have heard of him," Donald said, pressing the desk buzzer, summoning a dark, funereal figure in wide-brimmed hat, cloak, gauntlets and riding boots. "He's from the Old Country."

She froze. Oh yes, she recognised him all right. Van Helsing! The nemesis of all of her kind.

"It's been a long time, Ivana," the newcomer said, voice measured, eyes locking fearlessly on hers.

"Arguably, not long enough," she hissed, hackles rising. Spinning round to Donald, she demanded: "Why have you brought him here? Is this a trap? Are you trying to destroy me? What's going on?"

The billionaire shrugged sheepishly. "You know I love you more than anyone else on the planet, and I desperately want you to be my wife. But with who you are – what you are – I need to take a few precautions."

Van Helsing stepped forward. "With your reputation, it is only common sense to have safeguards," he explained, dumping his large canvas travelling bag onto the boardroom table. "I have been called in to ensure you never bleed Donald dry."

He reached inside, and Ivana stiffened. Shivering with fear she watched, transfixed, as he brought out the only instrument in the entire universe that terrified her. Not Holy Water, silver bullets or a weapon personally blessed by the Pope, but something immensely more powerful, something guaranteed to stop her dead in her tracks.

"We both know you've seen one of these before," the newcomer observed slyly, his Transylvanian accent suddenly more pronounced.

She couldn't help herself – Ivana flinched, repelled more effectively than if it had been a cross.

Staring furiously at the ancient parchment, she knew the game was up. Curse him! Curse Van Helsing! Curse all those sworn to thwart her sinking her teeth into a fresh victim.

"I suppose this is what they mean by raising the stakes," she ventured ruefully as, defeated, she turned to leave. "Well, it's been a good run. I almost pulled it off. Until next time…"

"I'll be waiting," the divorce lawyer agreed amicably, and stuffed the unsigned pre-nup agreement back into his battered voluminous valise.

In a Right Hump

Cursing and kicking the Cathedral cat, Quasimodo trooped dispiritedly down the 387 steps from the tower. It had been a pig of a day and he couldn't wait to clock off.

Friends told him he should be thrilled to be working at Notre Dame and being its top attraction. But he was sick of the tourists and their stupid questions, sick of signing autographs and most definitely sick of posing with them for sketches. God, he hated it!!!!

Limping along the dark Paris street, he thought about jacking it all in. Okay, he was misshapen and stooped – with a face that curdled milk – but this was 1482 and anything was possible for a man with a few good ideas, an engaging lisp and an entrepreneurial flair.

Perhaps, today – this most awful of days – was the time to finally take the plunge and start that beautician's business.

But first, he needed a drink.

Although the tavern was crowded he spotted a free space at the bar. At the fifth attempt he made it up on to the stool.

"You look awful," Pierre the bar-keep said, deadpan. "Bad day?"

"Like you wouldn't believe," Quasi grumbled. "A baying mob turned up this afternoon with pitchforks and flaming torches. They called me a monster; wanted to hang me by the gargoyles."

"Painful," Pierre observed sympathetically. "But why would they want to kill you? I thought you were the big star, a real draw."

"I am, but according to them it's…" The seething campanologist made quotation marks in the air. "…traditional at this time of year to lynch deformed dwarves."

Both men agreed it wasn't very politically correct, but could understand the argument for protecting the nation's customs and heritage.

"Still," Pierre consoled, "you've always got the love of a good woman. Your Esmeralda is a diamond."

"She left me," Quasi said sadly. "Packed her bags and went to her mother's. Said my constant moaning put her back up."

Yes, Pierre agreed with an expressive Gallic shrug, that romantic blow alone would be enough to make anyone bitter and twisted. There was nothing else for it. Only a stiff drink would do.

Reaching for the Johnnie Walker bottle the barman went to pour a dram, but Quasimodo waved his hand frantically at the whisky next to it – his favourite brand.

"The Bell's, the Bell's," he insisted.

Publish and be Damned!

A sudden commotion made Geraint jump; the hand scripted galley proofs he'd been scrutinising tumbling chaotically to the printing house floor. Outside, in the busy cobbled street, he could hear the air fill with shouts of anger and protest.

Bustling over to the mullioned window, the publisher took in the scene and immediately cursed.

It couldn't be! Not again! But yes, he realised wearily, the ecclesiastical whirlwind was returning.

Scything through the crowd, swinging his sharp-edged crook from side to side, Bishop John Henry was making a beeline towards Geraint's premises. Face crimson, voice tight and thunderous, he bellowed with every swipe: "Let me through. Let me through, I say. I am on the Lord's holy mission and I shall not be delayed for an instant. Stand aside."

Around him, like baby chicks clinging to their demented mother, several clerics flustered and fretted, shooing away those annoyed bystanders who'd taken umbrage and severe damage to their shins.

Geraint's spirits sank like a witch on a ducking stool. Placing his palms tightly together, he prayed that the pissed-off prelate was going to veer off at the last moment and let his biblical wrath fall upon some other unfortunate business owner. But the boom of the mighty stave bouncing off the front door put paid to any hopes in that direction.

"Master Geraint. I demand you open up immediately," the Bishop roared, with all the bluster and ferocity he normally reserved for his fire and brimstone sermons.

Fumbling with the handle, Geraint racked his memory to identify what cardinal sin he could have committed. Could it be the sign in the window sparking this old testament tempest?

Since gaining the exclusive rights to print and sell bibles across the city, the bookbinder had hung up a notice saying: 'We take Holy Orders'. It had raised a few eyebrows, certainly, but surely the witticism hadn't been bad enough to warrant this? If it was, he calculated, the follow-up – 'We're devoted to our customers' – definitely wasn't going to see the light of day!

"At last," John Henry snarled, as the door flung open and he marched inside, dragging the vexed vergers behind him. "At last we can gain admittance to this den of vice and blasphemy, and put an end to the assault on the morals of the God-fearing public."

Den of vice? Assault on the morals of the public? Had the priest been at the communion wine? Or had wearing that heavy pointy hat finally crushed his brain? Geraint feared it was both.

"You are always most welcome inside my unworthy establishment, your Holiness," he began, with an obsequious bow. "You honour us with your most saintly presence. What may I help you with today?"

The churchman gave him a withering look, signalling that at this instant he'd give anything to be a canon with a cannon.

"Enough with the flannel, master printer. Enough of the grovelling, humble shopkeeper routine. It won't wash this time. You are in the most terrible trouble and you know why."

Geraint really didn't. He shrugged helplessly. "If it's about the mixed-up pen portraits in the last edition of the I Spy Directory of Clergymen, I've already apologised about that," he reminded.

"Not much of an apology as I recall," his visitor snapped back. "You seemed to think it amusing to tell me that you'd simply got your vicars in a twist!"

The peeved parson breathed in heavily. "No, what has brought me here today is immeasurably worse. An insult of biblical proportions. Nothing less than the work of Satan himself!"

He plunged his hand inside his robes and brought out a thick leather-bound volume, throwing it down on the nearby table with an echoing crash.

"This FILTH, this PORNOGRAPHY is an abomination, the most depraved obscenity my eyes have ever had the misfortune to behold!"

His cheeks puffed, rage turning his complexion rouge. "It is a vile, corrupting, lustful, scandalous publication designed to tempt even the most righteous and holy towards base and impure thoughts."

Geraint blinked. Half of his brain was thinking; Wow! Now that's what I call a Five-Star review while the other half was puzzling over how he'd somehow managed to overlook producing a sizzling, salacious, guaranteed best-seller sensation.

"But it's just a history book," he said in puzzlement, as he craned over to read the title of the offending tome. "Third Instalment of our Ancient Classics Chronicles. It's innocuous. Completely innocent."

Around them the ring of anxious acolytes swallowed hard, crossed themselves and edged back a step from the inevitable explosion.

"There is nothing innocent in this Devil's digest," Bishop John Henry roared. "It is perversion in its rawest form. And I mean – raw!"

With that, the pontiff flipped open the book.

Geraint couldn't help himself. He'd uttered: "Holy Moly!" before he could prevent the stunned words spilling out.

If anything the angry cleric had understated the lewdness of the offending volume's contents. The sight that greeted the publisher's bulging eyes was unbelievable. Every drawing, every sketch, every image was unadulterated erotic titillation.

Page after page of bawdiness greeted him. Acres of bare skin, rude romps and carefree copulation adorned the parchment; each illumination shining a licentious light on activities that should definitely be kept in the dark!

"But I never authorised this," he gasped, as he studied the scenes of floosies and sandalled fighting men engaged in manhandling manoeuvres, and shuddered at the accompanying sex-filled storyline. "I simply told the author to make the Grecian era a bit more stimulating."

In that, the Bishop observed icily, the scribe had most certainly met his brief. "Who committed this foul act? Who is responsible?" he demanded.

Geraint sighed. "That will be Old Vic," he replied glumly.

"How can you be so sure?" the holy man demanded.

Geraint kept his face deadpan as he replied: "That's because, as all scholars know, history is always written by the Victor."

Closing the salacious hardback with a snap, jolting several of the gawping Reverends out of their reverie,

John Henry raised himself to his full height and instructed: "Then take me to him at once."

"You intend to communicate?" Geraint ventured.

"I intend to ex-communicate," the Bishop corrected menacingly.

* * *

They made their way in procession up the rickety wooden steps and along a dusty corridor until Geraint halted them before a door bearing the copperplate notice: *Vic's Heritage History Books – always busy making royalties from Royalty!*

None of the party smiled.

"Perhaps, I should go in first," the publisher suggested. "Just to have a quiet word with my employee, to get his side of the story. I'm sure there's a perfectly reasonable explanation for all this."

But John Henry wasn't having any of it.

"Stand aside," he commanded, pushing forward roughly. "I haven't time for your mealy-mouthed chats. I want an interrogation, a probing investigation. I want to get to the bottom of this outrage."

And letting a malicious growl enter his voice, added: "Indeed, when I get my hands and red hot poker on this heinous heretic, I intend to perform an outrage on his bottom."

Victor blinked in surprise as they spilled into his cramped writing room. He obviously wasn't expecting visitors, never mind an inquisition – Spanish or otherwise.

"W-w-what's the meaning of this," he gasped, as he navigated his way out from behind walls of precariously piled papers, mildewed maps and wilted wills.

The Bishop's eyes narrowed. "No, that's my question, scurrilous scribe. What's the meaning of…" He jabbed his ring adorned finger at one of the offending pictures. "…this!"

Victor flipped his spectacles from high on his forehead on to the bridge of his bony nose, and focused intently on the indicated coloured plate in the crisis-causing Chronicle.

"Ah, that's the fall of Troy," he reported, with a scholarly sniff. "The moment when the Athenian call girls seduced the guards, distracting them so that the city gates could be opened, allowing the invaders to pour in."

For a second Geraint thought the Bishop was going to faint. For that matter, the printer thought he might have a swoon himself. What was this rubbish?

"Call girls?" John Henry said, choking. "Athenian call girls!"

Victor nodded, beaming innocently.

"Seduced the guards?" the prelate repeated, aghast.

"Oh yes," the author agreed happily. "It was the turning point in the ten-year-old siege, when the courtesans were left on the beach. Agamemnon knew the Trojan soldiers wouldn't be able to resist the allure of these ladies of the night. One glimpse of their voluptuous bodies and the troops would instantly forget the old adage: beware the gift of bare Greeks."

Geraint didn't know whether to laugh or cry. To be on the safe side, he did a little of both.

"I have never heard such a blatant distortion of the facts in all my life," the stunned Bishop declared, as he shook his head and crook in perfect synchronisation. "This is some fantastical fiction; a fabrication. There was no fornication mentioned in Homer's Iliad, no hussies recorded in any other chronicle. How, in God's name, did you get the idea that this ancient war was ended by women of easy virtue. Who told you this nonsense?"

Victor pointed straight at his employer. "He did."

Geraint spluttered, mouth falling open.

What!

"N-n-o, I didn't," he contradicted loudly. "That's a lie. I did nothing of the sort." He held up both hands to show how vehemently he denied the very suggestion.

"Yes, you did. You specifically told me to include the jezebels." Victor turned to address the apoplectic apostle, revealing conspiratorially: "I remember it clearly, your Worshipfulness. He was very insistent. He wanted as many pictures as I could sketch. Every detail, he said, include every detail. Make it exciting… so I did."

Geraint gulped. The publisher didn't know what lunacy was at work here, but he reckoned it could only end in one way – with him being invited to the Bishop's poker night, where no amount of bluffing would be enough to save his rump from a roasting.

"I honestly have no idea what the senile old fool is raving on about," he protested desperately, looking round for a means of escape. "His brains must be addled. I never – repeat never – instructed him to include doxies in his drawings. I haven't a clue where he got that crazy notion from."

None of the churchmen appeared convinced. All glared accusingly at him, no doubt darkly imagining how satisfyingly the publisher's posterior would present as burnt offerings.

Then, suddenly, like a bolt from the very heavens, the answer struck him. Of course. It had to be!

Geraint groaned and covered his eyes as the hilarious solution to the rude riddle made itself blindingly clear.

And, grabbing the history scribe and pulling him close, the printer bellowed down Victor's trusty ear trumpet with enough force to send the cassocked assembly reeling.

"I was talking about a pony, you deaf sod. I didn't say whores – I said HORSE. Show lots of action of the guards celebrating with the Trojan Horse!"

Virgin Territory

Startled, Elaine grabbed the strap as the helicopter abruptly banked, plunging downwards towards the shimmering sheet of blue. She cursed, the unexpected motion making her stomach lurch violently.

God, she hated flying.

"Survey ship's about four miles away. Just over there. Due South. See." The pilot jabbed a gloved finger towards the distant shape silhouetted against the horizon.

Screwing up her eyes at the dazzling sunlight bouncing off the vast expanse of cyan, she recognised the familiar outline of Poseidon's Quest riding up and down on the gentle swell and felt some of her tension ease. Within a minute or two she'd be safely on the landing pad at the rear of the anchored research vessel – free of this rickety, rackety, levitating tin-can.

Even from this far out she could see the ship's crane swung out over the side, gingerly lowering the mini sub towards the waters of the Indian Ocean. It was nearly 4pm – the last dive of the afternoon; the last of five challenging daily submersions for the robot exploration pod, sending it hundreds of feet below the waves.

The derrick crew would be tired, but she knew they'd still be alert, cautious, taking huge care not to make any mistakes. Fatigue was dangerous and any lapse in concentration could bring the tiny craft – slowly swinging and rotating – smashing against the large ship's hull like a gleeful wrecking ball.

"I expect you'll be glad to get back to the action," the pilot commented, voice crackling on the headset microphone. "I really envy you. Searching for Atlantis. Wow, talk about a larger-than-life adventure. That must be mind blowing."

She nodded distractedly.

"It would be if we'd found anything," she agreed. "But so far it's been nothing but eight months of sweat, tears and frustration. Not a scrap of evidence, not a single artifact. Zip."

"But you're definitely on the right track? I heard it's only a matter of time. On the TV news last night they said your team is going to make a dramatic breakthrough any day now."

Despite her aerial jitters, and the acid churning in her belly, Elaine allowed herself a wry smile.

She'd heard that announcement too. Read all the upbeat, hyped, attention-grabbing write-ups. Alas, it was just publicity spin, something to keep the media happy and focused on the underwater archaeological expedition.

That was Richard's doing. The British tycoon wanted headlines and wasn't averse to putting a very rosy gloss on what was increasingly looking to be a PR disaster. He was paying for all this – to the tune of 2 million dollars a week – and wouldn't accept that the seabed scans and satellite imaging had come up blank; not so much as a sunken wreck, never mind a lost continent.

"But it's there," he'd told her just forty-eight hours ago at the crisis meeting in London. "Atlantis is down there. I just know it. It's simply a question of keeping faith. Widen the search area. Look harder. Work harder."

But they needed more than faith – they needed hard scientific proof. And as the chopper swung over the ship and began to land, Elaine told herself that this quixotic quest was rapidly turning into what the Brits called 'A Mug's Game'.

* * *

It had all seemed so different back in April when she'd been invited (she preferred to think of it *as summoned*) to the billionaire's Oxfordshire stately home. Then she'd been excited, optimistic and intensely curious.

Richard had been his famous charming, hyperactive, buoyant schoolboy self as he pumped her hand, dragged her inside and gushed: "Doctor Zuckerman. I can't begin to tell you what a real thrill it is to meet you. I've heard so much about your work on uncovering the treasures of ancient Troy. I've followed your career with huge interest."

"Call me Elaine," she'd replied, "and I have to admit I've heard a great deal about you too."

Mostly, she recalled, his exploits trying to kill himself in a series of increasingly dangerous daredevil publicity stunts – the last of which involved going over Niagara Falls in a barrel painted in his company's distinctive colours.

They'd taken afternoon tea in the huge wood–panelled library, she marvelling at the vast shelves of antique leather-bound books stretching thirty feet to the vaulted ceiling – and awed by how one of the world's richest men could be so badly dressed.

After twenty minutes or so of chit chat with him trying to convince her that hot air ballooning wasn't really as frightening or suicidal as she assumed, he got down to business.

"So, Doctor Zuckerman," he began, tone suddenly becoming firmer.

"It's Elaine."

"Yes, of course. Elaine. Tell me, how much do you know about Atlantis?"

She'd spluttered, almost spilling her cup of Earl Grey.

"Atlantis?"

"Yes. Atlantis. You know, the Lost Continent?"

Blinking, she'd studied his face to see if this was some bizarre test or that he was joking, recalling that Richard was almost as famous for his wicked sense of humour as his entrepreneurial genius. But he was deadly earnest, eyes shining brightly.

"Well, just what most classical scholars claim," she replied with a shrug. "That it was an advanced prehistoric civilisation, dating back to around 9600 BC. Legend has it that it was destroyed in a single day and night and disappeared beneath the waves never to be seen again."

"Yes, yes, the general myth is well known but what do you understand more specifically… as a scientist? As an expert in antiquity, an authority in early cities and ancient cultures?"

She made a dismissive face. "That it is a fairy tale, a fable. It never existed. It's a bedtime story dreamt up by Plato. He described it as the Isle of Atlas. I'm hazy on the exact details but there was some tie-up to Greek gods and magic. Allegedly, the inhabitants had advanced technology powered by some mysterious energy crystals."

She added: "Those who are gullible enough to believe the yarn claim the missing kingdom is located somewhere in the far northern Atlantic Ocean. But I've heard others put forward notions about it lying anywhere from the Azores to the Bahamas. And that's not including all the crackpot conspiracy theorists who will tell you it's everywhere from the North Pole to hidden underneath Central Park."

"And you don't buy into it – any of it?" he prompted.

"Sorry. I'm a scientist. I deal in facts. Verifiable facts. I put Atlantis in the same file as The Loch Ness Monster, UFOs and The Abominable Snowman. The one marked Freaky Fantasies."

At that the tycoon had suddenly laughed, and swung back on his chair. "Freaky Fantasies – I like that. That is so droll, so American," he chortled.

And, with an exuberant crash, he leapt to his feet.

"But what if I were to tell you that Atlantis really existed. That it isn't make-believe. What would you say if I told you that I have evidence that proves it; that I know where it is located?"

"I'd say," Elaine commented, refilling her cup and biting into one of the dainty cucumber sandwiches, "that you obviously had a bad bump on the head when you went over those falls."

* * *

Then he'd shown her the relic – had let her examine the intriguing tablet – and her whole world turned upside down.

The carved inscription wasn't Greek, wasn't Sanskrit, Latin or Egyptian but some strange hybrid – an ancient Esperanto. It featured many words she recognised, but many she didn't, and hieroglyphs, lots of them – arrays of small, crude, primitive pictograms.

"It's a hoax," she'd declared, unwilling to accept what her eyes were telling her. "It's impossible. I'm familiar with every known language of the Ancient World and I've never seen anything remotely like it before."

Running a finger thoughtfully over the bumps and dips of the stone, the billionaire nodded.

"That's what I thought at first," he confided, "I told myself it had to be a fake. It was too fanciful an idea to countenance. But then I let the lab boys loose on it."

"And?"

"And they were stunned. Completely bewildered. It passed every test they could throw at it – in fact, every test known to modern science."

The rock had been carved 10,000 years ago, using tools typical of the period, they'd deduced. The weathering was consistent with its age, and chemical erosion analysis showed the tablet had been immersed in salt water for millennia – then lain for further centuries in a hot climate, in sand with an acidic PH factor. And there were twenty-three other indicators to its provenance.

"The results were conclusive. Irrefutable," he gushed. "It's genuine. It's the real deal."

She couldn't accept it. Okay, so it was a clever fake, a clever old fake, but it still defied rational explanation. Surely Richard, with his legendary hard nose and business savvy, could see this.

"All right, then. Let's say that it is as old as you claim. Where was it found?" she challenged. "How did it come to light? I haven't heard anything about any centuries-old language tablet being uncovered. And, trust me, it's not something that would pass unnoticed."

He'd smiled mysteriously. "It popped up in the Middle East, about three years ago, on an old Grecian trade route. I won't go into details. It's best that you don't know the circumstances in which I acquired it. Let's just say that the downfall of a certain dictator helped a little."

Shaking her head, Elaine wondered who was more crazy – him for buying the counterfeit artifact or her, a serious scientist, for remaining there to listen to more of the madness. But, there were so many questions that intrigued her – nagging, puzzling questions – like what the Hell did the carving have to do with Plato's famous drowned-realm folk tale?

"That part is simple," he'd explained animatedly. "The language nerds have had a tough time deciphering the syntax and grammar, and some of the hieroglyphs are still a mystery, but the super computers have translated enough to identify that it's a set of directions. The tablet is a route map to the lost kingdom."

He pointed excitedly to a pictogram of a mermaid, the classic representation of the fabled sunken domain, then indicated the symbol next to it.

"It says Java," he said in an awed hush. "The location of Atlantis – lost to mankind for ten millennia – is off the coast of Indonesia. And guess what, Doctor Zuckerman. That's where you're headed. Freaky fantasy or not, you're going to find it for me."

Watching the chopper disappearing into the distance, Elaine rubbed her brow. Another headache was coming, a result of all the noise, vibrations and diesel fumes.

"London meeting go well?"

She turned and offered a sour grimace to Neil. Her deputy project leader, grunted knowingly.

"Oh, that bad," he surmised.

"Worse," Elaine replied, as they made their way from the swaying helipad and down the narrow gangway to the main deck of the survey ship. "Richard was doing his nut. He's a man used to getting his way. And he simply refuses to believe he could be wrong."

"So what do we do?"

"Keep looking," Elaine concluded with a sigh. "Keep scouring the area for any clue. Keep going until we either find something or he grows bored of the whole escapade and calls it off."

Neil looked at her as though she was a naïve child. "Call it off? He's not going to do that any time soon. His whole reputation hangs on us succeeding. Besides, I've heard he's already made plans to turn it into a vast sub-aqua theme park."

He put on a passable limey accent: "Bring the whole family to the historical holiday of a lifetime at Atlantis-land. The Underwater Magic Kingdom."

Despite herself, Elaine smiled.

"C'mon – let's duck into the control room," she suggested. "The camera link from the mini-sub should be online by now. Maybe just maybe, this time there'll be something – anything – that we can point to as progress."

The interior of the main cabin was eerily dark, the only illumination coming from the radar and the viewing screens. The slouching technicians nodded a greeting for an instant before returning to boredly scrutinising the grainy images coming from the depths. Visibility wasn't great; swirling sand and sediment making the water a cloudy, foggy mass of tiny dancing dots.

A shark swam into view, investigating the robot pod for a few seconds, before darting away. Two stray lobsters crawled across the undulating ocean floor.

Then nothing.

It was just the same as every other dive. No roadways or ruins, no temples or toppled statues. No sign of civilisation. Zero. Nada. Zilch.

Even the sound of the sonar pinging off the sub to the seabed seemed forlorn and dispirited, as though it knew how futile it all was.

Wherever it lay – fact or fable – Atlantis was obviously nowhere near Java, even if the jewel of the Indian Ocean was the most populated island in the world, sitting in the most densely inhabited region on the planet. Even if the isle was one of the most ancient sites of human activity.

"There's no point me waiting around here. I'm going to crash out for a few hours," Elaine announced with a loud yawn. "The jet lag is kicking in."

She turned to leave, when there was a noise. A loud buzz. A loud, insistent buzz – the satellite phone.

Groaning, she told Neil: "I can guess who that is. For Heaven's sake, what does he expect. I've just got back. I know he's frustrated with us but I can't perform miracles."

Aware that everyone was listening in, she said: "I'll take this in my cabin."

Safely alone, she dropped angrily into a chair and stabbed the button that activated the microwave video-link phone and its webcam.

Richard's face appeared on the screen, movements jerky through the time delay.

He had an expression she'd never seen before – a strange mixture of glee, disappointment, smug secrecy and open wonder. It was disconcerting. She wondered vaguely if the stress had finally got to him.

"Hi, Elaine," he said, voice sounding even more fatigued than hers. "I bet you weren't expecting to hear from me again so soon."

"No," she said, popping the ring pull on a Diet Pepsi and taking a swig. "I wasn't, and I know you're not going to be pleased but I have to tell you that I don't have any update. The status of the project is unchanged. Atlantis is not just a lost continent – it's a lost cause."

She expected some outburst, at least a curse, but the tycoon nodded as if it was exactly what he'd anticipated – and that he didn't mind.

"Yes, well, frankly that's not surprising. Not in the circumstances," he said, licking his lips both nervously and with excitement.

She stopped in mid slurp, puzzled. "Richard?"

"That's why I'm phoning. I've got some news." He smiled, sheepishly. "But you're not going to like it. There's been a… development."

For an instant, Doctor Elaine Zuckerman felt more alert, more tense and more worried than she'd ever been in her life.

"What kind of development?" she demanded.

"It's a breakthrough." He made a vague wobbling gesture with his hand. "Well, more of a re-evaluation."

At that moment, if she could have leapt forward, grabbed him by the throat and shaken him, she would have. Instead, she made do with hissing: "What? What are you saying? What am I not going to like? Spit it out."

He paused, breathed in deeply and said: "The language geeks have finally cracked the code on the tablet. And it's not what we thought."

Not, what you thought, she muttered darkly under her breath.

"The inscription is undoubtedly ancient. It does date back to when we calculated, but it isn't directions to Atlantis. In fact, it turns out it doesn't refer to the bloody place at all."

"So what does it refer to?" she said through gritted teeth, mentally adding up the man hours, the astronomical costs and the damage to her scientific reputation that the wild goose chase had clocked up.

"Well, this is the funny bit – and it will make you laugh. But it turns out it's actually a pre-history sales pitch, a sort of early newspaper advertisement."

An advertisement! An advert! She'd trekked half way across the globe and wasted most of a year for a bloody leaflet!

So what in the name of everything holy was the tablet advertising?

He giggled, then stopped suddenly and frowned. "Well, let's just say that a certain Seattle company hasn't exactly been telling the truth about when they first launched."

* * *

"I don't believe it," Neil gasped.

"Neither do I, but apparently it's the truth," Elaine confirmed minutes later. "And it all makes sense when you put it together – the mermaid picture and the symbol for Java."

"But the media are going to tear Richard apart when they get wind that the whole quest was based on a monumental mistake. He'll be ruined; a laughing stock."

Smiling ruefully, Elaine nodded. "Maybe, maybe not. Something tells me, he'll turn it round. By the time he's dropped his 10,000-year-old bombshell no-one will even care about the Atlantis fiasco. It'll be forgotten."

She leant across to switch on the TV. The newsflash was due any second. Richard was about to spill the beans.

It was destined to be the story of the decade. Something they'd all be talking about for the rest of their lives. Something that would rewrite the history books.

He was about to tell the world that the artefact actually said: *"Drink At Starbucks – best skinny latte in Antiquity."*

Poet Tree in Moh-Shan

The ride took three hard days – a bone–jarring 150-mile gallop across desert, scrubland and raging streams.

Under the merciless baking sun, Gregg had cursed for agreeing to the exhausting, quixotic trek through bandit country, and for what? A silly, senseless, romantic gesture.

But Li Yew had been insistent. His new girlfriend yearned to see the famed willow – to put its fabled talent to the ultimate test – and if he wanted her, he had to make the sacred pilgrimage.

"In the days of my ancestors, lovers would come to the tree to gain its blessing for their union," she'd explained. "And I cannot give my love to any man without us doing the same."

Okay, what harm could it do, he'd reasoned. They'd stare at the tree for a few minutes, leave some hokey token to the gods, and then he'd get roaring drunk.

She'd be happy, he'd be off the hook and maybe – just maybe – his fragrant, fragile, tiny, prudish blossom would finally let him into her bed.

Poor, silly, gullible, superstitious Li Yew believed that the mystical tree could see into your soul; that it knew your innermost thoughts and motives.

"And I suppose it talks," he'd teased.

"Yes," she'd replied softly. "In a way it does. It sings to you, in rhyme. As the wind rustles through its leaves, you can hear its message…"

The idea was clearly preposterous, a con to lure credulous tourists, but Gregg wasn't going to risk weeks of carnal delights by pointing this out.

And his lust surged as the horses rounded the bend and it appeared at last, bowed by the river's edge; the legendary Poet Tree.

Li Yew dropped from the saddle and ran forward, unable to contain her excitement.

Bowing before the delicate, revered willow she closed her eyes. For a second or two nothing happened, then the leaves rustled as though a mighty breeze had swept past.

Stunned, Gregg realised he could hear words, faint, whispered, lyrical words:

**Li Yew – gentlest heart, take care
beware the forlorn bliss,
revealing the tender betrayal
of a scheming lover's kiss.**

Shaking his head, Gregg told himself he was imagining it – hallucinating after days of sun. Yet no matter how crazy, how impossible, the tree was talking. And it was warning about him!

In an instant, everything he understood changed. Standing in this magical, bewildering, ancient spot, under the mighty willow's searching arboreal gaze, he felt reborn, renewed, all cynicism washed away.

Seeing the hope in Li Yew's face, he stepped forward, silently praying that the Poet Tree would find him worthy; would forgive his laddish, boozing, raucous, sexually obsessed ways and see the true beauty and compassion in his soul.

The willow swayed… and moaned… and creaked, the sad, drooping branches swishing backwards and forwards. It looked deep inside him and saw… and the whispering supernatural leaves spoke:

There was a young girl from Beijing
Who got knocked up in a fling…

Just Imagine

Murmurs of discontent swept the capacity audience. Peeping round the curtains, Roddy McPherson studied the anxious faces and grinned, savouring their tension.

The rows of annoyed delegates fidgeted, fearful that he wasn't going to appear – or worse, be so drunk he'd stagger across the stage and slur incoherently, unable to deliver his keynote speech.

After all, it had happened before…

It was that sense of danger, the unpredictability of what the bourbon-swigging hell-raiser would do or say, which had attracted so many to the symposium. That and the fact that the bad boy of speculative fiction sold more books than the rest of the genre's masters put together.

"Please, Mr McPherson – I'm pleading. The MC has announced you twice already," the organiser's voice grew so high-pitched that it could shatter glass.

"And he can do it a third time," Roddy replied, unconcerned. "I like hearing people mention my name."

"But the schedule! The delegates have planes to catch, hotel rooms to vacate. You're throwing the whole conference into chaos."

Putting an arm round the panicking official, he guided the man towards the crack in the drapes.

"See those people. My rivals. They'll wait. Trust me, for the great Roddy McPherson, they'll wait forever.

They want to know my secret. They yearn to understand how the Mozart of modern sci-fi does it."

"Yes, yes, I appreciate that. That's why we booked you – at such expense. But why the unnecessary delay in taking the stage?"

Roddy beamed. "Because it's showbiz. All part of the magic. I intend to make a dramatic entrance; to build up the expectation to bursting point."

The man frowned disapprovingly, but Roddy ignored him. Sensing the optimum moment had come, he was already striding towards the podium, waving to the hordes who leapt to their feet, exploding in spontaneous and relieved applause.

Bowing, he winked – giving them the full mega-watt effect of his famous Celtic smile.

"Please, please," he purred. "You're too kind. Please. You're making me blush. I'm just a humble writer…"

In a ten thousand dollar suit.

He waited until the delegates were back on their seats – on the edge of their seats – before saying: "Now, I'm going to ditch the pleasantries and the platitudes and all the other bullshit that you've been forced to listen to for the last few days and get straight to the point. I'll answer the big question. Why am I so successful?"

He leant forward conspiratorially.

"It's very simple," he said, barely above a whisper, causing the masses to topple alarmingly as they strained to listen. "I've liberated myself. I've thrown off the shackles, restrictions and formulas of orthodox storytelling. It may be ironic to reveal it at a narrative convention, but I've stopped obeying normal narrative conventions."

He scanned the hall for several long moments, enjoying the bafflement that radiated back.

Build up the tension, Roddy boy, tease their curiosity, make them sweat…

"I have abandoned using the 'what if?' principle in my work," he announced.

The next two minutes were bedlam as the audience reeled, unsure if he was mocking them or had simply lost his mind.

"But that's ridiculous," one voice shouted angrily. "It's impossible to write a sci-fi story without using what if?"

"It's the whole basis of what we do," another agreed. "It's the trigger question that fires the imagination; the crucial key that unlocks reality and makes anything possible in a fantasy tale."

Delighting at the stunned response and the headlines the controversy would undoubtedly generate, Roddy signalled for quiet.

"I can see I've stirred up a hornets' nest," he observed. "But I promise you it is possible to exist without it. Asking readers to imagine what if? is a cheap trick, a lazy device."

He sighed theatrically. "But, I can see you don't believe me, so indulge me in a small experiment. Close your eyes and imagine my world for a moment. Imagine – what if the what if? principle had never been invented."

There was resistance; many suspecting this was some huge practical joke, but gradually all complied. And Roddy closed his eyes too.

Silence fell across the hall.

A total silence.

An eerie silence.

Opening his lids after several moments, Roddy glanced out – into rows and rows of vacant seats.

His mouth fell open.

He was alone, but for an elderly man in a security uniform, hand half way to his holster.

"What you doing here, mister?" the guard demanded.

Roddy couldn't answer. His brain couldn't take it in.

Spinning round, first one way then the other, he stared frantically at the empty hall. It was impossible. Where were the people? And why was he now bafflingly dressed in threadbare jeans and sweatshirt?

"I'm – I'm here for the conference," he gasped, waving a hand helplessly.

The man had his gun out now, warily edging forwards. "Ain't no convention here, bud. Building should be all locked up."

"But – but that's crazy. It was here. Just seconds ago. I was the guest speaker, for Heaven's sake. I was talking to my fellow science fiction authors."

The guard's next three words were chilling as, eyes narrowing, he demanded: "What's science fiction?"

Roddy teetered on the edge of madness. Then he laughed – long and hard as he suddenly understood that the others had been right. They really couldn't exist without their precious what if?

Shrugging at the watchman, he considered the challenge of convincing anyone that there'd been a world where sane people earned a living from dreaming up stories about space ships, little green men, robots, time travel and alternative realities. A world that had vanished a mere moment before.

No-one would believe it. It sounded too far-fetched, too fanciful. But yet, the great Roddy McPherson thought he might just be able to pull it off.

"Look," he said, turning on the twinkle. "Just imagine for a moment…"

CS–Aye, Jimmy

There was no doubt about it, Frodo Baggins was dead. The diminutive fellow was both frigid and rigid – hairy bare feet sticking out from under the huge rock that had flattened him.

"Looks like mordor," DCI Matt Burke told his team of Caledonian detectives as they surveyed the crime scene.

"No, sir," DS Jackie Reid immediately corrected her boss, nodding to the otherwise idyllic fields and cottages. "I think you'll find this is The Shire."

Frowning in annoyance, the Glaswegian top cop adjusted his accent. "I mean, it's murrr-der," he explained. "There's nae way this could have been an accident."

His crack polis team all nodded in agreement. Partly because the way the tiny brutalised body was lying suggested Frodo had been the victim of considerable violence, partly because challenging the boss' opinion wasn't a good idea – but mostly because any suggestion of it being a death by natural causes and they were on the next bus home. And all had yet to visit The Mines of Moria, take holiday snaps on Mount Doom or sample a meal in the revolving restaurant at the top of Saruman's tower.

Admittedly, at first they'd been reluctant to take the posting, until the Super explained they were going to be assigned to Middle Earth – not Middle England. But now the tartan 'tecs were desperate to spin out their secondment to this blighted continent with its casual violence, bitter devastation, inhuman creatures and sudden death. It was, they agreed, a more genteel, conducive and welcoming environment than their normal Clydeside beat…

Years of intensively honed investigative experience meant the DCI's keen mind was already whirring wildly with questions. What was the motive? Who had the means? Were there any witnesses? And why was his show called Taggart when that wasn't his name?

"Was it robbery?" he asked, reminding himself wisely that it was probably better to be known as a Taggart than a Burke. "Somedae's nicked the wee yin's shoes."

"He didn't wear any," Sergeant Reid told him wearily, slowly letting her eyeballs rise skyward.

No shoes! Jezz, Burke told himself, now that's what I call a hard man.

"But he is missing some jewellery," the sergeant added and the DCI's estimation of Frodo dipped in an instant.

"Jewellery? What kind – gold chains? Bracelet? A watch? Not ear-rings – tell me it's nae ear-rings!"

She didn't answer, but led her superior officer to the group of suspects – a dwarf, an elegant elf, a goblin with a perm, a shifty looking nomadic wanderer and a hideous slime-covered orc. Burke couldn't explain why but the line-up reminded him of a boy band.

"These are his mates," Reid informed him, looking at her notes. "They call themselves The Fellowship of the Bling. They say he should have been wearing a ring of some sort. It's gone."

A missing ring, eh?

The DCI suspiciously eyed the rather colourful-looking fellows of the Fellowship. What a bunch of vain Jessies! Any one of these fancy dress poseurs could have nicked it, he told himself. Maybe jealousy over the jewellery had sparked a row amongst the group – a tiff over who wore the Tiffany?

"It was a very special ring," the Elf interrupted his musing, voice unexpectedly deep and mellow. "The one ring – the one ring to bind them all. The Dark Lord's ring."

Burke let that unexpected nugget percolate around his grey matter. This put a whole new complexion on the case.

"I see, so it was an engagement ring," he deduced, snapping his fingers triumphantly. "Frodo was supposed to marry the Dark Lord. And they had a lover's quarrel."

He nodded sagely. "Aye, that'll be it. Some men seem to think putting a ring on your finger means they can control you. The wee yin probably ditched him, called off the wedding, threw the ring back at him. The Dark Lord was crushed so he thought Frodo should be too."

A domestic crime, a gay domestic. Well, that shouldn't be too difficult to clear up, he thought with relief.

The Elf looked helplessly at DS Reid. She just shrugged back. She'd only had one grudging promotion in twenty-five years and more than ninety-five episodes. Why should she stick her neck out?

A scream broke the embarrassed silence.

"The precious! The precious! He's got the precious. Nasty, horrible brute… he's got the precious and we wants it!"

The entire team of detectives spun round to look at the pathetic, emaciated, stick-like creature that was jumping up and down in rage; lank strands of greasy hair falling down over his grey face and shrunken mad, sly eyes.

"Somehow I don't think this is going to make things any better," Reid groaned.

Gollum was pointing accusingly at Gandalf the Grey – who was walking surreptitiously in the opposite direction, whistling innocently, magical staff in one hand and the strap of his pull-along wheelie suitcase in the other.

"See, see. He's creeping away. Nasty, wicked wizard. Killed master Frodo, took the precious, he did. Took our precious. Give it back, give it back to Sméagol."

Shock swept across the mighty sorcerer's face, and switched instantly to fury.

"Sméagol? Sneak-le, more like!" he roared bitterly, quickly hiding the ring in his pocket. "You grass! Why couldn't you have kept your big trap shut? Another minute and I'd have been free and clear."

Turning the staff on the woe-begotten wretch, he hissed: "Well, I can make you quiet now. You won't be giving evidence against me."

There was a sharp, electric crack and the unmistakable odour of ozone. Gollum's mouth was certainly shut – it was gone, vanished. A blank space now sat on his face where his lips had been.

DCI Burke cursed. That bit of grievous bodily charm had silenced his only witness to the slaying. It would make the trial trickier, he realised, but they'd just have to worry about that problem when Gandalf was safely in custody.

With a nod, he signalled his men to make the arrest.

Alas, the booming, bearded, buccaneer of black magic wasn't coming quietly.

They barely had time to react before Gandalf used his sizzling cane again. With a non-audible eye-bulging yelp, Gollum was compacted into a tight ball and bowled straight into the detectives and the Fellowship of the Bling standing behind them.

"Stri-kkkke," the wizard shouted gleefully as the ten figures toppled in unison.

Picking themselves up, Burke and Reid surged forward but weren't quick enough. With speed remarkable for such an elderly figure, the enchanter swept the oversized wand in a circle – causing a three-feet-high wall of fire to surround him.

"You shall not pass," he warned, from behind the protective flames.

"Look, pal," Burke began, keeping his voice calm and soothing. "No-one blames you. It's tough when your pension doesn't go as far as you'd expected. We all ken that… but this isnae the answer."

"You could let me go," Gandalf suggested. "You have no DNA, fingerprints, fibres – no proof at all. Besides, this isn't really your jurisdiction."

The DCI shook his head regretfully. "Sorry, there's nae way. You've got to be stopped. You've killed one wee man. What if you killed another? And a third? Before you know it you'd be murrr-dering them every week. I cannae let you make a hobbit of it."

Nearby, Jackie Reid muttered: "Oh my Goad!" but Burke couldn't tell if it was in exasperation at the stand-off or the awfulness of the pun.

He didn't have a chance to ask.

Reaching into her bag, his sergeant produced a metal object and – without a moment's hesitation – threw it. Spinning end over end, the orange-coloured missile flew swiftly over the fiery barrier and hit Gandalf squarely between the eyes.

The can of Irn-Bru did its work and the concussed wizard went down like a Sauchiehall Street drunk.

"Magic," Reid said, with a self-satisfied smirk.

With Gandalf out for the count, the flames immediately died down.

"Get the cuffs on him," Burke ordered his officers, stretching his hand into the comatose magician's pocket and producing the cause of all the troubles.

The ring was so slight. Was it really worth killing for?

It looked normal, apart from some weird writing inside. But it felt… it felt different…

Strange thoughts raced through Burke's mind – long forgotten feelings of ambition, greed, ruthlessness. Why shouldn't he be Chief Constable? Commissioner of the Met? Overlord of all beings!!!!

"We'll definitely need to get a confession now that Gollum can't speak," Jackie Reid pointed out.

But Burke already had deliciously inventive, diabolical, sadistic ideas ricocheting round his brain. Locking up the wizard in a dark, deep, dank cell… playing him the bagpipes all night… forcing him to watch Monarch of the Glen… feeding him a merciless diet of haggis and deep-fried Mars Bars.

"Don't you worry," he informed his deputy with evil certainly. "I ken exactly how to make him crack. He'll be tolkien before he knows it."

Crazy Paving

Elsie stopped pruning her roses to watch the small flat-bed builder's truck cruising up the street. She trembled as it pulled up at the foot of her driveway with a menacing hiss.

"Watchya, grandma," a cheery voice called out from inside the cab. "Is your old man in? We need a word with him."

She shook her head. "N-n-no," she stammered. "He's gone. D-d-dead. I'm on my own now."

The truck doors opened and two young lads – Elsie guessed they were in their early twenties – leapt out.

"In that case," the taller one said, "it's you we want then. It's about your driveway."

Elsie frowned. "My driveway. What about my driveway?"

"It's dangerous," the second lad told her. "An absolute disgrace. Have you seen the state of it?"

"Dangerous?" Elsie repeated slowly. "Disgrace?"

"Yeah," the first lad told her animatedly. "Potentially lethal. We noticed it as we drove by. I said to Terry, that driveway is a potential killer. If some young kiddie was to trip in one of those potholes we could be talking about a death. Didn't I say that, Terry?"

Stern-faced, Terry nodded. "You did, Wayne. You most certainly did."

"So," Wayne continued, putting on his best sincere smile, "we thought to ourselves. How lucky. What a coincidence. We just happen to have a load of fresh tarmac in the back of the van."

"Ready for laying," Terry added helpfully.

"Ready for laying," Wayne agreed. "And we thought, why not see if we could do you a favour and repair your driveway at a very reasonable charge – making it safe for all the children in the street and saving you the hassle and inconvenience of having to phone round contractors for a load of stupid old quotes you don't need."

Elsie blinked. She didn't know what to think. The postman HAD tripped in the driveway just the other day. So had that nice woman from Age Concern who'd come to tell her something about bogus builders.

She stared at the pockmarked tarmac. The driveway did look awful. She'd let things go a bit since George had passed on. He'd handled all that side of things and now he was gone she was totally adrift – baffled by life's many complexities. Her gaze moved up to the two lads, both standing looking strangely angelic and caring.

She smiled. It would be great to get the driveway fixed, and having Wayne and Terry do it would mean that she wouldn't fall prey to those nasty cowboys who were touring the neighbourhood.

"Okay," she said after a few moments. "I don't see what harm it can do."

"Great," Terry said happily. "We'll get cracking, grandma. Why don't you nip inside and make us all a nice cup of tea?"

* * *

As she waited for the kettle to boil, Elsie hunted for her tablets. She was getting one of her headaches – the ones that came whenever she forgot to take her medication;

the headache she'd had when she pushed poor old George off the ladder.

The psychiatric report had been full of long words, words she couldn't understand. They'd said something about her being a pavement or something like that. She hadn't taken much notice.

The fresh-faced doctor, straight from medical college, had convinced the others that she was safe to rejoin society. There was no chance of her displaying any more anti-social tendencies.

"Elsie Watts is just what she appears to be – a sweet, silver-haired, pensioner," he'd said. "I'm convinced the whole business with the ladder was a one-off incident. She no longer poses any real threat."

Elsie smiled at the memory. The doctor had been a nice boy – just like Terry and Wayne. She wondered if the three lads knew each other.

"Coo-ee," she cried through the window. "Tea's ready. Would you like a chocolate biscuit?"

Wayne, and Terry, grinning widely, nodded back. "We're almost done," they answered. "We'll have a nice cuppa... and you can get out your chequebook."

* * *

Gazing forlornly at the black, smelly, lumpy mess, Elsie couldn't help feeling she'd made a mistake, a terrible mistake.

"It's awful. What have you done?" she asked, stunned. "Look, there are dips in it. It's not flat."

Terry sniffed: "That's your sub-strata."

Wayne nodded: "Definitely. The land is an undulating mass of subterranean layers. You're lucky we

247

got it as flat as we did. Normally we wouldn't tackle a tricky job like this one without a full survey team."

"And geological bore holes," Terry agreed.

Elsie wasn't convinced. The two builders had made the driveway look worse than before they'd started. Her headache pounded behind her eyes. She felt giddy.

Wayne waved a piece of white paper before her streaming eyes.

"What's this?" she asked worriedly.

"The bill," Terry replied, the helpful smile now vanished.

"For £4,000," Wayne told Elsie, his face coming up close to hers.

The world started to wobble in front of her. £4,000! She didn't have £4,000! They'd said it would be cheap. No-one said it would be that much."I haven't got it," she croaked. "I'm just a poor pensioner."

"Tough," the contractors chorused. "You owe it and we're not budging till we get it."

Elsie started to shake uncontrollably. "You'd better watch out," she gasped. "I'm a dangerous woman. I'm a… I'm a… pavement."

The lads sniggered loudly. "And I'm a dual carriageway," Terry told her nastily. "Now get the money."

Dazed, she gestured for the two lads to follow her back inside the kitchen.

Elsie's heart thumped so loudly against her chest that she thought it would burst through. The room spun madly, the wind rushed in her ears. She couldn't stop herself. Suddenly, she knew what she had to do. The bread knife was close… so close.

* * *

Even though she was no builder, Elsie thought she'd done a good job of levelling out the dips in the driveway. The two bodies had fitted the holes a treat.

Now that the task was done the tarmac didn't look too bad. No-one would be tripping over any more.

She hummed happily to herself as she washed the blood-stained bread knife in the sink. The headache had gone, just as it had done when George's nagging was silenced.

Without the pain in her head, Elsie could think a little clearer. She could remember what the psychiatric report had said. It hadn't called her a pavement – of course not. That would have been silly. It had called her a cycle path…

A Soonful of Spugar

The college doctor jumped. Who could be banging on his door at this time of night – and so insistently?

Hurrying to the porch, he was stunned to see the Dean there – looking pale and unsteady.

"My fear dellow, hank God you're tear," his caller gushed, grabbing his lapels, obviously dazed and confused. "I heed your nelp. I seem to be muffering from some sadness. I keep wuddling my mords."

The doctor blinked in surprise, not sure if his ears were playing tricks.He'd never heard anything like it. What strange contagion of the mind was affecting Reverend William?

"Good Lord, man. You look awful. You'd better come in," he said, catching his colleague as the man stumbled.

"Lanks a thot," the distressed cleric said gratefully as he was guided to a chair and given a large brandy. "You're kost mind."

The doctor listened carefully for several minutes as his distraught visitor babbled on bafflingly.

"It's a bizarre condition," he mused. "You appear to be transposing the openings to adjacent words. You're automatically creating a new vocabulary that is gibberish – but also comprehensible. I've never come across anything like it in all my years of medicine. What could have possibly caused this?"

The Dean pointed to the back of his skull. "I had a hump on the bed," he informed his host. "Then I found myself locking like a tooney."

Ah, a bump on the head, the physician thought excitedly. That might do it. The brain was a delicate organ, easily disrupted.

"Do you think you might be having a nervous breakdown?" he ventured.

"A bervous neckdown? I don't think so," the worried clergyman replied. "Apart from muddling my words, I feel quite normal."

The doctor did a double take and eyed his friend suspiciously.

"You sounded unaffected there," he said accusingly. "That second sentence was perfectly understandable. There was no transposition."

"It gums and coes," the Dean explained, exasperated. "It's rompletely candom. But I've found that eating chint mochlete seems to help."

For the first time, the doctor noticed blood. The cranial injury was more severe than he'd thought. Opening his black bag, he found a bottle of iodine and began dabbling it on — aware of the Dean wincing at each touch.

"Does that hurt?" he enquired.

"Lust a jittle."

So what caused the bump? It was a particularly nasty wound, he observed.

"It was my wife," Reverend William confessed, red faced. "She pit me with a hoker. She caught me with my fit of bluff. Texy Sina!"

"Fit of bluff? Texy Sina? Ah, I see — she caught you with your bit of fluff. Sexy Tina!"

"Rat's tight!"

"And what had you done? With Sexy Tina? To provoke your wife to such violence with the poker?"

The Reverend William Archibald Spooner paused for a second, let a lecherous smile cross his lips and, for a fleeting moment of normality, replied: "I told you, Dear Doctor. I had a hump on the bed!"

If You Pay Peanuts

Bill Shakespeare, playwright, Elizabethan poster boy and CEO of Sensational Sonnets PLC stared straight into the gorilla's inky back eyes, willing himself not to blink, not to show any sign of weakness.

"I thought we'd resolved all these issues weeks ago," he told the simian shop steward wearily. "You sat in that very negotiating chair and assured me that we had a deal. I'd allow every worker an extra ten minutes on their banana break and you'd ensure there'd be no more protests or walk-outs and what happens? Soon as my back is turned all this…" He searched for the right words. "…monkey business flares up again."

His hand waved towards the banner stretched across the scriptwriters' room, its message scrawled in untidy red paint: 'Tell the baldy bard where to stick his quill!'

"I mean, I'm a patient, sympathetic man. I understand that it's a demanding project and creative tensions are running high, but it's just one complaint after another," he pointed out. "What's their belly ache this time?"

The giant ape snorted and clambered over the desk, sending piles of parchment flying. His frown darkened, making the playwright decidedly uncomfortable.

"My members feel that you undervalue their contribution," he growled, "that you don't treat them with the respect that they deserve. Take that incident last week - you referred to the script editor as a big baboon."

"He IS a big baboon."

"Technically yes. But that wasn't the way you meant it," the union official countered. "It was just another blatant example of the distain with which you treat the workforce and their labours."

Shakespeare felt his blood boil. He chided himself for having listened to his over-greedy agent. Beryl had been wickedly persuasive, urging him to take the risk, to think big, that the rich rewards on offer made it worth living dangerously.

"We're snowed under with orders for new plays. The West End is crying out for fresh material," she'd explained with seductive logic. "You can't possibly keep up with demand on your own so let's use a bit of lateral thinking and call in some help."

The world believed that if you gave enough monkeys enough typewriters eventually they'd produce the entire works of Shakespeare, so why not put the theory to the test.

"What have you got to lose?" she prompted.

He didn't have a reply, but did have a question of his own. "What's a typewriter?" he enquired.

* * *

It turned out that a typewriter was 12 sovereigns. And despite buying them in bulk from the inventor, they still punched a huge hole in the bard's budget.

And they weren't the only items of equipment that the primate poets demanded. Climbing bars, tyre swings, rope hammocks, bowler hats, wrenches, hair care products. The list was endless. And that didn't include the gallons of tea they consumed - a top brand naturally. They refused point blank to consider Tesco Value bags.

Soon Shakespeare understood the true meaning of having a monkey on your back.

As for the disappointing quality of their writing? Huh! There'd have been more imagination, verve and quality control if he'd employed Marlowe - and that weak chinned wannabe could barely string two words together.

"But soft! What light through yonder window breaks?"

It was supposed to be a lyrical statement about the joy and longing of Romeo when he espied Juliet stepping out on to her balcony. The knuckle dragging hacks had made it sound like someone had hurled a brick through the glazing!

"There's something rotten in the state of Denmark."

He'd angrily scrawled in the margin: "This is ambiguous. By 'state' do you mean the condition of Denmark or the fact that it is a country? Playwriting requires precision."

And don't mention that doggerel: "Double, double, toil and trouble". The muddle-headed marmosets had actually repeated a word! They'd claimed it was for "dramatic effect". He'd immediately scored it out and inserted "Hubble, bubble, toil and trouble." THAT was a line that would please the punters!

* * *

And now, this latest go-slow was killing production. They were weeks behind. He'd already had to change one title to A Mid-Autumn Night's Dream!

"Look, old son," Bill said, edging backwards to a safe distance from the union rep, who was now beating his chest. "I have to be frank and tell you that I'm not happy about any of this."

Delving into his desk, he produced the flowing scroll that contained the legion of lemurs' CVs.

"For one thing, I reckon the entire troop misrepresented themselves at the interviews. They all claimed to be top-notch operatives. Award-winning writers."

"They are," the gorilla insisted.

"Only if you count *Tarzan on Ice* as a classic," Shakespeare replied. "From what I can see that's the only experience they've had - apart from the gibbons. Some of them appear to have worked on a stamp catalogue of some sort."

If he thought the hairy rep would back down at the accusation, he was greatly mistaken. Leaning over to ruffle Bill's ruff, it whispered in his ear: "Well, they're not alone in telling a few porkies, are they?"

"Pardon?"

"When you offered us the gig you claimed to be respected all over the Globe. It was only later we found out you meant a poxy theatre - not the entire planet!"

Bill coloured. Ouch!

Deadlocked, author and anthropoid folded their arms, both unwilling to give way. And that's the way the impasse would have stayed if Beryl hadn't walked in at that moment on one of her impromptu inspections.

"I knew if I left you two together there'd be plenty of rhyme and no reason," she scolded. "This is ridiculous. If no-one acts soon, we'll run out of... er... *Acts!*"

Ignoring her fuming business partner, she demanded. "We need to stop this drama turning into an almighty crisis. What will it take to get the chimps chipper again?"

The gorilla scratched his head - then his backside - before suggesting: "Perhaps a gesture of goodwill. A sign that they are valued, held in high esteem."

Beryl blew out her cheeks. "Is that all? Okay, you've got it."

* * *

The clatter of 20,000 typewriters being hammered at top speed was deafening but Shakespeare didn't care. To him it sounded like poetry. If they kept up the pace the backlog would be gone in hours.

And it wasn't just a surge in output, creativity had gone through the roof - the first draft of Macbeth had already been sponsored by a soap company who loved the slogan: *"Out, damn spot!"*

He allowed himself a wry smile. It was incredible that the solution to the dispute had proved to be so simple - and so cheap.

Gazing at his script team, he marvelled at the persuasive power of status and title.

Who'd have thought all it would take was giving each monkey a promotion, plus a rank badge emblazoned with the words: ORGAN GRINDER.

The Hex Factor

The unmistakable crunch of tyres on gravel alerted Marjorie that the police had returned. Tutting, she stopped stirring the large pot bubbling on the stove and went to the front window of the cottage.

Yes, the patrol car was there. And behind it were two large black official-looking cars. As she watched various men in suits got out and, together with two uniformed policemen, began walking towards the front garden.

Typical, she thought indignantly. I promise myself one day without any hassles then the whole world goes mad and beats a path to my doorstep.

Turning down the heat, she wiped her hands on her apron, ready to confront the forces of law and order for a second time. It wasn't fair. At her time of life she shouldn't have to be putting up with this.

"Believe me," she said darkly, "someone is going to pay for this. And it won't be pretty."

* * *

It had been only a few hours since the fresh-faced constable and grizzled sergeant had turned up at her door, looking for a young brother and sister who'd gone missing.

"Their parents are going frantic," the sergeant had told her. "We're doing door to door enquiries; asking if anyone saw the children today or might have spotted something out of the ordinary."

He'd said they were trying all the properties at the edge of the forest, but she'd known they'd come immediately to her door. It was inevitable. The superstitious villagers had sent them.

She knew about the rumours, the stories people told, the spiteful gossip. She was an old woman, living on her own with a black cat. She made remedies and potions from wild plants and roots in the woodland. She had a wart on the end of her nose. You didn't need to be a genius to jump to the obvious conclusion.

"They told you I was a witch, didn't they?" she challenged. "And you took them seriously. You listened to all their harebrained claims. It's ridiculous."

The young policeman flushed: "Well, one or two people might have said something…"

"Actually more than one or two," his older colleague agreed, "nearly the entire village. Our hands are tied. We're duty bound to investigate. Not that we believe it…"

"Not for a moment," the younger officer added, "but when two youngsters are missing we have to follow every possible lead."

Angrily, Marjorie had let them know how laughable it was. "This is the twenty-first century for heaven's sake - not The Middle Ages. I'm sick of all this stupidity. It's the same nonsense every Halloween. Go on - look round. See if you can find the children. And while you're at it, have a search for a broomstick, the place could do with a good sweep."

She supposed she didn't blame them. They were just two dim-witted wooden-tops doing their job. She'd shown them every room in the cottage. They'd found nothing, of course.

After ten minutes, they'd apologetically left her to get on with cooking her casserole.

"Smells good," the sergeant remarked.

"Goat-herd stew. It's an old family recipe," she'd explained, dipping in her spoon and tasting the bubbling, steamy concoction, "passed down for generations. I always make a huge load to freeze to see me through the winter. Only trouble is…" She sighed. "…it does need such a lot of fresh meat."

* * *

Marjorie knew it was naïve to think the police would leave it at that. But she hadn't expected them back so quickly or in such numbers.

Breathing deeply, she composed herself for a moment. It didn't pay to let her simmering fury show.

"Hello again, officers," she said, opening the door. "Did you forget something?"

The sergeant shook his head.

"Ah, there's been a development?" she suggested. "In the search? The little loves have turned up?"

"No," he replied somberly. "No such luck. The children are still missing. We're really concerned now. We're widening the search area and bringing in more men. And the force helicopter is going to fly over the woods with a thermal camera."

He jerked his head over his shoulder at the silent group of pin-striped individuals who were staring uncomfortably at their shoes.

"I'm afraid we're here about a different development."

He made a sour face. "These gentlemen are from the council planning department. It seems that you don't have planning permission for this cottage."

Marjorie was momentarily taken aback. She hadn't been expecting that!

"Ms Marjorie Weatherwax," the lead official began, clumsily opening his briefcase, letting a flurry of papers fall to the path, "we've written to you countless times about this property but you've never replied to our letters. Or answered the door when we've called. Or responded to any of the messages we've left on your answer phone."

Marjorie gave him her most direct malevolent stare, the one guaranteed to turn heroic champions into water-kneed, lily-livered scaredy-cats.

"That's because I don't like being pestered," she whispered icily. "Specially not by busybody twerps from the council with their meddling rules and regulations."

The man swallowed hard, but wasn't giving up. "That may well be, but the planning law is quite clear in this matter and it's our duty to enforce it. You don't have permission for this structure. It's an unauthorised development… in the green belt."

The other officials, who'd all heard the disturbing rumours about the old woman, nodded to give their colleague moral support - from a safe distance.

"I'm not harming anyone being here," she pointed out, folding her arms defiantly. "It's just one little cottage."

"And," he pressed on, "there's also the problem of the materials used in its construction."

Ah, that! Marjorie saw where this was going. "What's wrong with gingerbread," she demanded. "It smells nice, it tastes nice. It keeps me warm at night and it doesn't let in the rain."

"Yes, maybe so, but it's not…" The council man struggled for the right words. "…usual. Not… approved."

"It's eco-friendly," she pointed out, "bio-degradable."

But the argument was lost. She could see that. He held up a court order and waved it weakly.

"These police officers are here to make sure you take this document. It gives you two weeks to vacate the premises after which time…" His face blanched as he realised he'd inadvertently uttered the 'w' word. "…after such time the property will be demolished by our contractors."

It was long past the time for pleading, Marjorie understood that. Sighing, she reached into her apron pocket and brought out the wand. Why did it always have to come to this?

The ebony stick twitched and there was a loud electric crack and a smell of ozone. Marjorie cackled as she gazed down at the bemused looking toads that had suddenly appeared at her feet.

"That's the way to deal with busybodies," she declared and bustled urgently back inside. What a day! So many interruptions when she was trying to cook. It would be a miracle if the casserole hadn't spoilt.

One last taste. Ahhh… lovely goat-herd stew. Very flavoursome. Very satisfying. Especially when it was packed with plump vegetables, just the right herbs and spices and, of course, plenty of kid.

Exit, Stage Left

Cinderella blew a kiss to the panto audience and three hundred kids cheered loudly enough to blow the roof off the theatre. With regal grace, she swept to her dazzling glass coach.

Just three feet away, Lucy Bateman regarded Cinderella's shining beautiful face with sheer, unadulterated hatred.

Lucy - described by the Thorpington Evening Gazette as "an adequate but uninspired Prince Charming" - tried hard to force a smile but the effort nearly cracked her face.

"Here," she purred venomously, "let me help you up, Cinders." Grabbing a handful of the voluminous dress, she roughly shoved the startled pantomime star into the coach.

Samantha Black - darling of the TV screens and the secret love of a million men's hearts - fell ungraciously into the crystal carriage, curly blonde wig slipping askew.

Blinking in surprise, she hissed: "What are you playing at?"

"Just helping you on your way," Lucy snarled back. "We wouldn't want you to be late for your wedding, now would we?"

Samantha's sudden look of terror made it clear that she understood what was going on.

"Look," she whispered anxiously, "we can talk about this. Later. After the show."

But Lucy was in no mood for chit-chat. Ignoring the other actors' puzzled looks and the audience's restless murmuring, she patted Cinderella's cheeks menacingly.

"This is going to be one performance that's going down in theatre history," Lucy warned. "You're going to find out just how unprincipled this Principal Boy can be!"

* * *

It seemed like all Lucy's life she'd been living in Samantha Black's shadow. No matter what roles Lucy tackled, Samantha always effortlessly upstaged her. Lucy won a BAFTA - Samantha won an Oscar.

Lucy was cast in a six-week sit-com, Samantha got her own three-series cop show. Samantha advertised luxury cars while Lucy - dressed as Mrs Mop - extolled the virtues of a pine-smelling toilet bleach.

Even in this third-rate panto, Samantha had succeeded in making Lucy look like an ugly sister rather than an attractive thigh-slapping fantasy figure.

Perhaps, Lucy told herself, she could have learnt to be philosophical, learnt to admire Samantha, but losing Terry had put paid to that. Not content with having everything that Lucy so dearly wanted, superstar Samantha had stolen Lucy's boyfriend as well.

Shaking with rage, Lucy remembered the look of pity in Terry's eyes as he'd hugged her and said: "We can still be friends."

"But why?" she'd bawled. "What has Samantha Black got that I haven't?"

Terry had shrugged apologetically. "Poise, class, looks, talent, money, prospects, sex appeal..."

He'd been ready to go through a long list, but Lucy's wail of despair cut him short.

"Okay," she'd yelled, "run off with Little Miss Perfect. I don't care. Go away and play at happy families. You'll come crawling back to me as soon as she's had her fun. She'll grow bored and ditch you. You don't fit her goody-two-shoes image."

But eighteen months on, the lovers were still together and the front page of that evening's Gazette announced: "Thorpington Panto Star Plans Fairytale Wedding."

Lucy wanted to explode with rage. At that moment Lucy had known that she couldn't let Samantha get away with it. She had to murder the blushing bride. And what more fitting time than during the panto - right in the middle of Cinder's big wedding scene.

* * *

"She's mad or she's drunk. Get her off," Samantha pleaded with the show's mousy producer. "She'll ruin everything."

But the man merely wrung his hands, saying: "We haven't got an understudy. Just keep going. Pretend nothing's amiss and the audience won't notice."

At that, Lucy smiled broadly. It was going to be difficult to pretend nothing was wrong when Cinderella fell down dead centre stage.

Lucy knew that she wouldn't get away with it. You couldn't commit murder in front of sixteen school parties and a coach-load of old age pensioners and hope to stroll away whistling innocently. Yet, she didn't care.

She realised now that losing Terry had been the end of her life. What did it matter if she spent the rest of her natural days behind bars? Perhaps Terry would come to visit her - when he'd got over his grief. Perhaps, he'd come to understand how much he'd really loved her and what a fool he'd been...

"Places everyone!" the producer's voice snapped her back from her reverie.

As the wedding scene started, Lucy sidled up to Samantha, smugly noticing that Cinders was trembling.

Swallowing hard, Samantha turned to the audience and said: "Today I marry the man of my dreams. My Prince will take me away to his castle and we'll live happily ever after."

Lucy didn't know if it was years of panto training or the burning jealously inside her that made her suddenly blurt out: "Oh no, you won't."

The audience, unaware of the diversion from the script, responded on cue. A chorus of voices echoed back: "Oh yes, she will."

"Oh no, she won't," Lucy promised. "This is one Cinders who won't get a fairytale ending. Not if I have anything to do with it."

Grinning, she spun to watch Cinderella drink her wedding glass of champagne. Any second now, she told herself, and goodbye forever.

Samantha's hand shook so much that the contents slopped over the sides. Careful now, Lucy thought, don't waste it. That poison cost a packet!

She didn't know if Samantha tasted the bitterness of the drug or was alerted by the triumphant gleam in Lucy's glare, but the actress refused to drink the doctored liquid. Pretending to trip, Cinderella made sure the champagne ended up on the floor.

"You bitch," Lucy growled, "I ought to snap your neck." She lunged forward but Samantha - a highly accomplished tap dancer - neatly sidestepped the attack.

Lucy went sprawling, sliding across the now slippery stage. Up ahead she could see a large black square - the trapdoor open waiting for the Fairy Godmother's final appearance.

She stopped an inch from the edge and breathed in a huge gulp of air. That had been close. Another second and she'd have plunged down thirty feet to her death.

Brushing herself off, Lucy got back to her feet. The stage erupted into chaos. Actors screamed, stage hands hurriedly tried to bring down the curtain, musicians clambered over their instruments.

Glancing round desperately, Lucy searched for Samantha. She couldn't let that scheming cow get away with it. She had to die.

"Where the hell is Cinderella?" she screamed, fists balled.

Two dainty hands suddenly pushing into her back told Lucy what she wanted to know. She tipped forward into the sinister gaping hole.

Plunging through the darkness, the last thing Lucy ever heard was the audience yelling loud enough to shatter her eardrums: "BEHIND YOU!!!!"

Suits You, Sire

Stefan chortled tipsily, swinging his flagon so hard the ale slopped on to the sawdust-covered tavern floor.

"It's got to be the con of the century. The most outrageous caper of all time," he giggled. "And we pulled it off. We did it. Us, Freddy boy, us! We're geniuses."

He punched his companion hard on the arm, making Frederick wince.

"It's a classic hustle I tell you, a bloody classic. Mark my words, people are going to be talking about this scam for years … for decades to come. We'll be legends."

He hiccupped. "Who knows - maybe they'll write a song about it. Let's see - *the King was in the altogether, the altogether, the altogether –* "

Frederick's fast fingers grabbed him round the throat, squeezing off his boozy ballad in mid chorus.

"Shuttup you fool," his partner-in-crime hissed, eyes flashing. "Keep your voice down. Do you want to get us strung up!"

He jerked his head at the other dark, menacing, unsavory drinkers dotted around the shabby inn.

"Any one of them would turn us in for a shilling," he warned. "And by now we'll have been rumbled. There'll be a reward out, bounty hunters searching for us, not to mention the palace guards."

Stefan tried to focus on what Frederick was saying, but he couldn't get over the audacity, the sheer unadulterated cheek, of their grift.

"But the invisible clothes ploy, Freddy. The old birthday suit routine. It's a tough number to pull off, and we made it look easy. We got him hook, line and scepter!"

"It was very satisfying," Frederick admitted grudgingly, faint smile playing across his lips. "Just proves the bigger they are the harder they fall… for it."

His amusement vanished as swiftly as it appeared. "But we can keep the gloating and self congratulations for later. Just now, we need to lay low and wait for the stage coach. Okay?"

Stefan made a mock salute. "Anything you say, partner." He took another slurp of beer, a trickle running down his chin.

"Yeah, but… but when you asked him if he liked the colour and he said he preferred a lighter shade. And you said that would cost more! That was bloody brilliant. I nearly wet myself!"

This time Frederick wrenched him so close that their noses were touching.

"Will you keep quiet!" he snarled, waving away Stefan's 36% proof brewery breath, "I won't warn you again. You've got a real drink problem, you know that?"

Stefan felt himself blush like a naughty schoolboy. God, he'd never seen Frederick look so threatening!

"And don't think for a moment I haven't forgotten how you nearly blew it back there - jabbing him in the Regals with the measuring tape."

The bitter words cut through Stefan's grog-induced grogginess. "My hand slipped," he replied defensively. "It could have happened to anyone."

"Any drunk, you mean!"

He was about to fire back a hazy, hops-fuelled retort, but became aware that Frederick wasn't glaring at him any more - or trying to choke him. Instead, his fellow huckster was spinning round towards the door.

There was a noise outside, clattering across the cobblestones.

"The coach?" he asked hopefully.

"No," Frederick answered, voice tense. "There are too many horses. It must be soldiers. It's the palace guard. They've found us. Shit!"

Both bolted for the door, almost forgetting their bag of ill-gotten gold. But they were too slow.

It opened, and framed in the doorway the burly Captain of The Imperial Guard stood - sharp, gleaming sword in hand.

"Ah, just the two characters I'm looking for," he said, voice deep and menacing. "We've been looking for you all over."

Signalling to the troopers to seize the double-dealing duo, he added: "You're coming with us. The Emperor wants a word with you. And, believe me, he's not happy."

* * *

It was amazing how quickly he'd sobered up, Stefan realised. It might have been the bumpiness of the hurried horse ride back to the city, the look of terror on Frederick's normally unruffled face or the knowledge that they'd both better start thinking up a world class alibi pretty damn quick.

Of course, the sight of the gallows being tested played its part.

The wooden scaffold platform came into view just as they entered the inner courtyard. It was solidly constructed, made of finest Dark Forest oak, and raised ten feet up so that the crowd could get an unrestricted view - and the condemned were ensured a fast, effective and terminal plunge.

Busy at work, a hunchback figure in a hood was manhandling large sacks of grain into the nooses and giving the trapdoors underneath a quick sharp stomp to make sure they worked smoothly. He stopped to wave as they drew level.

"Would you like a demonstration?" he offered, mellow voice missing the lisp that most people would have stereotypically expected.

"N-n-o… no… t-t-thanks," Stefan stammered, heart shuddering and his guts twisting into an ale-flavoured pretzel.

"I've never had any complaints," the hooded figure assured him, "but of course, I can't really get testimonials from my customers."

He pointed to his wagon. On the side, in crude lettering, was painted: *Speedy Executions - we never leave you hanging about.*

"I'm better than my rivals *Capitol Punishments,* and they charge double what I do."

"M-m-maybe later," Stefan told the hunchback, trying not to hurt his feelings, then immediately regretted it when the implications sank in.

Frederick gave him a withering look. "For a conman you have a lousy way with words," he whispered tartly.

"Enough blabbing," the Captain of the Guard snapped, "get moving. We haven't got all day. The

Emperor is waiting and he hates it when the executions don't start dead on time."

That, Stefan told himself worriedly, was just what he was afraid of…

* * *

"Any chance of using the restroom, just before we see the King?" he asked, as two stern-countenanced troopers dragged him along the long marble corridor. "It's just that when the bottom falls out of your world, you feel the world is going to fall out of your bottom. Know what I mean?"

Neither responded, just kept clomping onward with military precision and a decided lack of compassion.

Damn. Well that put paid to the old *going-to-the-restroom-slipping-out-the-unlocked-window-and-shimmying-down-the-drainpipe* plan.

Ahead he could see Frederick being lugged along by another pair of chocolate box squaddies. He wasn't having any more success trying to finagle his way of his predicament.

"Look lads, gentlemen, it must cost a packet to provide your own uniforms," he was telling them. "If you let us go, my companion and I could quickly knock you up some amazing threads, just like the King's. Just as classy - and just as cool."

But the soldiers weren't fashion fans, or else weren't as gullible as their esteemed ruler.

Gulping, Stefan realised that this was it - they were in as much trouble as it was possible to be. They were dead men walking. Well, dead men dragging…

With a rough shove he was sent flying, landing in a heap on top of Frederick, and immediately before two massive, tall, imposing silver-plated doors.

"Get on your feet, "the Captain of the Guard barked at them. "Smarten yourself up. And bow your heads. We're going into the throne room…"

With a well-oiled squeak - like a very polite mouse trying to attract attention - the doors opened and they shuffled forward, eyes cast downwards.

"Your Highness… I have apprehended the *tailors* you so desperately wanted to get your hands on," the officer announced.

And, trembling, Stefan looked up and saw something that took his breath away…

* * *

The King - his mighty Majesty, the Regal ruler, the Emperor of all the lands from here to the Sardonic Sea, the head honcho, the big cheese, the grand gaffer - was stark, raving, starkers!

Parading in front of a full-length mirror, the country's figurehead was displaying all of his figure.

"But he's still bare–" Stefan blurted, before Frederick's hand shot across the space between them, and clamped his mouth tightly shut.

"Bare…ly had time to try everything on," Frederick corrected. "My word, Your Highness, you look magnificent. So poised and elegant."

Unable to do more than mumble, Stefan took a second to mentally catch up then twigged what his smarter friend had immediately sussed. The King hadn't found out yet.

Even for an inbred Royal this one was slow on the uptake!

"Yes, it's exciting," the King said, beaming. "So many outfits to wear. I can't make my mind up what to sport to the executions."

Going straight into hustle mode, Frederick rubbed his hands subserviently, with just enough smarm to act the totally authentic tradesman.

"But if I may enquire, Sire. The Guards said you were unhappy, and we were summoned back here rather... *robustly*. I thought something must be amiss."

The Emperor made a 'what can you do?' face, explaining: "Soldiers! Eh! They are always so rough and overzealous. I merely said I wanted to catch you both before you disappeared off - so you could make the alterations."

"Alterations?" Stefan asked, bemused.

On make-believe, non- existent, garments?

"Yes, alterations," the Monarch replied, beckoning them both forward.

"I'm afraid I've been overdoing things," he confided. "Too many banquets. Too many civic receptions. I've put on a pound or two and, fabulously fashionable as your delightful apparel is, it's getting a bit snug. It really needs letting out a bit. Can you do that? Is that possible?"

Stefan fought the urge to laugh out loud. This was ridiculous! This was madness! But what the hey...

"That would have to be extra," he said, ignoring the daggers look Freddy flashed at him.

"Extra?"

"Yes, sorry. It would have to be another bag of gold. What with the additional material and the thread and the man hours."

The King stroked his chin thoughtfully. "Yes... I can see that. It is intricate work, and you two are such *artistes*. It would only be fair."

He smiled. "And if we're doing that I'll get you to run me up some robes in the darker shade of blue you suggested. I was thinking I was a bit hasty insisting on the lighter hue. Do you think I'd look good in it?"

"You would look sensational," Frederick promised.

"Really? You think so?"

"Of course!" they chorused.

"Sensational? You're not having me on?"

"Oh Sire," Stefan assured him with a wicked smile. "That's the absolute truth. You might say the *naked* truth..."

* * *

From high in the tower King Rudolphus the 16th watched the two hucksters swagger out of the palace gates, laughing and swinging their matching bags of gold.

He shook his head. Clowns! Amateurs! They definitely deserved to die. But not quite yet. Let them have a few weeks to feel safe, to wallow in their ill-founded, deluded smugness. Then he'd enjoy springing the trap and watching them swing.

He tutted. The sheer effrontery of them trying the old birthday suit hustle on him. They must have thought he was just off the boat.

Still, it had been fun, he conceded. Playing the part of the clueless victim had been hilarious – a delicious break from the boredom of his normal Court duties.

There was no greater pleasure in life than conning a conman.

Apart, he thought with a shiver of delight, from indulging his naughty naturist fantasies in public for a while… with the perfect cover story!

Hotel Babylon

From the HQ of Travel Rest Inns
Holy Lands Division
Palestine
29th December 0000AD

Dear J. Carpenter

I'm writing in response to your letter of complaint about the unfortunate events which took place while you and your wife were staying as guests at the Bethlehem Travel Rest, and to address the various points highlighted in your recent one star TripAdvisor review.

I wish to assure you that we at Travel Rest Inns take all customer feedback seriously and I have spoken at length to the duty manager to ascertain what exactly transpired that night. He accepts that a certain number of snags did occur. However, while admitting that you did experience some measure of inconvenience, he feels it a tad unfair for you to have headlined your review with the words: "A Cock-Up of Biblical Proportions."

To deal with each of your main points in turn:

The unavailability of a room

As we point out on our website, rooms are booked out on a first-come, first-served basis. The annual Census is always an extremely busy time for the hospitality trade in this part of Judea and in all our promotional materials we urge potential guests to "Book Early For Yuletide". You arrived late on Christmas Eve without having made a prior reservation.

Our staff did their utmost to find you suitable accommodation, but your insistence on a non-smoking room, with whirlpool bath, temple view and mini-bar made this impossible. We did, nevertheless, suggest a generous alternative - space in our animal-themed budget annex, including free parking and feed for your transport. This offer you accepted. We also supplied you with complimentary cookies, toiletries and fluffy slippers.

The lack of cleanliness

While I agree that the annex doesn't offer the same level of amenities as our deluxe rooms, I dispute that there were any issues with the general hygiene or presentation of your accommodation. Housekeeping were scrupulous in ensuring that the straw was fresh, all animal waste had been carefully removed, the manger was freshly rinsed and that the entire area had been well aired. We cannot accept that there was "an unholy stink."

Slowness in summoning a doctor

We are always happy to summon medical assistance for our guests 24/7 and have a number of physicians whom we regularly call upon in times of emergency. Although we noted that your wife was displaying signs of plumpness, we didn't realise that she was pregnant, having unfortunately misinterpreted your comment that she had been sitting on her ass for days.

Had we understood that you and you wife were expecting an imminent joyous arrival, we would naturally have had one of our in-house healers give her a full examination.

Substandard catering

I'm surprised that you found our room service menu limited and unappealing. As you can appreciate, we have a large number of Roman visitors so it makes perfect sense to offer a wide range of pizzas and pasta dishes. We're sorry if that wasn't to your taste, but I dispute your assertion that you were forced to eat field mouse dipped in honey. That was your choice. Other side dishes were available.

You could, of course, have availed yourselves of our "all you can eat" loaves and fishes package, but you turned it down stating that the accompanying wine was - and I quote - "a lot of watery piss, only fit for a philistine. Like that slop we had at that wedding in Cana."

Unwelcome noise

Frankly, Mr Carpenter, we find your claim about the hotel being so noisy that you couldn't sleep quite puzzling. Granted, reception did receive many complaints during the evening about loud heavenly music and general raucousness, but it transpired that the disturbances actually emanated from your section of the annex.

Upon investigation, staff discovered you and your wife hosting a fancy dress party attended by a number of individuals who weren't registered as guests. The information you offered about the identity of these persons seemed sketchy at best, at one point describing them as wise men, then kings, then shepherds. We were particularly perturbed by your admission that before the party you hadn't known any of these people.

Now, without wanting to be critical of anyone's alternative lifestyle, we pride ourselves on being a respectable, family establishment and take a dim view of unsuitable gatherings being held on our premises, especially late at night.

We are happy to accept your protestations that this was an innocent "baby shower" and nothing untoward was taking place, but the discovery of certain resin substances - in particular myrrh and frankincense - does prompt some worrying questions. As does the large amount of gold that seems to have changed hands.

Slowness in checkout

In your review you state that our staff were criminally slow in processing your bill, putting your family - especially your newly born son - in great danger. Our receptionist is adamant that she checked you out as swiftly as possible in the circumstances, but this was naturally problematic because of the dispute over the missing bathrobe, which later turned up in your baggage.

She found your reasons for demanding to use the express checkout - a facility normally reserved for our Platinum Loyalty Members - far-fetched and implausible. King Herod is a non executive director of our company, and held in great esteem in these parts. The idea that he would order a mass slaughter of all first born babes doesn't strike me as likely - or logistically possible. The King is very PR conscious and this type of infanticide doesn't play well on social media.

In view of this, and having looked at all the facts, I and other senior managers at Travel Rest Inns consider our staff did everything in their power to make your stay as pleasant, relaxing and comfortable as possible. For this reason, I'm afraid we cannot agree to your request for a full refund.

That being said, we are keen to ensure that all customers feel they had great value for money and would want to stay with us again. And as such we would like to offer your group one night's complimentary accommodation in an executive suite at one of the other hotels in our chain. We can particularly recommend our newly refurbished Jerusalem Rest Inn featuring delightful views over the gardens of Gethsemane.

If this is acceptable, please contact us to confirm. How does Easter sound?
Sincerely

Charles Bishop
Customer Relations Manger

In The Beginning…

"**D**octor Roberts, Doctor Roberts, you've got to come quickly. They're waiting for you in the lecture hall. The telemetry's due on stream any second."

Diane rolled her eyeballs in exasperation as the nervy voice whined through the restroom door. Even in here she wasn't free of Simon's constant nagging.

Washing her hands in the tepid water, she thought mischievously about pretending not to be there. That would send her fretting, hyperactive assistant into a total nervous meltdown. But it would be unnecessarily cruel.

Besides, he was right. The experiment was too important to disrupt at this crucial stage, especially not for something as mundane as a comfort break.

"Be right with you," she shouted back, and for the tenth time that day wondered how she could stay so calm when everyone else on the research team was beside themselves with excitement; stomachs in knots, eyes dark from lack of sleep.

Maybe, she told her reflection in the mirror, it was this unflappable manner that made her ideal to be the leader of Project Prologue. But deep down inside she knew the real reason - the multi-billion costs involved were so huge, so astronomical, that they simply had no meaning for her. She just couldn't equate the mountain of dollar bills NASA had spent on the deep space probe with anything in the real world. And all to capture a few fuzzy sound effects…

"What's the word from Mission Control?" she asked as Simon hurried her down the corridor towards the large auditorium.

"They say the hyper drive is functioning better than expected - it's achieving 90% efficiency."

"And the microphones?"

"Picking up every radio wave, every tiny audio disturbance."

Diane allowed herself a small smile of satisfaction. Maybe it WAS going to work. Maybe all the hundreds of thousands of man-hours were going to pay off.

The room burst into excited clamour as she walked in. As well as her staff, there was a mass of faces: NASA executives, invited VIPs, representatives of the media, scientific observers from nearly every country on the planet - and of course, the President's top advisors.

"Doctor Roberts," one of the quickest reporters yelled, leaping to his feet. "How do you respond to the claims of the leaders of the world's main faiths that what you're doing here is blasphemous?"

Taking position at the plinth, Diane replied: "I'd respond that the claim is total nonsense and they have nothing to worry about. We are simply trying to understand what happened at the very moment the universe was born."

"But aren't you setting out to disprove the existence of God?" another challenged.

"What we're setting out to do is learn more about the forces unleashed at the instant of the Big Bang. This is an exercise in studying the physics and the astro-mechanics of the creation - not the possible divine spark behind it."

"But I don't understand it," a third pressed her, frowning. "Why are you firing a microphone across the galaxy, why not a video camera? Why not film the Big Bang instead of merely listening to it?"

Diane sighed. No matter how often she explained the physical and theoretical operating restrictions of the experiment, there was always someone scratching their head.

"The reason we don't send a video camera is that it would be utterly pointless. It would simply take pictures of the planets and stars - as they are now," she explained, hiding her annoyance. "To film the Big Bang event we'd need a time machine to take us back billions of years, and I can assure you, we haven't invented one of those. There's a limit to even my ingenuity and budget!"

The audience laughed dutifully.

"No," she went on, "we don't have a time machine, but we have the next best thing. Sound waves. Perfect permanent audio records of events, moments of time captured in the noises they made - echoes living on, being shot endlessly across the vast heavens, travelling through space for all eternity."

The older the noise, the farthest it would have travelled, she informed them. When the Big Bang occurred it not only flung out material but sound vibrations - the first broadcasts ever created - and these waves would have hurtled outwards with the stardust and the gases and the other life-creating elements to the very edge of the universe.

"So that's where we've sent our microphone," she said, with a flourish. "To the very boundaries of known space. Using the fastest projectile ever devised by mankind."

"What do you think? Beautiful isn't she?"

Even distorted over the noise of the helicopter's madly spinning blades, the pride in Chief Engineer McCallum's voice had been obvious.

And Diane couldn't help but whistle in appreciation, replying that it was incredible.

It had been 18 months before, her first glimpse of the Prometheus intergalactic rocket, and the visage before her was breathtaking – the missile a stunning, soaring shaft of gleaming stainless steel projecting 400 feet into the air, like an enchanted arrow from some ancient Greek fable. And as the chopper banked for another turn around the gantry, she'd gasped as the sunlight reflected momentarily off the nosecone, almost blinding them with its brilliance.

It was, she'd realised with emotion, a work of art, the absolute pinnacle of design and engineering, perhaps the most phenomenal machine ever made.

And that was before considering the unbelievably powerful engines - the revolutionary hyper drive that had taken twenty years to conceive and build, mighty engines that could provide enough thrust and motive force to not just propel the ship faster than the speed of light, but outstrip the wildest imaginings of science fiction.

McCallum had toiled all his adult life on perfecting the drive, but even now that it was installed and ready for blast off, he still couldn't outline the principles behind its operation without resorting to concepts that bent accepted mathematical dogma and made mincemeat of applied quantum physics.

Each time he tried to explain it, Diane ended up completely bewildered and needing a drink. It was enough, she conceded, to make Einstein feel like a dunce.

"Look, I'll make it easy for you, Doctor Roberts," the designer had finally said, with a troubled sigh that suggested he was compromising his intellectual purity by deigning to simplify the complexities. "You've watched Star Trek, right?"

"Yes, but I don't see -"

"And you know the USS Enterprise had warp engines?"

"Yes, of course."

"Well, just imagine that our rocket has them too, but refined, upgraded and with more oomph."

"How much more oomph," she prompted, raising a questioning eyebrow.

He'd grinned like a naughty schoolboy. "It's impossible to be totally accurate but I estimate that with the hyper drive, Prometheus will have a cruising speed of about warp 35!"

* * *

She smiled at the memory, noting that the briefing room was now silent, excited ears all turning to the large loudspeakers, willing the towering black boxes to explode into life. There was a reverence in the air, a tangible sense of awe and expectation.

Looking down Diane found her knees were now shaking. So much for your famous icy, logical, rationality, she told herself wryly. You're just as hyped-up as everyone else; as excited as a child on Christmas Eve.

The first crackle issued, a coarse splutter, and she shuddered, stealing a glance at Simon. He peered back, almost dancing on the spot with excitement.

"This is it," his wet, shining eyes seemed to tell her. "The moment of defining, absolute truth. Either it will be the most momentous microsecond in the history of mankind or the instant all our careers evaporate in the heat of public derision."

The epoch-shaping words that came from the other side of the cosmos were distorted, gruff and echoing, but thankfully still comprehensible... "Your President is no crook... there will be no whitewash at The White House..."

Seeing the look of bemusement and surprise sweeping the audience, Diane held up her hand in reassurance.

"I know what you're thinking, but don't worry," she told them, "Richard Nixon wasn't around at the beginning of time. Thank heavens! It's simply that the probe has caught up with broadcasts from the 1970s. We'll get sound clips from even further back as the rocket's velocity picks up acceleration and it continues its journey."

As if to prove this, the speakers vibrated again. "...A House divided against itself cannot stand..." - Honest Abe's solemn tone discernible even through the rustling and distortion. The 1860s. The probe was picking up speed.

"...I know I have the body of a weak and feeble woman, but I have the heart and stomach of a King, and King of England too..."

Elizabeth 1st, 1588, Diane informed the VIP listeners, Good Queen Bess making a speech to her troops on the eve of the arrival of the Spanish Armada.

The next words weren't in English but even in Latin they were clear to many in the room. "...I come to bury Caesar, not to praise him...the evil men do lives after them, the good is oft interred with their bones..."

Some 2000 years covered in as many seconds. The rocket propelled onwards, speed increasing inexorably...

There were bursts of ancient Greek, followed by languages none could recognise, before the discharges from the speakers became no more than Neanderthal grunts. Then, Diane noted with satisfaction, the sounds transformed to chattering, monkey-like shrieks - they were listening to the exact point in pre-history when man evolved from tree-dwelling apes.

Millennia became millions of years in the blink of an eye. A loud roar made everyone jump, then another snarl rumbled - even more fierce and aggressive. The T-Rex sounded, to everyone's jovial surprise, exactly as it did in Jurassic Park. So Spielberg had got it right, Diane observed to the smiling faces.

The next five minutes were unremarkable, except for the crash of waves, crushing rocks and strange hissing, popping noises.

"This is the planet forming," she explained. "The sounds of mountains being thrust upwards by the force of crashing tectonic plates, lava boiling and bubbling, the oceans swirling in torment."

If possible, tension in the room doubled. They were almost there - to the point before Earth and the other planets and stars in the solar system existed. A few more seconds of nail-gnawing anticipation and they'd arrive finally at the incredibly violent, apocalyptic, mystical start of the universe.

Even though Diane and her audience had been briefed on what to expect, the detonation of the Big Bang was hundreds - thousands - of times more startling, ear-splitting and humbling than any had dared imagine.

The devastating din shook her to the very core, as though a rampaging army had marched straight into her ear and was frantically slashing and gouging at her brain. The booming, thunderous, cacophony of destructive force went beyond pain, beyond agony, beyond human experience and endurance. I'm going to die, Diane thought through the crimson dots dancing before her eyes, the ocean of acid churning her guts, the atoms in her bloodstream jarring and colliding.

This must be what it is like to travel through a black hole, she told herself, between Technicolor flashes of excruciating fire and light.

Then suddenly, abruptly, mercifully, it was over.

* * *

"Is everyone all right?" Diane croaked.

Glancing swiftly around the room, she saw that all had shared the same bewildering, life-altering, ordeal. Sprawled, shaken, dishevelled and white-faced, the scientists, delegates and press men got unsteadily to their feet, clearly stunned.

"It worked," Simon yelled, his expression sheer manic delight. "It actually bloody worked!"

The audience, unsure how to react, sighed, gasped then burst into a round of ecstatic applause.

Blushing, Diane took a bow and signalled to Simon to join her in accepting the acclaim.

But he didn't get the chance.

For at that very second a noise, a new mind-teasing sound, inexplicably burst out of the speakers…

Diane couldn't believe it. Wouldn't accept what she was hearing.

It was a voice. A deep, authoritative, commanding voice older than time itself - its ancient, echoing timbre resonating, majestic … God-like.

The tone was wearily exasperated as it boomed: "No dear, I don't need to read the instructions. It's perfectly straight-forward. Nothing can go wrong. I simply plug the wire in here like this…"

Upper Crust

"What in damnation do you mean, there isn't any food! I've never heard anything so outrageous in all my life!"

Lord Montague knew he shouldn't be shouting at the servant, but he couldn't help himself. After ten gruelling hours at the card table and a losing streak that threatened to double his already nightmarish gambling debts, the depleted nobleman desperately needed sustenance and plenty of it. Not excuses.

The footman sighed, carefully avoiding eye contact. "Cook is adamant, your Lordship," he said apologetically. "She says that if you choose to miss meal times, that's your affair. But you can't expect her to rustle up a repast at all times of the day and night."

He gulped before adding: "She also told me to inform your Lordship that she's fed up with him treating the place like a common coaching inn and she's not going to stand for it. Breakfast will be in two hours and at that point she will be delighted to serve yourself and your illustrious guests a wide selection of delicious egg, bacon, sausage, fowl and blood pudding dishes. Alas, for now, the kitchen is closed."

Lord Montague's mouth fell open. He couldn't believe it. He was First Lord of the Admiralty, for heaven's sake. A man of standing and reputation, a confidante of the Prime Minister, Mr Pitt. The leading lights in 18th century society bent over backwards to indulge his every whim. How could he be thwarted by a mere functionary. And in front of his friends. Oh the ignominy of it!

"Need I remind you that I am master of this household and can terminate a servant's employment at any moment that pleases me," he hissed.

The footman shrugged, making his powdered wig slip perilously. "Cook thought you might say that and instructed me to remind you, with all respect, that several other noblemen have enquired about her availability to run the kitchens in their country houses; all at a higher rate of remuneration."

Scowling, Montague understood that it had been a mistake to allow Mistress Delia to produce the lithograph sheets of her favourite recipes. His cook's foray into the fledging world of pamphlet publishing had been a surprise sensation and she now boasted having something bafflingly called a 'three-book-deal' and a fan club; an army of adoring young debutantes who had her beaming countenance engraved upon their fans.

He should have seen it coming. Mistress Delia had inevitably developed what that engineer fellow Mr. Stephenson would have called "ideas above her station".

"Any trouble, old bean?"

Spinning round to his fellow card players, Lord Montague shook his head. "Just a little local difficulty," he assured them, wishing they hadn't mentioned beans, as his stomach rumbled alarmingly."It appears that Cook is indisposed at the moment," he reported. "But that won't prevent me from providing my friends with proper hospitality. I propose that we embark upon an adventure - a culinary quest. Our merry band shall go scavaging."

The twelve well-plucked eyebrows that shot up told him the idea wasn't the hit he'd expected.

"It'll be fun," he promised.

The six gamblers were unimpressed.

"I'll do all the work," he promised. "The preparation of victuals shall all be done by my fair hand."

The frowning statues offered no response.

"All right, all right - I'll break open the best vintage claret."

The instant stampede caught Lord Montague by surprise and sent him flying. Picking himself off the floor he reflected that the last time he'd seen his companions so excited and mobile had been when the grand fountain went out of control, and several buxom wenches had unwittingly taken part in what was later described in the parish newsletter as a scandalous 'wet bonnet' competition.

Chasing after the rapidly disappearing frock-coated sprinters, he shouted: "No, no, chaps - the kitchens are the other way!"

* * *

Scanning the desolate, deserted serving area, Montague felt his heart sink even lower. He'd assumed there would be a cauldron of broth slowly simmering away, a chicken turning on a spit, juicy oysters piled high with ice from the cold store. But the larder was bare.

Well, not quite bare. There was a misshapen, sad-looking loaf of bread, some cold cuts of meat, a meagre scraping of butter and a spoonful of pickle. Not exactly a banquet.

Everything else was safely under lock and key. And Cook was the only one with access to it.

"Looks like she's bested you, old man," his nearest guest said with a sigh. "There ain't a dashed morsel worth eating."

He let his head dip. Percy was right. He shuddered as he imagined what a laughing stock he'd look when word of this dinner time debacle got out. It would be the end of him. He'd never be able to show his face in polite society again.

His hand shook as he took a consoling sniff of snuff and felt its tingling reassurance in the back of his nostrils. As he exhaled explosively into his fine lace handkerchief a stray thought raced across his mind. What was the expression? Not to be sneezed at? Maybe these unpromising scraps of food shouldn't be sneezed at. Perhaps - just perhaps - they could be turned into something edible.

"Damn it, I shall not be defeated by a glorified pot stirrer," he promised, and turning to the pitiful ingredients declared: "Watch, my friends. Watch as I employ every scintilla of guile and resourcefulness I possess. I am going to invent a completely new dish, hitherto unheard of in the length and breadth of the land."

And grabbing knife and plate, he set to work.

* * *

"Dash it, John. You are a veritable magician," Percy said half an hour later, cramming the last of the sliced bread with meat and pickle filling into his mouth. "This new culinary concoction is quite simply delicious."

The other card players all nodded happily, raising their claret glasses in salute to the founder of their feast. "We've never tasted anything like it. Or seen anything remotely similar. It's damned ingenious."

"It's going to change how the world eats," they declared, munching happily. "Be assured, M'Lord, you're going to make history. This is the stuff of legend. Your name will become forever synonymous with these doughy delights."

Shuffling the deck, their host smiled indulgently. It was a lovely thought, but Lord John Montague, 4th Earl of Subway seriously doubted it would ever happen.

Wisdom of Our Four Fathers

"Wake up! Wake up! You've got to wake up!"

It was a child's voice, the small hand tugging at her shoulder, rocking her slumbering body with a panicked urgency.

For a moment Shyster was dazed, part of her mind still in the dream, remembering the rockets filling the skies, their white vapour trails connecting the clouds like a gossamer spider's web, then the first flashes of blinding crimson as the missiles plunged to earth and their payloads exploded.

"What? Who? Whatya want? Leave me alone," Shyster groaned, as she opened one eye.

It was one of the settlement kids, a ragged, underfed, dirt-faced girl of about nine, What was her name? Faith? Hope?

"You've got to come. You've got to come now," the urchin insisted, her anxiety growing. "It's the holy men. They've got Maxine. They've ordered a stoning. It's going to start any minute."

Shyster was instantly alert. Damnation!

Swinging out of her rickety cot and grabbing her goggles and heavy woollen overcoat, she paused only for a moment to take a swing from the near empty bourbon bottle before hurrying outside the shelter.

She blinked for a moment. The air quality was good today, no trace of mist or toxins, and she could see far up on to Capitol Hill and its damaged dome, looking for all the world like a cracked egg shell.

"Hurry, please," the child urged, grabbing her arm again and pulling her towards the path.

Nodding, Shyster let the child lead her up the steep incline, going as fast as her elderly legs would allow, walking stick hitting the ground in a tattoo that sent up swirls of grey dust.

Even from this far away she could hear the excited yells and catcalls, the agitated voices echoing off the walls of the crumbling buildings. It sounded as though there was a large mob, whipped up into a malicious fervour.

It was getting worse, she told herself, things were beginning to spiral out of control. It had only been three weeks since Kardinal had been proclaimed as tribal shaman, yet in that short time his reign of terror and religious intolerance had taken hold like a cancer.

All feared him but none dared question his authority, for was he not the voice of the Gods? Did he not speak for the deities that lived far above where the electric storms danced and crackled in multi-coloured splendour? Did he not venture into the sacred senate, there to hold blessed congress with the divine?

Only I dare, Shyster thought, as she neared the plateau. And I risk all in doing so. He treats me with caution and wariness now but his boldness grows and soon even my status as keeper of the ancient laws won't be enough to protect me.

Shivering at that realisation, she quickened her pace and, reaching the brow of the hill, gasped at the violent sight that befell her eyes.

Almost everyone in the tribe was there, a crowd of wide-eyed men and women posed in a tableau of hate, all clutching rocks – frozen suddenly like statues in mid hurl. And before them Mad Maxine – the miller's deranged daughter – was huddled in a ball, hands palms outwards trying to protect her face.

The mob eyed Shyster anxiously, waiting for a sign from her, a word of encouragement or condemnation.

"Go away, old woman. This is none of your concern. This is a Holy matter," Kardinal warned, stepping from their midst and making a mystic gesture of defiance with the carved totem hanging around his neck.

"If it is the dishing out of punishment, it is very much my business," she told him levelly, drawing closer. "You are not a judge. You have no jurisdiction. Only I can determine if Maxine has transgressed."

The shaman curled his lip. "She is guilty of heresy. This shameless hussy has defied the Gods and must pay. She must be stoned to death."

"And what was the girl's crime," Shyster demanded.

He shook in anger and disgust, gesturing towards Maxine. "Look, look at how she is dressed. It is an outrage. A blasphemy!"

To Shyster, Maxine's garb seemed acceptable, if a little thin and inadequate to keep out the chill. The tee-shirt especially was threadbare.

Then Shyster groaned as it dawned on her. The silly girl wasn't wearing the protective coveralls.

"See how she defies the will of the Gods?" Kardinal boomed theatrically to the onlookers. "How she flaunts her body, scorns the sacred coverings."

The crowd murmured at this, whispering excitedly, obviously wondering how the law-maker would respond.

Shyster kept her own counsel for a moment, trying to discern if the shaman was cynically exploiting the situation or did indeed believe that the radiation suits were garments of supreme religious significance. Who could tell? There were so many hucksters and false prophets, quick to exploit the gullibility of the weary and superstitious survivors.

Shyster had to admit that she herself could be viewed as one of their number. Before the attack decades before she had been a mere secretary to a small time attorney. She had no legal training - only the presence of mind to jot down what she could remember of the many laws that had once governed the land.

Her memory had been poor even before the apocalypse, and the initial sickness and fever had made her recollections even more fragmented but it had been enough until now. But would the half remembered regulations be up to this challenge?

Breathing in deeply, she told herself that they would have to be and, shouting to the assembled congregation just as loudly as her rival had done moments earlier, declared: "This poor addled child has done no wrong. She will not be harmed. She has broken no laws and I can prove it."

And stepping boldly forward, she produced a tattered piece of parchment from her satchel and thrust it into the shaman's hand.

Kardinal looked down, eyes going wide as the knowledge that he'd been outfoxed finally became clear. His anger surged but he knew he was beaten.

Tossing the paper back to her with distain, he hissed: "Now I can see why they call you Shyster, old crone."

Ignoring him, the keeper of the laws hurried forward and pulled Maxine to her feet. "We have to get away quickly while we still can," she urged.

Maxine may be eccentric but she certainly wasn't as delusional as the others believed and immediately did what her rescuer instructed.

Staggering hurriedly back to Shyster's tumbledown dwelling, she asked: "What did the magic parchment say? I don't understand. What made him back down?"

Relief and a sense of triumph made Shyster grin. "I simply showed him a section from the old constitution," she replied mysteriously. "A fragment of one of the wise men's Amendments."

The girl still seemed baffled.

"It's the section that guarantees our most basic freedom," Shyster explained sagely. "I'm hazy on the exact words but it's the statute that says all the citizens in this great land have the right to bare arms."

Getting Wood

Geppetto's wrinkled hands shook as he poured brandy into the cracked porcelain cup, the alcohol sloshing over his carpenter's workbench making the sawdust turn a soggy, muddy brown.

He frowned, downing the drink in a single gulp. He'd never been so nervous. And it was going to take a lot more Dutch Courage to help face up to what he had to do.

Refilling the cup, he told himself it was ridiculous to feel so embarrassed and afraid. Yet, never in his wildest imaginings had he dreamt he'd ever be having the awkward, intimate conversation with his enchanted son that all fathers must eventually have.

After all, he reasoned, Pinocchio wasn't real, he was made of oak. Geppetto had himself fashioned the magical lad from a hunk of tree trunk 18 years before. But the puppet had always yearned to live a normal life and recently Geppetto had noticed that although Pinocchio's carved features hadn't altered, his attitude and behaviour certainly had. His boy was becoming a man… well, a mannequin.

All these women callers at the humble puppet shop. All the giggles and squeals coming from Pinocchio's bedroom. And all that sap…

A knock on the door made the elderly woodworker jump. Draining the cup, he croaked: "Come in."

Pinocchio entered, cap in hand, head slightly bowed. "You-u-u w-wanted to speak to me, Father?" His stammering echoed the old man's discomfort.

Geppetto motioned to the chair beside him. "Yes, my son. I think it's time we had a chat about the... um... birds and bees."

The puppet blushed, turning redder than the darkest mahogany stain.

"Do we have to?" he pleaded. "Please, please, can't we just forget what you saw yesterday? Pretend it never happened?"

Geppetto shook his head. "I'm afraid it's not that simple."

He shuddered, trying to blot out the shocking memory of walking in on a scene of total debauchery. Pinocchio had been lying on the floor, face hidden under the skirts of the blacksmith's daughter as she moaned and writhed, yelling: "Lie to me, big boy. Tell me some fibs. Oh yes, yes, I want a whopper!"

At that instant, Geppetto had comprehended that his son's famous elongating snout - normally a curse which caught out the puppet in every falsehood - was now proving to be a blessing in disguise. Overnight the marionette had gone from knotty to naughty!

"We can't risk there being any accidents," the woodcarver said, avoiding eye contact. "After all, we don't want the clatter of tiny feet, now do we?"

And coughing, held up the cedar condom.

"I'll show you how to use this," Geppetto promised. "But first, I'll impart a piece of wisdom that all men should know. A fact of life my father told me and his father told him - and is especially relevant to you."

His voice dipped to a conspiratorial whisper. "Never, ever - under any circumstances - stick your nose in a woman's business..."

Spreading the word

If you've enjoyed this book, please, please climb to the top of the nearest tall building and yell excitedly that everyone should read it too or risk forever having empty lives. Alternatively, if you don't have a head for heights, simply approach hundreds of strangers at bus stops and urge them to buy this humble collection.

If you're less outgoing, online reviews are always welcome. Paranoid authors check their Amazon pages every hour, on the hour, and a few words of praise helps prevent them from falling into terminal despair or down the steps of basement drinking dens.

Put my name, Iain Pattision, into the Amazon search bar, to find all my books.

Many thanks.

Disclaimer

No animals were harmed in the making of this comedy book, but some puns were forced into very awkward positions.

Printed in Great Britain
by Amazon